ATMAN CITY BOOK 2

M.I.A.

Missing in Atman

MICHELLE E. REED

Month9Books

M.I.A. (Missing In Atman) by Michelle E. Reed

Published by Month9Books
Cover designed by Stephanie Mooney
Cover Copyright © 2014 Month9Books

For Aldo, from your G.R.
I miss you every day.

ATMAN CITY BOOK 2

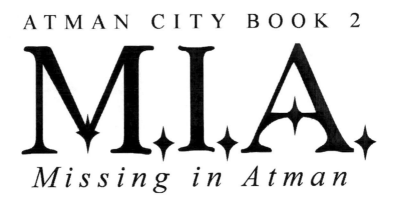

M.I.A.

Missing in Atman

MICHELLE E. REED

CHAPTER ONE

"Thinking about her again?"

The grass prickles me through my thin cotton shirt as I roll onto my back and take in the sky's churning array of blues peeking through the treetops. My thoughts drift back over a span of months, coming to rest on a farewell still tugging at my heart.

"Of course I am."

"What do you suppose she's doing right now?" Charlie asks. His fingers trace a meandering trail up and down my arm.

"I have no idea, but whatever it is, it's probably amazing."

Three months. That's how long Hannah has been missing from my life.

Well, my afterlife.

She was my first friend, and my first goodbye. Our worlds intersected for just a week, but that's all it takes. Bonds form fast and strong here, and when you're stranded in limbo, never quite sure who will be the next to leave, you have a steady reminder that the end of life does not mean the end of loss.

My bracelet taunts me, an unwanted reminder of exactly how long I've been here and how far I am from leaving. LEVEL 02-068-098.

I scroll through the menu to the time and groan. "I have to go."

"Want me to walk you to Admin?" Charlie sits up, chivalry at the ready.

"You'd better try and find Pip before work." I point to the bag of grapes sitting next to him. "He's going to want those."

"He's just a bird, Dez."

"But he's Hannah's bird. And we promised to take care of him."

"That was before I knew how high maintenance he is." He holds up his hand for inspection. "My finger still hurts."

"You're the one who was teasing him with that banana. Besides, if you can jump out a ninety-five story window without a scratch, I don't think a toucan is going to hurt you."

The day I met Charlie, he set our relationship in motion by plummeting from a library window in an ill-conceived attempt at humor. It was then I learned of his early, dark days at Atman when he tried in every conceivable way to kill himself, from hanging to stepping in front of high-speed trains. Through this terrible process, he learned the physical pain we feel and injuries we sustain in this transitional existence are all in our heads. Charlie is the only underage soul I know of who is immune to pain.

"Still, his beak is really sharp," he says.

"Poor baby." I kiss his fingertip. "Well, I've got to hurry up and get to my meeting before work. I'm running late as it is."

"At least you get a short work day."

"I'd rather scrub dishes than deal with Kay." I stand. "See you at open rec?"

"Count on it."

✦✦✦

A receptionist sits at a small desk before the only other door in the room where I sit, impatient. Drab, run-of-the-mill décor adorns the walls, which are painted in a revolting shade of dull. As I survey the clean lines of the minimalist furniture, I can't help but wonder how gigantic the afterlife's IKEA must be.

I chuckle, just loud enough to attract the attention of the new receptionist.

She's a plump woman with graying hair and a shockingly pink pantsuit. She looks up from a small stack of paperwork to give me a polite smile.

"Don't worry, Desiree, she'll be with you shortly."

"Dez. No one calls me Desiree," I say for what seems like the millionth time. My mood is in rapid decline. This looming therapy session allows no happiness to overlap from my picnic lunch with Charlie.

"What's that, dear?"

"Nothing."

I hate pink.

She returns her attention to the stack of paper on her desk. Her smile becomes a small but noticeable frown. My attention turns to the task of identifying the familiar melody piped in from a speaker overhead.

What's the point in not letting me remember? It's a love-hate relationship I have with this existence. Mostly hate. My fingernails *tick tick tick* against the slim metal arms of my chair.

Pink Pantsuit looks up again from her collating. "Can I help you with something?"

"Depends. Can you get me on the next train out of here?" I plaster an angelic smile and hopeful look on my face.

She scowls and returns her attention to her paperwork.

"That's what I thought."

The door behind Pink Pantsuit opens, and Kay Robinson's tall, lithe frame breezes into the waiting area.

"Hi, Dez. Come on back." Her voice is warm and soothing.

A feeling of serenity washes over me, and I don't bother fighting it. Her greetings always have this effect on me. It's what follows that sends my mood plummeting.

She leads me down a narrow corridor to her cramped office, where I plunk down in my usual spot, facing her desk.

"You know, Dez, you're actually one of the lucky ones."

My reply comes out as a single, disgusted snort. I grab a stress ball from her desk and toss it in the air. It sails up, arcing slightly, and lands back in my hand.

The corners of Kay's mouth curl up just a bit, and she does a poor job hiding the amusement dancing in her eyes. This is how our relationship goes. Mutually aloof, but secretly friendly. I can't say I really get her, but I guess that's not the point. She's my Station Guidance and Assistance rep, so she's here for me.

"Lucky? Yeah, sure. Lucky me," I say.

"Grumpy again?"

"Is that the clinical term? And what do you mean, 'again?'"

"I'll take that as a yes. You're going to love what's on the agenda for today."

"Great."

"We'll start with something easy. Tell me about adoption."

"I thought I was here for your 'guidance and assistance,' Kay."

"Yes, that's exactly why you're here. You know that. Now, if you don't mind, allow me to guide and assist you."

I shrug. "Adoption in general, foster adoption, multi-racial adoption, or my multi-racial adoption? There are lots of choices."

"Whatever you feel like. Just go for it."

"Fine. You're getting my sophomore year Honors English informative speech."

"You remember a speech from a class you took two years before you died? You're good."

"You want to hear this or not?"

Kay raises her hands in surrender.

"I'll just nutshell it for you." I clear my throat and begin reciting. "My mom was always certain it was fate that brought us together as a family. The infertility treatments, miscarriages, tests, and endless months spent as a human pincushion were all for a reason. Adoption wasn't a distant second choice—that's just how things shake out. You decide you want a baby, and you try to have one the way most people do. When it doesn't work out, you find yourself consulting specialists, going to appointment after appointment, trying all sorts of crazy medical procedures in order to—"

Kay holds up a traffic cop hand. "I was hoping you'd share

your feelings on adoption."

"You said, 'whatever you feel like.'" I toss the stress ball to her.

"Speaking of a deeply personal matter in a detached, sterile way does neither of us any good." She tosses the ball back to me. "You tend to de-personalize the deeply personal, Miss Donnelly."

"What's that supposed to mean? And what's this 'Miss Donnelly' crap?"

"You balk at sharing feelings and experiences in a personal way. You detach in what I believe is an attempt to avoid the risk of being exposed to painful emotions."

I glance around her small office. "You'd think that for an eternity, they could spring for better digs."

"You're also a master of deflection."

"So are you," I retort. "You called me lucky." I throw the stress ball at her, a little harder than necessary. She catches it with ease, her coordination matching her graceful, willowy frame. "Last I checked, I've been attacked by a madwoman, stalked and assaulted by a murderer, had some mystery staff member linked to my brain without my consent, and had my roommate unceremoniously snatched from this limbo-verse a week after I got here. How, exactly, am I lucky?"

"Because you're not as complicated as you think you are."

"Gee, thanks."

"What I mean is you're not going to be at Atman so terribly long. Moving on is really up to you, and you have an uncanny ability to make things far more difficult than they need be." She raises her eyebrows, daring me to challenge her.

"That's comforting. Glad to know it's my fault I'm stuck here, because, you know, it's not bad enough just being stuck here. It's not enough to die at seventeen and never really get a chance to live. I need guilt, too."

"You've found yourself a great support system. In your short time with us, you have developed strong bonds with several floormates and a particular member of our staff."

"Fine, you've got me. I'm lucky. Charlie's awesome. Bobby's a genius. Crosby's the best mother hen a girl could ask for. Hannah, however, is gone, and thanks so much for that. Can we move on, please?"

"What has you in such a mood today, Dez?"

"Do I have to have a reason? Isn't being dead enough?"

Kay lets me sit in silence and stew in my anger. I focus on a granite plaque on her desk. Each time I've been here, it has displayed a different quote.

Chaotic action is preferable to orderly inaction

"That's helpful, as usual. Last time it was some Confucius crap."

"It was good advice. 'It does not matter how slowly you go so long as you do not stop.' Haven't you found that to be true since you've gotten here? Be honest." She narrows her gaze and leans forward in her chair. It squeaks, marking another entry in the long, long list of things here that make no sense.

A chair in need of a blast of WD-40 in the afterlife?

"You remind me of my mom," I blurt out.

Kay waits a moment before responding. "You're changing the subject again, but let's go with it. I think this could be important." She tucks a strand of hair behind her ear and leans forward to rest her elbows on her desk.

It's not just those left behind who grieve; the dead feel the agony of loss as well. We worry about the living and how they're coping, how they're getting along without us. We feel the sharp, raw pain. The same suffocating fear crushes us. Those we leave behind suffer a single loss, but the dead? We lose everything and everyone who ever mattered to us.

"Do we really have to get into this right now? I think I need to go partake of some chaotic action."

"I think you've had your fill." She glances out her small window toward the skyline of Atman City. "Enough to last quite some time, even in the span of eternity."

An immediate longing pulls at me as I take in the off-limits city I'd snuck into three times during my first week here. The final visit nearly cost me my freedom in a dangerous confrontation with a lunatic. Despite the pointed lesson, I know I'd go back in a second if I could get away with it.

"Never going to let that go, huh?" I ask, drawn from my daydream of adventures never to be.

"Let's not get off track." She clicks the top of her pen. "Have you seen your mom in DSR lately?"

In the days following my funeral, my mom's sorrow and pain left her contemplating suicide, a scene played out for me in Dream-State Reflection. Fearing the worst, I made that fateful third trip to Atman City, hoping to use the communication pods at Nero's Tavern to contact her.

"It seems like she's doing a bit better, from what little they show me. She's been working on her garden. I think it's therapeutic."

Kay nods as she takes notes. "Returning to activities she enjoys is a good sign, and I'm glad to hear she's progressing through her grief." She looks up from my file. "I want to get back to what you said, though—that I remind you of her. Can you tell me what it is about me that lends itself to that comparison?"

"I…maybe nothing. Maybe I'm just grasping." I pick at my fingernails and focus on my cuticles to avoid her gaze. "Is it ever going to stop hurting so much?"

"Think of how far you've already come, and you'll find your answer."

My hands drop into my lap. "Talk about clinical."

"You're in a much better place than you were upon arrival, are you not?"

"I suppose."

"Of course you are. Don't be afraid of progress, Dez, and don't be afraid to feel. Own the pain. Allow yourself to experience the loss you've suffered. It is the only way to move forward."

"Could you be more vague?"

Kay smiles. "Well, now you've stepped in it. You want specifics? I have a perfect assignment for you."

Fantastic.

CHAPTER TWO

I stand before Crosby's desk, arms crossed, glowering.

He looks up from his computer, smiling. "What's with you, cranky?"

Crosby is my self-appointed mother hen, mentor, button-pusher, and occasional butt-kicker—the latter a skill at which he especially excels. Our relationship was forged in fear and rebellion, but has become one on which we both depend. After a rough start, he took me under his wing, and I've more or less been there ever since.

His eyes sparkle with mischief, which means one thing: button-pusher.

"Was it your idea?" I demand.

"Was what my idea?"

"Don't play dumb. Nothing happens around here without you knowing about it, especially when it comes to me."

He scratches his chin, trying his best to look puzzled. "You had a meeting with Kay this morning, right?"

"Forget it." I spin on my heels and head for the exit.

"Aw, come on. Don't be that way." He jumps up from his desk to follow me and drops a hand on my shoulder before I open the door.

"Abbey?" I turn to face him, my hands planted on my hips. Waves of contempt dance off me like flames. "Is this some sort of joke? Because it's not funny."

Crosby raises a hold-on-a-second finger before reaching to his head and tapping a miniature earpiece. He begins talking into the air, his other hand still clamped on my shoulder.

"Hey, Lillie. Can you watch things out front for a few? Hurricane Dez just blew in." He smiles as I shoot him a withering glare. "Thanks, hon. Will do."

He pulls me through the door and into the hallway. We walk in silence down the winding corridors on a familiar route to our favorite meeting spot. He opens the door to a small room furnished with a single couch, a pair of chairs, and floor-to-ceiling windows that taunt me with sweeping views of the city.

Crosby motions to me to take a seat, but I refuse to budge.

"Would you just sit?" he says.

"Fine." I flop onto the couch.

"What's this about Abbey?"

"Like you don't know."

He pulls up a chair and sits, his feet propped up on the couch next to me. "I've been in meetings all morning."

"My assignment? Telling Abbey about my final, dying moments?"

Abbey and I got off to a rough start, to say the least. Getting into an argument on our first encounter was only the beginning, as I soon discovered she'd been spying on me per the request of Atman Staff. Despite her small efforts to repair the relationship these past months, she's still far from my favorite person. Opening up to her, of all people, is about the last thing I'd consider doing.

"That's news to me," he says.

"You didn't put Kay up to this?"

"I don't put Kay up to anything. You need to learn a thing or two about the pecking order around here."

"Please, everyone knows you're Atman's Queen Bee."

"You're too kind." He smiles. "I may have heard something about you getting an assignment, but no specifics."

"What's the point, anyway? I already did the full disclosure session. Why do I have to do it again?"

"They call it a full disclosure session for a reason. Its purpose is to share with your floormates the most intimate details of your death. It's cathartic. But it doesn't work when the subject spends the entire session hiding in her room."

"I wasn't in there the *whole* time." My stomach ties in knots at the memory.

Franklin, our floor adviser, directs me to a chair. The group sits before us in a semi-circle, respectfully quiet in anticipation of what's to come.

Franklin flips open a file folder and begins to read aloud. "It was early in the morning of April thirteenth, the seventeenth year, tenth month, and fourteenth day of your life. You were driving to cello practice on a rural route you routinely took through the Wisconsin countryside. It was cloudy and cool, but road conditions were clear."

My heart begins to race. I swallow back bile.

Charlie, sitting only a few feet away, gives me an encouraging smile. "It's okay," he mouths.

"Your phone rang, distracting you," Franklin says. "Would you please share with everyone what happened next?"

My throat constricts.

The race to my suite is a blur, and the next thing I know I'm huddled under the covers of my bed.

"I can't believe you're doing this to me," I snap, pushing aside the humiliating memory.

Crosby leans back in his chair and crosses his arms over his chest. "It wasn't my idea."

"So you think it's stupid, too?"

"I didn't say that. In fact, I wish I'd been the one to come up with it. You're on, what, day ninety-nine?" He glances down at my identification bracelet.

I yank my wrist from view. "Ninety-eight."

"It's high time you deal with this," he scolds in his uniquely Crosby way—stern enough to get his point across yet soft enough to make the point tolerable.

I try to calm the too-familiar surge of anger and adrenaline. The peaks and valleys of the rollercoaster ride that is this existence have smoothed out considerably in these past months, but every once in a while, the bottom still drops out.

Crosby nudges my elbow with his foot. "Come on. It's not so bad."

"Have you met Abbey? Dying in a car wreck was bad enough. I don't need to tell her about it."

"It might help."

"How, exactly? How is it going to do anything but humiliate

me?"

"You have been resistant in sharing anything meaningful, which is hindering your progress, as is your act-before-thinking, jump-down-everybody's-throat attitude."

"Gee, thanks. You sure know how to flatter a girl."

"Kay feels—and I agree—that forcing you to share something this personal with someone you aren't exactly close to might be just the thing to get you started down the right path."

"So you did know."

He shakes his head. "Not the specifics. But this will be good for you. If you can share with Abbey, you can share with anyone."

"I tell you plenty."

"You do, but usually only after I drag it out of you, or catch you in the act." He glances over his shoulder and out the window at the cityscape before fixing his stern gaze back on me. "And I'm not Kay. You need to open up to her."

"You don't know what it's like."

"What do you mean?"

"You're here because you want to be. You come and go as you please. You don't have every aspect of your death dictated to you."

"You've made some good friends here."

"Amazing, considering my horrible attitude, right?"

"Come on, it's not so bad. You've got Charlie."

"For how long?"

This is a conversation I'll have to navigate with care. It's one, truth be told, I'd rather avoid altogether. The fact is, romantic involvement is more than just frowned upon. For tower residents, it's forbidden. Charlie and I have been keeping our status under wraps—sneaking off to the park or to quiet corners of the library, spending free time at the cafeteria in a neighboring tower to avoid familiar faces—while maintaining a friends-only public appearance.

I've already lost Hannah. What would happen if I let myself fall into unflinching, unreserved love with Charlie? He's been here over a year, now, and he's doing so well, despite getting knocked back to level two when he followed me to the city. In the months since, he's earned back his levels and then some—he just hit level five last week. We can't possibly have much time left before he leaves, too, and I can't bear the weight of another albatross around my neck.

I have to choose between love and sanity. There's no other way.

I will myself to hold it together.

"What aren't you telling me?" Crosby asks.

"Nothing."

He pulls his feet down and leans forward in his chair. "This attitude of yours isn't just about Abbey."

Guilt and fear hit my stomach like a phantom fist. "I can't."

"Thus the need for your assignment."

"Anything but this, Crosby. Please."

"You know I'm not letting you out of this room until you tell me."

"You have to swear this doesn't leave the room. You can't tell Kay or anyone. Especially not Charlie. Promise me." My throat constricts around the words. My voice shrinks along with my courage.

"You know me better than that."

"You promise?"

He holds his hand up in a pledge. "I swear on my death, this stays between us."

"Can you sit over here?" I motion to the cushion next to me on the small sofa. "I can't look at you. Not if I have to tell you this."

Crosby obliges and pivots into position next to me. "You're in love with Charlie," he says, matter-of-factly.

"What?" Panic grabs me. "What are you talking about?"

"Please." Crosby rolls his eyes. "Everyone knows."

"I…we're just good friends," I sputter.

"Just tell me what's on your mind."

"But—"

He holds up a hand to stop me. "I'm going to let you in on a little secret. You and Charlie aren't the first to break the no dating rule, and you won't be the last."

"But nobody's said a word to us."

"When the inevitable happens, we keep an eye on things and only step in if it gets too serious. Which, depending on what you tell me, might be called for. Spill it."

Arguing with Crosby is useless, a point I still haven't entirely come to terms with. In life, I relished my stubborn resolve, but he has proven to be a challenge like no other. Fighting him, on this point, especially, is like shoveling during a blizzard.

I brace myself and confess. "When we first got together, I was scared. I was homesick, and Charlie was there for me. He was everything, you know?"

"Your feelings have changed?"

"I love being with him."

"You're just not sure if you want to *be* with him?"

"Maybe."

He shifts slightly on the couch and begins a stare down I want no part of. "What else?"

"What do you mean?"

"We could play the 'what' game all afternoon, or you could cut the crap and tell me what else is going on. Up to you, kiddo."

"He's going to leave soon," I blurt out.

"As are you, in the grand scheme of eternity."

"I'm going to be stuck here without him."

"Not for long. Don't let attachment fears keep you from feeling, from finding support from your peers."

My eyes burn. "What's wrong with me, Crosby?"

"Nobody said being dead was going to be easy. Everything hits you harder here. Your emotions, especially. It's all magnified. Even doubt. And that's why we want you to avoid getting involved like this."

"But Charlie's fearless."

"That doesn't mean you have to be."

"I really do care about him."

"Then just let it be. Officially, I'm telling you to stop seeing each other and reminding you that romantic involvement is forbidden. Unofficially, I'm looking the other way—for now— and telling you not to stress yourself with what might or might not happen later."

"I'm not so sure it's that simple."

"It's exactly that simple." Crosby slides back into the chair facing me. "Stop over-thinking everything."

"Next you're going to tell me I make things harder than they need to be, right?"

"I should make you wear that on a sign around your neck."

"You're not funny."

"Good, because I'm serious."

"And you say you and Kay aren't conspiring against me?"

Crosby lets out a deep sigh. "When something is painfully obvious, it isn't exactly a conspiracy, sweetie."

I let his dig slide, knowing full well how much I owe him. For keeping my secret. For keeping me safe and relatively sane. "Please don't say anything to Charlie."

"You know I won't."

"Thanks." I nudge my foot against his. "Sorry I was so…"

"You? I'm used to it."

"I know, but thanks."

"I'm always here, anytime you need me." He swings back into mother hen mode without missing a beat. "You okay, now?"

"As okay as I ever can be, I guess."

Crosby stands and gestures toward the door like he's trying to get rid of me. "I hate to ditch you, but I have another meeting I have to get to."

"What's up?"

"Never you mind, young lady."

"Relax. It's not like I'm planning to barge in or anything."

"Damn right, you're not."

"Fine, bossy. And you think I'm touchy. I've got plans, anyway. I have to get to work, and if there's time after, I need to go hang out in my room and sulk for a while."

"Have fun with your assignment."

I scowl. "Thanks for reminding me."

CHAPTER THREE

I step off the elevator and spot Charlie alone at the foosball table, practicing. With a smile and an improved outlook, I cross the vacant common area and join him at the table.

He glances up, and a smile spreads across his face. "Hey."

"Hey, yourself," I reply, brimming with wit and eloquence. I glance down at the little soccer men. "You still think you're going to get good enough to beat me? That's just sad."

"You win a couple of games, and you get all cocky." He wraps his arms around my waist and pulls me close. His fingers trace the curve of my back as his lips press to mine.

My breath catches in my throat and I pull back. "Charlie," I say, glancing around the rec room.

"What? There's nobody around. Everybody went out to the park for open rec. Soccer match."

"Well, in that case," I run my hands across his abs and up his chest as he kisses me again. His lips are warm and eager.

"I was wondering where you were."

I rest my head on his chest. "You don't want to know."

"Yes, I do. That's why I asked."

My shoulders slump. "Things weren't great with Kay. She gave me this assignment. I got really pissed about it, so after work, I went to find Crosby."

Charlie gives me a puzzled smile. "Crosby again? I'm starting to think you're obsessed with the guy."

I lean back against the foosball table. "What? It's Crosby. If you knew what Kay is making me do, you'd want to vent to him, too."

"Crosby and I don't exactly spend a lot of quality time together. He's kind of got his hands full with a certain someone I know. You're a full-time occupation." He smirks.

"Funny guy," I say, my voice flat. "Did you feed Pip?"

"I did and even managed to keep all my fingers."

"Learned your lesson, huh?"

He shakes his head. "Honestly, I don't know why we keep feeding him. There are plenty of fruit trees for him. Besides, we're dead, right? Does he really need us?"

"Maybe I need him."

"You need a greedy, vain bird?"

"He was Hannah's greedy, vain bird, and I miss her, remember?"

"You make it pretty hard to forget." He takes a step back and sizes me up. "What's with you, anyway?"

"It's pretty simple. I'm less than thrilled about the assignment Kay gave me, and I have a lot on my mind. Is that okay with you?"

Irritation darkens his eyes. "How about you let me help you through it? Or is that too much of a commitment for you?"

"That's not fair, and you know it."

"You want to talk about fair? Really? So, it's fair that you won't share anything that matters with me?"

"I tell you everything."

"Yeah, you did. Three days after you got here, but it's been pretty superficial since Hannah left."

"You don't understand."

"You're right, I don't. I have no idea if I actually matter to you, or if it's just convenient to have me around."

"Where is this coming from? Why are you acting like this?"

"Are you kidding me?"

"You know you matter, Charlie."

"No, actually, I don't. I thought I might, but lately, I have no idea. Maybe you can clear things up for me. Will I ever matter? There's a big difference between being important and being convenient. So which is it?"

"Charlie..."

"If you have to think about it, you've just answered my question."

I run my fingers down his arm and reach for his hand, but he pulls it away.

"Don't bother." He pivots on his heel and walks away.

"Charlie, wait," I call after him, but he ignores me.

CHAPTER FOUR

Stunned and stinging from my fight with Charlie, I slink back to my room to hide.

The entryway is bathed in the bright flashing light of the message center located just inside the door, alerting me in no uncertain terms to the fact that I have mail.

I try to shake off the rising gloom as I tear into the envelope in my hand.

Hi Dez,

Please stop by my office when you get a chance. I need to discuss the rooming situation with you.

Thanks,

Franklin

Just what I need piled on this already crappy day. I've been flying solo since Hannah left, and I'm none too anxious to have a new roommate. I look over at her bed. Dread fills my thoughts at the prospect of someone else occupying her space. Clutching the note in my hand, I move across the room and open her closet doors. The light comes on and reveals a sterile space devoid of clothes or even hangers.

On top of everything else, the last thing I need is a new arrival to deal with. The dread of newfound death is too fresh in my mind to make me of any use to someone new. I've only been here ninety-eight days. How helpful can I possibly be? I am, after all, the girl who needs an additional staff member just to get by. What wisdom could I possibly have to offer? It gets better? I'm not sure it does. It gets marginally less terrifying, I suppose, but I'm not sure that's what they're going to want to hear.

I glance down at the note again and decide it's best to rip off the Band-Aid, especially since the alternative is tracking down Abbey.

I head two doors down to Franklin's room and knock.

"Come on in," he calls out.

With a resigned sigh, I enter his suite.

He looks up from the book he's reading. "Hey, Dez. Thanks for stopping by."

I glance at the hefty tome he's holding. "Wow, some actual free time?"

"Happens once in a while."

"No fires to put out?"

He moves over to his desk, a weary smile on his face. "Not at the moment, but we'll see." He points to a chair sitting in front of his desk. "Have a seat."

He sits and grabs a file folder from the top of a stack of paperwork.

I brace myself for what I know is coming. "I take it my solo ride is over?"

He flips open the file and scribbles a few notes on the front page. "It is, and that's what I need to talk to you about. We have a special situation, and I'm going to need to shift things around a bit."

"New arrival?"

"Arrivals. Plural. And that's where things get interesting. We have two girls down in orientation right now."

"More twins?" We already have one set of twins on the floor, and after three months, I still can't tell them apart. Another pair would make my head spin.

"No, not twins. They're best friends who died together. They're only thirteen—barely—they each had their birthday within the past month. We're afraid separating them will be the last thread that completely undoes them. So…" He looks at me with trepidation.

"I'm not so sure I'm up for dealing with a severely traumatized girl. I'm still pretty traumatized myself."

"You won't have to. We're going to keep them together. Not just on the same floor, but in the same room. We feel the benefits of having a roommate with some experience at Atman will be greatly outweighed by the trauma of separation, even if it's only into different rooms."

"But there are no free rooms on our floor."

"There will be if we combine—"

"Wait a minute. You mean Abbey? Are you kidding me?" I stand. "I really don't need this right now."

"Dez…" My name is enunciated as a warning.

I pace in front of his desk. "First Kay, and now you? Did Crosby put you up to this?"

"Sit down." Franklin points to the chair. His tone does not invite argument. "Nobody put anyone up to anything. These girls just got here. There may be a lot we can control, but what happens in life and what ends it is beyond our reach."

"Fine."

"You and Abbey are both without roommates right now, and we believe these girls will be best served by staying together. The only logical move is to put you two together to free up space for them."

"Fantastic."

"What's going on with you? I thought you and Abbey had put your rocky start behind you."

"Coexisting on the same floor is not the same as sharing a room."

He flips the file folder shut. "Have you forgotten so soon?"

"What?"

"What those girls are feeling. And let's not forget they're five years younger than you." He glances back at the file. "If you had any idea what they'd just been through, I doubt you'd be acting this way."

"This is a big place. You're telling me this is the only floor in the only tower they can go to?"

"Would you listen to yourself? When did you get so selfish?"

"That's not fair."

"Isn't it? I know it's going to be a major adjustment, but I think if you give it a chance, you and Abbey might actually like each other."

"Abbey the drama queen? I doubt it."

"You may want to take a look in the mirror before tossing

labels out there." His expression softens. "Just give her a chance. You're not the type to discount the feelings of a couple of scared kids."

"Don't be so sure."

Irritation clouds Franklin's face. "You can forgive Herc after everything that happened, but you can't get over a silly squabble with Abbey?"

"It's a lot easier to forgive someone whose been banished to another tower. Besides, I saw what his dad is like. He can't help the way he turned out."

He throws his pen down on the desk. "Yet you can't be bothered to learn if Abbey might have reasons for her behavior. You're willing to make a couple of terrified new arrivals suffer, just so you can avoid the inconvenience of rooming with her?"

I slouch down in the chair. "Franklin…" I search for words that aren't there.

"Just go. I'll talk to you later."

My gaze is glued to the floor as I leave his suite, and I nearly crash into Abbey exiting my room. Our room, that is.

"Hey, Dez." Her smile is guarded, cautious. Her normally perky, bouncy demeanor is scaled all the way back to subdued, making her nearly unrecognizable. "I guess we're roomies now, huh?"

"Sounds that way."

"Franklin told me to move into your suite to make it easier, but I can only imagine how it went over."

"It's fine."

"Somehow I don't believe you." She stares down at the handful of clothes hangers she's holding.

"It would have been nice to have some sort of say in all this. It's not like anyone asked me how I feel about it, or ever seems to care what I might want."

"Wow, okay." She stares daggers at me. "I guess it's a good thing the suites are big. I'll do my best to stay out of your way." She walks back to her old room and shuts the door with a bang.

Rather than subject anyone else, even Crosby, to my presence, I retreat to the sanctity and solitude of Jhana Park.

CHAPTER FIVE

It's been forty-two days since I've missed a session or meeting. Forty-two days of cooperation—as cooperative as I get, anyway—and now I'm blowing off Sharing Circle. When you miss one session, the rest tend to fall like dominos, but maybe they'll let Active Body, Active Soul slide, since I'm going to the park.

That's active, right?

Punishments vary based on the infraction, but at a minimum, I'm looking at a lecture from Franklin—and they're the stuff of legends, long winded affairs brimming with guilt and disappointment. Worst case scenario, I could face a loss of privileges and even see a delay in attaining my next level. The mood I'm in, though, I can't be bothered to care about consequences or rules.

I walk the meandering path deep into Jhana Park, out of view of the distant city skyline and the residence towers at the park's perimeter. The surrounding trees are abuzz with the chatter of birds, but even Hannah's beloved Pip, always hungry and ever greedy, seems to be ignoring me. He makes no appearance even after I call out to him.

Dejected, I sit at the bank of the nearby bubbling stream, trying once again to drift away. Escapism, for the moment, wins out over wallowing in self-pity. The sunless light filters unnaturally through the copse of pines towering over me, leaving odd shadows native only to this weird existence—a little too angular, a bit too dark.

I flop onto my back, stretch out my arms, and run my hands through the soft grass. I pull a few blades from the ground, put them to my nose, and inhale the strong, earthy scent. What should be fresh and lightly fragrant is cloying and off-putting. My upper lip curls, and I drop my hand back to the turf.

In a moment of stubborn, foolish resolve, I pretend that sleep is possible in this existence.

I miss naps.

"Dez, what a most pleasant surprise."

I open my eyes to the familiar mop of unruly curls and the lean frame of Bobby approaching. He's our floor's resident genius, the prodigy who took his own life a day shy of his eighteenth birthday. His denial of the afterlife has persisted even after seeing it for himself, which has left him stranded here for what must be a record for underage souls at eighteen years. Bobby and I have formed an unexpected bond over these few months, and he even served as my unofficial tour guide on my first two visits to the city.

My failed effort to convince him this limbo existence is real led to a project I proposed, in which he gave himself over to the schedule and the staff and conducted an experiment of full cooperation. After a few weeks, though, Bobby became bored and restless. He fell back into his old ways within a month.

"Hey, Bobby. Find any new species today?"

He glances down at his journal. "Sadly, no, but the search is nearly as enjoyable as the discovery, is it not?"

"I wouldn't know. I've never discovered anything. Haven't really searched, either."

He sits down beside me. "I detect a subtlety of discontent. Is there a matter you find troubling today?"

"Several, but you probably shouldn't get me started. I haven't exactly been the most pleasant company."

"I find that highly unlikely. I, for one, consider your companionship to be most enjoyable. While certainly not an exhaustive survey, nor a measurable sample of the population, I feel qualified to conclude as much without hesitation."

A reluctant smile spreads across my face. "You always know just what to say. Undeserved buttering-up never fails to soothe my ego."

"Please don't hesitate to unburden yourself, if the mood strikes you. I find your unhappiness quite distressing."

"You don't need to hear me whine about my problems."

Bobby's cheeks bloom in a subtle hue of pink. "I have to inform you…" He looks away, the flush of color spreading to the rest of his face.

"What is it?" I sit up and scoot close to him.

"I presume most who encounter me find me distant and incapable of forming meaningful bonds with others, but that simply isn't true. There are those for whom I care a great deal, and you are chief among them. I would be remiss not to invite you to share whatever burden weighs upon you. You matter immensely to me, Dez."

"You mean a lot to me, too, which is why I don't want to bother you. I dump my problems on enough people around here."

"You couldn't be a bother if you tried."

"You'd be surprised what I'm capable of. You might just want to get up and run."

He puts a gentle hand on my arm. "Everyone is entitled to the occasional day of being less than their best self."

"I haven't been my best self since before the accident." I toss a pebble into the stream. It shimmers upon entry and leaves a rippling wake behind. "I'm losing who I was, Bobby."

"What do you mean?"

"Before I died, I had it all figured out, you know? I had my whole future planned. College, grad school, a great career. I could see it. I could feel it. I knew exactly who I was and where I was heading. And now…"

"You've come a bit unstuck."

"Unstuck?"

"I speak metaphorically, of course. You had your anticipated position in the world, but that all went out the window when your life came to an abrupt and untimely end."

"Literally." I lean my head on his shoulder and am assaulted by the memory of my final moments.

He puts a hesitant arm around me. His embrace is calming, strong—exactly what I need.

I slip my arms around his waist, drawing comfort from him.

The fact that I don't have to worry about what it all means or where we stand is a relief.

A pang of sorrow hits me as I remember Charlie's words.

"Will I ever matter?"

A sense of guilt creeps in, like I'm betraying Charlie, like we're drifting apart and I'm letting it happen.

"I should go."

I pull free from his tender embrace, my limbs clumsy and leaden. I lurch to my feet.

"Dez, what is it?"

"I don't know. I…it's just too much right now."

"Stay. Talk to me."

"I…"

I can't do this.

"Dez? I don't understand."

I take in the sight of my friend—confused, and worst of all, disappointed. "I'm sorry."

My body takes flight. I stumble back to the path and deeper into the park. I run until my legs give out. Exhausted, I collapse at the foot of a tree in a distant corner of the park.

A familiar squawk beckons from the nearby bushes. With a flurry of screeches and feathers, a beautiful toucan lands at my feet.

"I don't have anything for you, Pip."

He looks at me and lets out another piercing squawk.

"I told you, I don't have anything. Now get."

He taps his beak on my shoe and flaps his wings. I try to shoo him away with my foot, but he hops to the side. His head bobs up and down in a strange dance.

"Just go."

He stands his ground and stares at me.

I can't even manage to be nice to a bird.

"Fine, have it your way. I'm out of here."

Lucky for me, the afterlife is a big place. I let my feet and my shame carry me all the way to Shanti Park. It's the last outpost before the vast wilderness that spreads out in all directions from the center mass of the city, station, towers, and parks. Shanti is much the same as Jhana, but it has the benefit of being far enough away that I have little chance of encountering familiar faces.

I come upon a narrow gravel path off the main trail. It's so overrun with tropical foliage that I almost miss it, but a small sign, barely visible, catches my eye. I pull away overgrown vines and uncover its message:

PEACE COMES FROM WITHIN. DO NOT SEEK IT WITHOUT.

Despite the Kay-like nature of the quote, curiosity wins out, and I decide to press ahead. Leaves and branches slap against my arms and face as the trail snakes through a thick forest, where soft beams of light filter down to the mossy ground. The gravel below my feet gradually thins out until all that remains is a dirt trail.

It proves to be a long walk, and I begin to question my decision to take this trek to who-knows-where when a large frond smacks me square in the face.

I seek solitude, not punishment.

The path widens and begins a gentle downward slope, alleviating my feelings of claustrophobia and regret and heightening my curiosity as to what lies ahead.

I've been walking for at least half an hour in total silence, leaving even the birds behind when I departed the park's main trail.

The forest finally opens up into a large, circular clearing ringed with manicured birch trees. A path of stepping-stones leads up a steep incline into the woods and out of sight. At the center of the clearing is a stone carving embedded in the earth—a circle with eight spokes, almost like a ship's wheel, carved into black stone. My fingers trace the outline, sliding across the smooth-as-glass surface.

I sit cross-legged on the ground and take deep, slow breaths in an effort to push out thoughts of this awful day. Guilt creeps around the edges of my consciousness, nagging and needling me.

The crack of a nearby twig makes my breath catch in my throat.

My eyes spring open and my head jerks in the direction of the sound.

The tip of a black nose and two quivering nostrils lead the way as an inquisitive doe breaches the solitude of the clearing. Her ears flick forward and back. She lets out a snort. Her big, brown eyes stare at me as she approaches, her movements elegant and fluid.

I don't dare move for fear of scaring her, knowing how quickly deer can move. Where I grew up, they're as abundant as squirrels.

Snapping twigs echo from all directions, and four more deer soon join me. The last of them is an enormous buck. They all take the same approach, slow and inquisitive, until all five of them have joined me in the clearing, standing around me in a circle.

"Hello." My voice is soft and gentle as I appraise my visitors.

The sound of melodious chanting drifts like a dense fog from the hills along the stepping-stones. The deer all turn in the direction of the sound, staring up the incline and into the woods.

The first doe turns her gaze back to me.

"Okay, I can take a hint."

CHAPTER SIX

The steady, rhythmic chanting grows louder as I scale the steep hillside. Each stepping-stone brings me closer to the otherworldly chorus. At the crest of the hill is an overlook with panoramic views of a vast valley of rolling, forested peaks and open fields.

A pang of homesickness hits me as I survey the familiar landscape below, identical to the countryside of western Wisconsin which was carved out by glaciers more than ten-thousand years ago.

I push ahead, continuing my journey of self-imposed exile. The chanting spurs me on to a small wooden footbridge crossing a brook. A white marble statue of Buddha acts as a gatekeeper of sorts, a coy smile spread across his face. I reach out and rub his round belly as I pass.

The wooden boards creak under my feet as I cross the brook. The water's laughing melody sings me a welcome and, for a moment, drowns out the sound of the chanting. The exotic scent of jasmine wafts from nearby shrubs decorated with delicate, white flowers.

I follow a stone path to the grounds surrounding a temple.

Eucalyptus and bamboo form a border around the vast space. Neatly manicured hedges and shrubs line the marble walkway passing through a stone gate and leading to the sanctuary.

At the temple's center is an enormous, intricately carved obelisk. A stone railing runs along its perimeter with a smaller tower at each corner.

A dozen monks dressed in vivid orange and crimson robes sit on a platform before a gold Buddha statue at the center of the courtyard. Buddha's expression is the placid look of a man with all the answers and no regrets. Wisps of sweetly scented smoke snake and twist around the men and into the air, combining with their unified chorus in an intoxicating display of scent, sight, and sound.

Part of me feels like I'm intruding on something sacred and private. Even so, I proceed across the courtyard, closer to the ancient ceremony.

I sit next to a column under an awning, hiding in the shade and trying to join the incense drifting in the wind. I can't manage to shake this funk, but the serene chanting and rich scent of exotic spices set me in a contemplative mood.

There are no do-overs, even in the afterlife. Flashes of the morning play through my mind, pummeling me with waves of frustration, guilt, and regret in equal measure, carrying me back across these days of my life, A.D.—after death—to my first.

It was over in a flash. A phone call and my own stupidity met head-on, ending my life in a violent collision of car and fate. Whisked aboard a train and shuttled to Atman Station, I stumbled off, afraid, confused, and hoping for a miracle that wouldn't come. I was destined to join the ranks of the flagged—those denied passage to what lies beyond. As those first desperate hours passed, hope seeped away like a balloon with a pinhole leak, until I drifted down in the weeks that followed, deflated, to begin the work of accepting my death.

Hannah would have been the one person who could talk me through this awful day. Our start was rough, but our bond was quick and deep. A friendship bloomed that neither of us expected, but both of us needed. She helped me through those early, dark days when I was unable to so much as get out of bed, and, in return, I helped her find her confidence. Together we could face this place.

I open my eyes to an empty courtyard. My ears lock in on the silence. The palpable absence of chanting echoes in the quiet. One monk remains, sitting cross-legged on the platform. He radiates contentedness as he looks down at me.

I scramble to my feet. "Sorry, I shouldn't be here."

"Quite the opposite, child." His smile is as warm as his thickly accented voice is soft. He raises a wrinkled hand, beckoning me to step forward. "Come, come."

"No, really. I barged in, and all of this"—I gesture to the Buddha statue and the shrine—"it's not really my thing."

My clumsy fingers scroll through my bracelet's menu in haste. 19:40:05

Free time is almost over.

Missing a session isn't great. Missing two is bad. Three in a row? *Franklin is going to flip out.*

"I should get back to the towers," I say.

"One can neither rush, nor run away from, eternity. Have you not grown weary from the effort of both?"

"Tell that to my floor adviser and his schedule." My shoulders slump. I kick at the hard packed dirt, which sends up swirls of dust.

"Come," he says again, his words gentle and inviting. He pats the open space next to him on the platform. "Unburden yourself."

"The last person who told me that wound up regretting it."

"It is a risk I am willing to take."

I trudge to him, my weight seeming to have doubled in the span of a minute. I sit at the edge of the platform facing the statue of Buddha and his benevolent disciple. The monk's eyes are alight with happiness, a joy like nothing I've ever possessed.

Jealousy rises in me, burning hot and angry in the back of my throat. "Are you here by choice?" It's an accusation more than a question.

"We all are. Every soul whose path has crossed this plane has done so by his or her own hand."

"No, I'm not allowed to leave. There's nothing I wouldn't do to move on."

"If that were true, you would have already done so."

"It's not that easy."

"The road to enlightenment is long and treacherous. We must all choose how we travel and in what way we face the challenges."

"Enlightenment? This isn't exactly Nirvana, so what are you doing here?"

"We are each our own path. Focusing on the journey of another distracts you from your own."

I let out a long, slow breath, trying to rein in my irritation.

"I'm not a fan of fortune cookie soothsaying. No offense."

He laughs and claps his hands. "It may have been centuries since I walked the earth you so dearly miss, but your words are not lost on me."

I tap my feet on the platform. The hollow thud of my rubber soles hitting the wooden planks only increases my anxiety. My drive to escape everyone and everything, including myself, is suffocating.

"I came out to the wilderness to be alone."

"Yet here you are."

"Touché. You have an answer for everything, huh?"

"With a few hundred years practice, you might as well."

My hands form tight fists, which I bounce off my thighs. "Look, I'm not exactly having the greatest day, even by Atman standards. The last thing I want to think about is being here for hundreds of years."

"Perhaps a change of focus is in order. Energy flows through us and surrounds us—"

I wave my hand to stop him. "I think Yoda already beat you to this speech."

"You are quick with your words."

"Is that a polite way of telling me to shut up?"

He shakes his head, smiling. "It is a good thing we have eternity. I believe you and I have much to discuss."

"This isn't the best day for it. I'm not so good at conversation. I can't even pull off self-exile."

"You are on your own path, but you do not have to face your journey alone. Fellow passengers surround you in this existence. Find comfort and strength in them."

"Nobody wants to comfort me right now, believe me."

"Then you need to focus on centering yourself and casting out negativity. What you do not have is not what matters. Accept now. Be present in your reality."

"We'll see what happens." I slide down from the platform. My feet hit the ground with a solid thud. "Thanks for the serenity break, but I've got to get back to my dorm."

"Such haste." A flash of sorrow darkens his eyes. "You are running in quicksand. To resolve your anger, you must first slow down. Rushing through death is counterproductive."

"I know you're trying to help, but I can't do this right now. And I really am going to be in trouble for skipping out on my sessions this afternoon."

"It would do you good to stay, but the choice, as always, is yours to make."

"Maybe I'll come back some time."

"As you wish."

"The chanting was really beautiful." I wave farewell as I make my way back to the path.

"Come see us again, Dez," he calls after me.

How does he know my name?

I spin back around to face the temple, but it's gone. All that remains is an empty field.

Well, screw you, too, Atman.

✦✦✦

I waste no time making my way back to the Administration Building, my surroundings passing by in little more than a blur.

My feet carry me through Admin and back to Crosby's office.

May as well let him get his lecture over with.

Crosby is nowhere to be seen. I stand before his desk and wait for someone—anyone at this point—to come out from an adjacent office. I'd even settle for a new arrival bumbling through the door, because at least it would be someone unhappier than me.

And then I spot it.

His appointment book.

I step around his desk and snatch up the little black calendar. After glancing around to make sure I'm still alone, I begin to thumb through the pages. Finding today's date, I skim the entries, ignoring the alarm bells going off in my head. I've blown right by guilt and landed square on don't-give-a-crap.

08:00—STAFF MEETING—CR1228

10:30—JULIE KALINSKI—MR106

12:00—KAY ROBINSON—OFFICE

I glance up at the clock. 21:00.

He must be gone for the day.

I'm about to return his appointment calendar to his desk when I notice the final entry, scribbled in a hasty print near the bottom of the page.

15:00—GWENDOLYN JACKSON—A.C.—USUAL

The room begins to spin.

CHAPTER SEVEN

It can't be a coincidence. It has to be her.

The appointment book falls from my hands.

Time blurs.

I weave down the path through Jhana Park, sprinting toward the dorm, desperate in my effort to outrun the truth. My brain races as fast as my feet, my thoughts needling me with doubt.

She's here. She's in the city.

How long has Crosby known?

Who else knows?

Betrayal burns my skin like wildfire. My afterlife savior, my confidant, the one I've thought deep down in my soul I can trust—everything we've shared is a lie. I bumbled off the train and into Crosby's world on my very first day, and he's the only reason I've made it this far. What does any of it mean, though, if this has been hanging over our every meeting, our every encounter? My thoughts boil, toxic and venomous.

How could he keep this from me?

I speed through the lobby and make my way to the bank of elevators. Rage and nausea conspire to render my limbs useless, but I manage to quell the trembling in my hands long enough to press the "up" button on the wall.

I pace the elevator, a caged animal. I glance up at the numbers clicking off one by one, then back at the polished metal doors, willing them to open.

23

24

25

The reflection staring back at me is almost unrecognizable. Wild, frantic eyes, a body trembling and on the verge of complete meltdown—I don't know who this is.

40

41

42

Arms across my face, I lean against the doors for a moment and try to slow my breathing and my whirlwind mind.

75

76

77

Will Charlie even speak to me? I may have been awful this morning, but there's no room for shame in my overwhelmed heart. I need him to not be angry.

93

94

95

I burst from the elevator and run toward the suites with

complete disregard for avoiding Franklin and his wrath.

I reach Charlie's door and raise a hand to knock. But I can't do it. I feel ill, shaky, afraid. Backing away, I retreat to the solace of my own room, saying a silent prayer that Abbey will already be in DSR.

I make a beeline for the bathroom and slam the door behind me. At the sink, I turn the cold water on full blast, waiting for it to get an icy chill. My head is spinning. I lean forward and splash the bracing water on my face. One hand fumbles for the tap as the other grabs a towel. I scrub my face dry, the velvety soft material gentle against my skin despite the vigorous pressure I apply.

I cannot wipe away this awful day.

Out of view of prying eyes, I collapse to the floor. It's no use trying to pull myself together.

There is a soft knock at the door. "Dez? Are you okay?"

Abbey.

Just what I need.

"I'm fine."

"Can I come in?"

"I just need a few minutes alone." I lean back against the wall. The towel dangles from my hands as I rest my arms on my knees.

"What's going on?"

Just go away.

"I'm coming in," she says.

The door opens, and I can feel her looking down at me.

"I can't deal with you right now, Abbey."

"Well, we're roommates, and we can't keep this up. There's

got to be a place between angry silence and being at each other's throats. We need to find a way to get along."

"You pick the worst time to—"

"Would you just get over yourself?" She sits down next to me. "Look, we got off to a bad start, and for that, I'm really sorry. I know you were angry with me for spying on you, and I get it. I really do. But that was months ago, and you haven't given me a chance since."

I cover my face with my hands.

"Do you even remember what that first fight was about, Dez? Why you were so pissed at me?"

"I really—"

"It was because I made assumptions without knowing anything about you. And you know what's funny? I mean, think about it. What have you done ever since?"

I lean my head back against the wall.

She's right.

"Can we please just start over?"

"Fine, whatever," I mumble.

"Good. Now, what's going on with you?"

"I don't want to talk about it."

"At all? Or with me?"

"I don't know."

"You want me to get Charlie?"

"I don't think he's really in the mood for me right now."

"I doubt that." She gives me a worried appraisal. "You look awful, no offense."

"Just having a bad day."

She steps back toward the door. "I'm going to get Charlie."

"No." I wave her off. "I'll go."

She holds out a hand to help me up.

"Thanks," I say, surprised by the strength she has in her tiny frame. She pulls me to my feet and follows me out of the bathroom and into the hallway.

I make my second appearance at Charlie's door, this time with Abbey leaning out ours, watching me. I raise my hand again, and this time, I knock.

"Come on in," he calls out.

I gulp in deep breaths of non-existent air and dig deep to find the courage to face him. Blinding fear replaces my anger at Crosby. I may not know much in this crazy afterlife, but I know, without a doubt, that what lies ahead isn't something I can face without Charlie, whether I'm in love with him or not. I need him with all the selfish, thoughtless desire I possess. He's safe. He's familiar. He's strong. He's everything I'm not right now.

I open the door and slide in, slinking despite the invitation.

Charlie glances up from the book he's reading. The quizzical look on his face turns to confusion and something else—*betrayal, is it?*—before going blank. He marks his place and puts the book down on the nightstand next to his bed. His movements are slow and careful, his expression unreadable.

"Hey." My voice trembles. "I'm sorry about this morning." Shame wells up and grips my heart. I feel ice in my chest and trickling down my veins. "I need to talk to you."

He turns his flat gaze on me. "Crosby work his magic? Fix everything for you, so now you can be bothered with us?"

"It's not like that, Charlie."

"It's exactly like that. I will never matter to you the way he does."

His words are a slap in the face that knocks the breath from me. I fall into a chair. "I can't do this right now, Charlie." I try to wish myself away from this room, this dorm, this existence.

"So, now something's wrong that the almighty Crosby can't fix? And I'm your backup plan; is that it?"

"You don't understand."

"You're right. I don't. You've been drifting for weeks, pulling away from me, pushing me out while you cozy up to him. I don't know what else I can do to earn your trust. I need to be a priority. I'm tired of second place, Dez."

My hands fall to my sides. "That's not how it is."

"Really?" His vivid blue eyes are filled with anger and pain, his voice ramped up to a razor sharp pitch. He crosses the room, stopping a few feet from where I sit. "You know what? I'd be lucky to come in second. Between Crosby and Bobby, I'm probably third at best."

"I should leave."

"No, you can stay."

I take a desperate, hopeful breath.

"On one condition. Tell me you love me."

I stare at the floor. "Of course I do."

"No. Say it. Say 'I love you, Charlie,' and you can stay."

"I came here to tell you…" Nausea pulls at my gut. "Crosby's been lying to me, and it's big."

"Damn it, Dez, I don't care about Crosby! Just tell me you love me. Tell me this means something to you. Tell me I matter, more than him, more than Bobby."

"Please…"

He shakes his head. "You can't do it."

"It's not that simple."

"That's only because you're making it complicated. You thrive on chaos, don't you?"

"Charlie, I—"

"Go." He raises a shaking hand and points to the door.

I stand. "No, please. Let's talk about this." I reach for him and try to wipe away the tears streaming down his face.

He bats my hands off and takes a step back. "Just go."

"You don't mean that."

"Go run to Crosby, or Bobby, or whoever your savior of the moment is, because we're done. You've made your choice, and now I've made mine. It's over."

"Charlie, no. We can fix this."

He turns his back and walks to his bed. "Get out of my room."

CHAPTER EIGHT

Curled into the fetal position on my bed, I await the arrival of Dream-State Reflection—the nightly ritual all transitional souls experience at Atman Station. It's a period in which Atman itself shows you the critical life events that have led you to this stranded-between-worlds existence.

On the day I stepped off the train, I was subjected to a procedure that linked my DSR visions with a senior staff member. The nameless woman with dark, cascading hair and a bright blue uniform appears in my visions each night to guide me through the evening's reflections. She's also been known to scold me when I've had a less than stellar day.

Tonight should be a real picnic.

"Desiree," she says, "a minor slip should not become a pattern of behavior. I am confident today's lapse in judgment is one you will not repeat. I needn't remind you of the importance of each and every session.

"In happier news, you will be pleased to hear you've made significant progress in these past months, sufficient enough that tonight will be our last session together. Beginning tomorrow night, you will view DSR entirely on your own. Congratulations.

"Tonight we will focus on what lies ahead, what you're working toward."

It's late autumn. I'm twelve and climbing the towering willow tree in my front yard. My best friend, Aaron, is right on my heels. We shimmy out a thin branch, tempting fate. My fingers are cold and clumsy, numbed by a chilly November wind.

I lower myself onto a thick branch where I sit and stare into the steel gray sky.

Aaron sits next to me, breathing heavy. He follows my gaze. "Gonna snow soon," he says.

"No way." I elbow him. "Not for another couple weeks, I bet."

He grunts at the light impact and rubs his ribs.

"You okay?" I ask.

"I think Grandpa Roy gave me his cold."

"His stupid dog ate through your screen door, and now your grandpa got you sick?"

Aaron gives me that mischievous grin of his. "He and Grandma never go anywhere without their *Shih Tzu*."

We both laugh at his purposeful pronunciation of the dog's breed.

"When do they go back to Florida?" I ask.

"They leave on Monday for St. Louis."

"What's in St. Louis?"

"The Arch."

"No duh, Aaron. What else?"

"My great aunt, Carol." The smile fades from his face. He wipes the back of his hand under his nose. His glove is streaked with blood. He slumps against me, his breathing labored. "I don't feel so good."

"Mom," I scream toward the house. "Something's wrong with Aaron!"

"It's just Grandpa's stupid cold," he murmurs....

Aaron and I sit at the bank of the creek that runs along the back of my parent's property. The mosquitoes haven't yet come out for the season, making for a perfect early summer day.

"It's not fair," I cry, wiping away angry tears.

Aaron's arms are stick thin, his hair long gone. Despite the warm day, he's bundled up in a fleece pullover and a stocking cap. His face is bloated, another side effect of the chemo, the bully that ran wild through his body, beating up everything in its path.

"I just don't get live as long as everybody else. But at least I got to be here," he says.

"Don't say that. There has to be something else, some other doctor. Something they haven't tried yet."

"You have to promise to take care of Boz for me. Mom won't remember to give him his favorite treats."

"I will," I say, gasping against tears.

"Promise?"

I nod.

He tosses a stone into the water and counts as it skips four times before vanishing into the creek. "I'm going to miss this."

"How can you be so brave?" I wrap my arms around myself and fight against the awful truth.

"I don't want to spend the little bit of time I have left being scared. And I don't want you to, either."

I gulp deep breaths of air and try to calm myself. "But I am scared. I can't help it."

"I am, too." He puts his arms around me, and we both cry.

CHAPTER NINE

"Dez?"

Abbey has found me hiding at a corner table in the back of our dorm's cafeteria, face down on my crossed arms.

The metal legs of the chair next to mine drag against the linoleum floor as she sits down. "I wasn't trying to snoop last night, honest. I wanted to be sure you went in to talk to Charlie, and I was waiting in the rec area. I could hear him yelling. And you ran out of the room so quick this morning that I didn't get a chance to talk to you."

"I can't do this, Abbey."

"Look, I know I'm not Hannah." She exhales a slow breath. "But I know what it's like to feel alone."

"Why are you doing this?"

"What?"

"Why are you even bothering with me? It's not like we're friends."

"Could you sit up and talk to me instead of the table?"

I oblige, blinking at the flood of light. "Happy?"

She leans back in her chair and crosses her arms. "Not really."

"I didn't ask you to come after me."

"You're right, you didn't. And you can be as bitchy to me as you've been to everyone else. That's fine, and it's your choice."

I press my palms to my eyes until I see stars. "I'm really not in the mood—"

"You asked why I bother? That's easy. Life is short, but death is forever. If you want to go through this alone, well, that's up to you. Personally, I'm tired of it, so I'm reaching out. You want to do the same? You know where to find me."

The legs of her chair groan against the linoleum as she pushes back from the table. Without sparing me another glance, she walks away, passing Franklin on his way in with two girls. He shepherds his tiny flock to a table near the door. They pull their chairs close to each other, their arms linked, and nod as he talks to them.

After a quick trip to the drink machine, Franklin returns with two sodas. He hands each girl a straw and a drink, and he begin to scan the room.

Our eyes meet, and he strides across the cafeteria toward my table.

This morning just keeps getting better.

Without asking, Franklin pulls back a chair and sits. "I heard you were down here."

"And here I am. Good to know the rumor mill is a reliable source of information."

"Is that where we are? Still mad at everyone?"

"You have no idea."

"Well, you're going to have to suck it up. I have a job for you."

"As I'm already employed in this very cafeteria, my plate is full. I'd suggest putting up a want ad. The lobby gets lots of traffic, so I'm sure you'll find someone in no time."

"Enough!" he bellows. He bangs his fist on the table. His outburst gets the attention of everyone in the immediate area, myself included. "I've had it with your attitude." He glares at me, daring me to respond.

My feet begin to twitch. My knees bounce up and down beneath the table, but I remain silent.

"You are in serious need of some perspective, Dez. When you wind up at Atman, it's pretty easy to feel special, like you're the only one this is happening to." He raps his knuckles on the table and points an accusing finger at me. "But you're not. There's nothing special about dying in a car crash. It's scary, it's hard, but it is not unique. Happens thousands of times a day. You are not the first, nor will you be the last to feel what you're feeling.

"Until you learn to get realistic about what's wrong and why you're here, you're not going anywhere. As bad as you think it is, there is always someone who has it worse. Always. Take those two." He gestures to the girls. "The one on the right? Hasn't said a word since stepping off the train. She's been terrified into silence. And that is why you are going to come with me. You're going to introduce yourself to those two girls, and then you're going to spend your Saturday showing them around. You are surrendering your day off to someone other than yourself, something aside from your own problems."

"I don't get it," I say.

"I thought I was pretty clear."

"No." I swallow back a lump in my throat. "I don't get you. You have it out for me, and I don't know why. Everyone else gets business as usual, but me—"

"No. My approach with each individual is unique. I speak and act in a way that is very deliberate. And I know for a fact that kind and delicate won't work with you, so you get what you get. Now come on."

He stands and walks back toward the girls on the other side of the cafeteria. I consider my options for a split second and realize compliance is the only one that doesn't terrify me with its potential consequences.

I hurry after him and reach the table just as he glances back over his shoulder to make sure I'm following. He pulls out two chairs and we sit across from the girls, who stare at me with matching green eyes and twin looks of stunned detachment. I remember all too well the feeling of my mind retreating, fighting against the crushing, oppressive reality of Atman Station.

"Jenna, Erin, this is Dez." His voice is low and calm in the particular soothing tone reserved for new arrivals. They must have staff meetings to practice that voice. Not that it helps much.

"Dez is going to show you around. We have a beautiful park just outside the dorms, and she'll show you the Administration Building, where you'll have your first meeting with your SGA rep. That will probably happen tomorrow morning."

"Everyone on our floor has Kay," I tell them. The oddity of sitting on this side of the table, looking at the frightened faces of new arrivals, leaves me searching for a foothold.

Franklin stands. "I'm going to leave you ladies to it, but I'll check on you later."

Jenna and Erin nod in unison, their arms still intertwined.

"Saturdays are free days, so take the time to get settled in. No rush." He gives them a warm smile before his hard stare falls on me one last time.

Message received.

I try to gather my thoughts. Focus. Push out Charlie, Bobby, Abbey, and most of all, Crosby. Yesterday was a nightmare, but it's one I don't have time for. Not now.

My final living moments flood my memory and return me to the side of the highway, my mom's car a crumpled wreck, my body a broken mess.

The train. The station.

"You died today, Dez."

It was too much. I couldn't process what was happening. It left me overwhelmed, just as they are now.

I have to help them. Or at least try.

I sit up straight, forcing everything from my mind except the two souls sitting before me. "Okay, well, like he said, I'm Dez." I smile, trying to connect in some way with these terrified girls. "So, which one of you is which?"

"I'm Erin, and that's Jenna," says the girl sitting on the left.

"I know it's a lot to take in. I was where you are just a few months ago, and I remember exactly what you're going through. We're going to take things slow. I think the park's a good starting point."

On our way out of the cafeteria, I grab some grapes from the fruit station and fill my pockets. The girls don't seem to notice. They stick close together, practically glued to my side as we pass through the lobby and out into the park.

"Is this really happening?" Erin asks. "I know we've been here almost a whole day, but it still doesn't seem real."

I guide them over to a nearby bench, and we sit. "It wish it wasn't, but it is."

"We were getting pretzels in the food court." Erin says. "It sounded like firecrackers. Jenna was…she was the first. The blood was so red in her hair." Tears spill down her cheeks as she reaches over to touch Jenna's blond locks. "And then it was me."

Jenna puts her arm around her. They huddle together.

"I'm so sorry that happened to you. I know you're scared, but you're safe now. Just let yourselves feel the peace. The stillness. The calm. It really does help."

They close their eyes.

"Slow your thoughts down," I say. "Try and push everything else out. Just be here in this second. Listen to the birds, the breeze in the trees, the water, all of it."

Their shoulders drop. Erin inhales a deep breath through her nose, blowing the air out her mouth. She reaches for Jenna's hand as she opens her eyes. "Talk to me, Jenna," she pleads.

Jenna opens her eyes, her muscles tensing as fear grips her once again. She shakes her head. Her lower lip trembles.

"You have to say something," Erin begs. "I'm scared too."

Jenna stares at her lap and shakes her head in slow motion.

"She just needs some time. Everyone reacts differently. Some of us scream and yell, some can't stop crying, others"—I turn to Jenna—"go silent." My hand slides into the overflowing pocket of my cargo pants. "Let's walk some more. It'll be good for you, and I want you to meet somebody."

They give me a cautious appraisal.

"You'll like him, I promise."

"Okay," Erin sniffles.

"Let's try something," I say. "Erin, you walk over here." I point to my left side. "And Jenna, you come over to this side." I point to my right.

They freeze in their tracks.

"Just for a minute, okay?"

They manage to untangle from one another and fall in place to either side of me.

"That's not so bad, right?"

Erin's gaze darts around, tracking every sound as we make our way down the path and deeper into the park. "Where are we going?"

"Not far, I promise."

We walk to a clearing by the river, and I reach into my pocket to grab a handful of grapes. "Pip," I call out. "Come on, buddy. I have some new friends for you to meet."

"Who's Pip?"

"You'll see."

As always, Pip makes a grand entrance, landing on a shrub in a flurry of feathers and squawks, startling the girls. They jump and grab my arms.

"It's okay; you're safe." I disentangle from their grips and step up to Pip. "There you are." He gobbles down the first handful of fruit and lets out a screech. "I know, buddy. I'm sorry about yesterday." I run my fingers down the top of his beak.

Jenna and Erin ease toward him.

"He's pretty," Erin says.

"This is Pip. He's the prettiest bird in the afterlife," I say, stroking his head. He preens, soaking up the compliment as though he understands what I'm saying.

"Is he a toucan?"

"He is." I hand each girl a bunch of grapes. "Go ahead. You can feed him."

They stare wide-eyed at Pip as their trembling hands hold out the fruit. He must be able to sense their delicate state, because he takes the grapes carefully, eating with slow, deliberate bites and not his normal, vacuum cleaner inhalation.

Jenna holds up her hand, hesitant.

"Can we pet him?" Erin asks for her.

"What do you think, Pip?"

He rubs his head against Jenna's hand like a cat.

"I know you two just got here, but I have something I need your help with." I give him one last pat before I step back, letting the girls take over. "Pip was my roommate Hannah's bird, and he's very special. She moved on, but Pip stayed, just like all the animals. He belongs here in the park. He was here long before Hannah and will be long after we've all moved on. For now, though, he needs someone to take care of him. I've been doing it for the short term, until we can find him new caretakers. I think you might be perfect for the job, but it's a lot of responsibility. Do you think you could come feed him every day for me?"

They look up at me, tiny sparks lighting up their dulled eyes. They each give me a solemn nod.

"Are you sure? He's pretty high maintenance. He's really finicky, so you'll have to be sure to bring him a variety of fruit."

"We can do it," Erin says.

"You'll have to come every day and spend some time with him."

"We will. We promise."

"What do you think, Pip?" He screeches and nudges Jenna's hand. "Looks like a yes, to me."

He takes off into the trees, as loud going as he was arriving.

✦✦✦

Erin and Jenna, back to arm-in-arm travel, stick close by my side as we make our way down the corridor toward Kay's office, their mouths agape as we navigate the labyrinth that is the Administration Building.

"They didn't show you around yesterday during orientation?"

They shake their heads in unison. "No," Erin says. "They just gave us these big manuals, told us the rules, told us we'll be feeling a lot of emotions in the first few weeks, that kind of stuff. Isn't that what happened your first day?"

"I didn't go to my orientation. I have no idea what they tell you."

"You didn't? Why not?"

"I went to the SGA Assignment office after ticketing told me I was flagged, and I sort of freaked out."

"Really?" Erin looks impressed.

I nod.

"Where is that, anyway? We were sent from ticketing right to orientation, 'cause it was just about to start. Otherwise, we would have had to wait for the next session."

"It's not that far. A few minutes' walk."

"Can you show us? The guy running our orientation said we need to know where it is, 'cause the staff there is going to be helping us with the day-to-day stuff or something."

My hands tighten into fists. "I'll walk you by after I show you where you'll be having your sessions, but then we should head back to the dorms."

We stop outside Kay's office. I reach for the door just as it starts to open.

And out walks Crosby.

A tremble runs from my scalp to my toes.

"Hey, you." A smile spreads across his face. He nudges me with his elbow. "Showing around some new girls, huh? Check you out."

"Don't touch me," I warn through clenched teeth.

His smile fades into bewilderment. "What's going on?"

I turn to the girls and plaster a reassuring smile on my face. "I need to talk to Crosby for a second. Wait here. I'll be right back." I storm a safe distance down the hallway, out of earshot, with Crosby close on my heels.

"What's wrong?" He grabs my elbow, and I spin around to face him.

"I told you not to touch me." Rage burns at the back of my throat. "Don't you ever do that again."

"What's going on? What happened?"

"You happened, Crosby," I say a little too loud. I glance back at Erin and Jenna and lower my voice. "You and your lies, pretending like I mean something to you. After everything I've shared, after you tell me I matter to you."

Mouth agape, he stares at me. "What are you talking about?"

"You're a liar."

"What? I…what do you mean?"

"Does this ring a bell? Gwendolyn Jackson, fifteen-hundred, usual. Or is the name just a coincidence?"

All the color drains from his face. His shoulders slump. "Dez—"

"Go ahead, deny it. I dare you."

"I can explain." His voice is thin, stretched to its limit.

"Really? Is that why you were in such a hurry to ditch me yesterday? That was your important meeting? With her?"

Crosby hangs his head. "Dez, I—"

"How could you keep this from me?" Violent fury fills me. I lash out, my hands shoving against his chest with all I have. His powerful frame towers over me, yet he stumbles back, making no effort to resist my attack. "Were you ever planning to tell me my birth mother is here?"

"Please just let me explain."

"Don't bother. I'm done."

CHAPTER TEN

I barely recall leading the girls back to the dorms and giving them a quick, inadequate tour. They deserved much better than me today. Somehow, they've wound up back in their room while I sit alone in a distant section of the library, hiding out where there is little chance of being bothered. Sitting on the floor in the Hellenic languages section isn't high on my list of ways to wait out eternity, but it's quiet. And it's lonely. Who knows? Maybe I deserve alienation, having thrown my selfishness around like confetti these past twenty-four hours.

My birth mother is in the city.

I have one single, fleeting memory of her. Just her face, hiding behind her hands, her smiling eyes peeking between her fingers. That's it. I have no recollection of the crash that took her life and gave me a new family—parents who would raise me, adore me, give me all their love, and hope for a future I'd never get to enjoy.

I close my eyes and stretch back across time to a distant voice singing. A mobile hangs over me, vivid pinks and greens turning in a lazy circle.

"Lullaby and goodnight, thy mother's delight
Bright angels beside my darling abide."

"Dez?"

I'm pulled into to the present by my name, a rope tied around my waist that drags me back to reality. Franklin stands before me at a respectful distance, as though I might lunge at him like a rabid animal.

He might regret not arming himself with a tranquillizer dart.

I lean my head back against the wall as I heave out an enormous sigh. "Crosby, right?"

"He's worried."

"He should be."

Franklin comes closer and sits down, his back to a bookcase, facing me. "Look, I understand you're having a bad couple of days full of upheaval, and knowing what you think you now know isn't helping."

"What I think I know? So, you mean he hasn't been hiding the fact that my biological mother is in the city? Is it a different Gwendolyn Jackson he's been meeting with in their 'usual' place?"

"It isn't that simple."

"She's here. He didn't tell me. Period."

"And how exactly did you make this discovery?"

"It doesn't matter."

"Have you considered that there may be reasons beyond his control which have kept him from telling you? That he lobbied heavily for this information to be shared but was prevented from doing so?"

"He's a big boy. It would've taken two seconds to say, 'Oh, by the way, Dez, your birth mom is here. Thought you might want to know.' And death would go on. I'd still be here, but I'd be a lot less pissed off than I am right now."

I glare at Franklin, daring him to interrupt my rant. He doesn't. He simply watches me with placid eyes.

"Why does everyone think they know what's best for me? All you volunteers, you have no idea what it's like for us, do you? Is it fun to watch us suffer? To make us jump through all these hoops so we can maybe, someday, get to whatever's next, which you conveniently refuse to discuss with us?"

"Are you done?" Franklin's voice is low and even, almost disinterested.

"Not by a long shot."

"Well, then, go for a walk. Blow off some steam. Have a relaxing evening. Do whatever it is you need to do to get it together, because tomorrow morning at ten o'clock, you have a meeting in Kay's office. You, me, Kay, and Crosby. And you'd best be there."

"Crosby? Are you kidding me?"

"This is not open for debate."

Every inch of me hurts, as though the tectonic plates of the universe have shifted, landing all their weight upon me. It's suffocating. Stifling.

"What did I do, Franklin?"

"What do you mean?"

"To deserve all of this? Did I upset the balance? Enrage some higher power that now has it out for me?"

"Deserve has nothing to do with it. None of us can control

the challenges thrown at us, but we can choose how we face them. That should be your focus. We each leave a footprint, and you have to decide what yours will be. Do you want to rampage through death, tromping on everyone and everything in your path, or do you want to be thoughtful and deliberate, stepping with care? Life isn't fair, and neither is death. It's just something you're going to have to get used to."

"I can't do this anymore."

"There's no other choice. You've got to shift your focus. Where you should be, what you wish was different, those things don't matter. They're only going to hold you back."

"I worked so hard. I did everything right. Star student. Athlete. Never stayed out past curfew. Never got in trouble. And for what?"

"Chin up, Dez. It's going to get better." He reaches over and pats my shoulder, then stands.

"It's not like it can get much worse."

He walks out, leaving me alone with the books and the oppressive thought of sitting in a meeting with the trifecta of doom: Kay, Franklin, and, worst of all, Crosby. Meanwhile, the one person I spent my life wanting to meet, to talk to, to ask a million questions of, is in the city I've been forbidden from setting foot in again.

All the adults who arrive at the station and discover they're flagged are housed in the regulated sections of Atman City, where they stay in apartments and meet with counselors, much like we do here in the dorms. But Atman City is dangerous, brimming with criminals, from petty con men under minimal supervision to closely monitored murderers and rapists, all hoping for a shot at redemption. Despite the perils I know all too well, the city has an allure, an intrigue I just can't shake. And now it has my birth mother.

I run my hand across the spines of the books on the shelf nearest me, comforted by the feeling of the collected knowledge passing beneath my fingers.

"I would have imagined you a follower of the romance languages." Bobby looks down from the end of the row. He holds an enormous book to his chest, a sad smile on his face.

I struggle to my feet, my back pressed against the cold cinder blocks of the curved wall. "Bobby." My mind scrambles to find words that simply don't exist. "I'm so sorry about yesterday."

He slides the tome carefully into its place on the shelf. "You have nothing to apologize for. I'm sorry if I did something to upset you. If I've overstepped the boundaries of our friendship in any way—"

"Don't say that. I already hurt Charlie, and I don't think I can undo it. I…" The words pile up into a jumbled mess in my throat.

He closes the distance between us. "Do not concern yourself with fears of where we stand. You are my friend, and that will not change."

"I don't know what to do, Bobby." I lean against him. My cheek rests against his chest, and I listen to the beating of his long-dead heart.

"Shall we try again?" he asks. "You can tell me anything, you know."

"Thank you."

"I have an idea," he says, glancing out a nearby window

that looks onto the park. "Care to join me tonight for some stargazing?"

I stand up straight, puzzled. "How?"

✦✦✦

"What, exactly, are we doing out here?"

I help Bobby spread a blanket out on the soft grass in Jhana Park. His trusty electric lantern bathes us in warm light, cutting a small path through the black night.

"You need to unburden yourself. We'll stargaze, and you can tell me about your troubles."

"But there are no stars to gaze at."

"A minor detail we can easily work around."

"I haven't been so good at expressing myself, lately. You might want to rethink this whole 'unburden yourself' plan."

"It is a risk I am willing to take." He holds his hand out and motions to the blanket.

I sit down, reluctant.

Bobby sits next to me and pulls a flashlight from his messenger bag. "It is July, correct?"

"It is. Not like it matters, though."

"It matters a great deal." He lies on the blanket and flips on the flashlight. "Ursa Major is right there." He points the beam of light to the northern sky and traces the outline of the Great Bear. "See?"

I lie back, letting my imagination play along. "And the Big Dipper's handle makes up his tail."

The beam is guided by Bobby's deft hand to the imaginary position of each star. "Alkaid, Mizar and Alcor, Alioth, Megrez, Dubhe, Merak, and Phad." He flickers the flashlight off and on again to the right of the Big Dipper . "And there is Ursa Minor."

"Polaris," I say, pointing to the end of the Little Dipper's handle.

"Quite right." He sweeps the flashlight across the sky, to the right of Ursa Minor and down a bit. "There's Cepheus the King."

I shift on the blanket to face him. "You got to see Halley's Comet, didn't you?"

"I did."

"Lucky guy."

"It was actually the worst viewing in two-thousand years, so one could say I was decidedly *un*lucky."

"I thought for sure I'd be there to see it come back around."

"Given life expectancy parameters, it was an entirely reasonable assumption."

"I never got to see the Southern Cross." Regret and longing pull at my heart.

"Allow me to show you," he says. "Alpha Crucis." The flashlight's beam slashes into the black as Bobby traces another imaginary constellation. "Gamma Crucis." The fingers of his free hand brush against mine as he draws the stars I'll never see. "Delta Crucis." His arm sweeps to the final point of the cross. "Beta Crucis."

"Thank you," I whisper as I slip my hand into his.

"You are most welcome."

"Charlie broke up with me." The stinging words tumble out, hurried and clumsy. "Whatever we had, it's over."

"I am sorry to hear that."

"It seems like everything is falling apart."

"Tell me."

I fight back tears as I tell him everything, from the ugly details of my fight with Charlie to the painful lie Crosby has been harboring.

He puts a comforting arm around me. "That is a lot for anyone to take in the span of a single day."

"And that meeting tomorrow. That might be the worst of all. I wish I didn't have to go."

"The choice, as always, is yours to make."

"Franklin was pretty clear that attendance is not optional."

"We should really do something about that."

"Like what, stage a coup?"

He smiles. "Too drastic?"

"I don't think our rebellion of two would fare well, and I'd rather not be remembered as the Bonnie to your Clyde."

"Quite right. We'd be much better as the Curies."

"I don't know what I'd do without you, Bobby." I sigh. "I don't even want to go back to the dorm. I can't take running into Charlie again, not right now. And DSR is going to be a nightmare, I'm sure."

"Well then, let's stay."

"What, here? In the park, all night?"

"I know the perfect spot."

I reach for him and he takes my hand, our fingers twining around one another in a delicate knot.

He leads me by lantern light to a secluded stand of evergreens on the bank of the stream that winds a lazy, crooked path through the park. The lantern's soft glow is our small oasis in the dark, our shelter from the troubles of the day.

We sit in contemplative silence, our backs against the trunk of a towering pine as a strange feeling builds between us. I lean against his shoulder but then sit back up, hesitant.

"I don't mind." He puts his arms around me and holds me close. I huddle against him, for the first time noticing the taut muscles hiding beneath his loose-fitting shirt.

Nerves play at my stomach, charged by the spark of an unidentified, yet very real, change passing between our two souls.

"Do you still think all of this is your imagination?"

"I'm not certain what I believe anymore." His trembling hand moves in slow motion, coming to rest on my cheek.

A sudden, invasive image of Charlie fills my mind.

The pain on his face.

His trembling hand pointing to the door.

His angry words.

Our first kiss that took my breath away.

His arms, his love, sheltering me from the pain, pulling me back from the abyss.

He was my everything.

What have I done?

What am I doing?

I wince, pulling away from Bobby.

Bobby looks away, ashamed. "I'm sorry. I presume too much."

"I'm the one who should apologize." I rest my head on his chest, selfish for the comfort of his embrace. "You don't deserve to be dragged into my mess."

"There is nowhere I would rather be."

"Asking you to wait out the night with me is too much, Bobby, especially after—"

"I won't leave you alone. Not like this." His finger traces the contour of my back, sending shivers up my spine. "I will stay with you until your meeting, and after, if you'll have me."

CHAPTER ELEVEN

Knowing Bobby will be waiting for me on the bench just outside Kay's office is only a small measure of comfort. My knees bounce up and down in a nervous rhythm as I wait in the reception area for Kay to call me back. Sparks of energy dot my darkened vision. My hands tingle. I can only hope her calming influence will have some effect on my current state—equal parts fear and fury. It's all I can do to resist the urge to flee.

After several agonizing minutes have passed, the door behind the reception desk opens, and Kay steps into the waiting area. "Hi, Dez. Come on back." Her breezy demeanor is subdued, but she still offers up a warm smile.

I force myself from my seat and follow her through the door.

"Thank you for coming back this morning."

"It's not like I had a choice." I stop as the door closes behind me.

Kay turns around, a puzzled look on her face. "What is it?"

"Well, since Franklin demanded I show up for this meeting, I have some demands of my own."

Her eyebrows dart up. "Let's hear them."

I survey the hallway before us. "For one, I want no lectures about skipping Morning Meditation and Three P today."

"Fair enough," Kay says. "You've been in upheaval since Friday afternoon, so we will let it slide." Her eyes lock with mine. "What else?"

"There's a big conference room back here somewhere, right? Isn't that it?" I motion to the door just to our left.

"Yes. Why?"

"If you want to talk, we're doing it in there. I am not going in your little office with Crosby. It's too small, and if he comes within ten feet of me, I'm going to scream." I open the door without knocking. Finding the room empty, I flick on the light and shut the door behind me.

The room is filled by a long oval table and cushy office chairs, several of which are set against the back wall. I choose one in the corner, where I sit. There are no windows, no beautiful views to occupy my mind as I wait. I tilt back and lean my head against the wall, my eyes closed as I try to slow my pounding heart and calm my trembling hands. I take deep, deliberate breaths, and turn my thoughts to Bobby and our quiet spot by the stream. My mind drifts back to the comfort of his arms.

There is a soft knock at the door. Kay enters, with Franklin right behind her. He closes the door.

"Crosby is in the hallway," Kay says. "We want to talk to you before I bring him in."

Franklin takes a seat at the table and pulls back the chair next to him. "Why don't you sit by me?"

"We don't want to make this any harder on you than it's already been," Kay says.

With a snort of derision, I give in and sit beside Franklin.

"Before I bring in Crosby," Kay says, "I'd like to tell you a few things. First, he feels awful about what happened. He is beside himself over this."

"Good."

Kay sighs. "I know you're angry, but please know that not notifying you of your birth mother's presence was my decision, not his."

"And who are you to decide that? I have a right to know about her, to know she's here. No matter what you told him, he should have told me anyway."

She places her hands on the table, almost as though she's trying to physically steer the conversation. "We'll delve into all of this once Crosby joins us, but first, I want to discuss a few ground rules. There is to be no screaming or yelling, and no interrupting. Let him say what he has to say, and you will be given the opportunity to do the same. I want to keep this discussion civil and productive. And keep the sarcasm to a minimum."

"Fine, whatever."

Kay steps back into the hallway.

"You're going to be okay," Franklin says.

"You don't know that."

"It's better than average odds, though." He reaches over and squeezes my arm.

He's being too nice.

"Just remember to breathe," he says.

"We're dead, remember?"

Kay returns with Crosby. They sit across the table from us within my ten-foot bubble, but I couldn't scream if I wanted to.

Kay clears her throat and flips open my ever-growing file.

"Hey, kiddo," Crosby says. His voice is hoarse, unsteady. He reaches across the table toward me.

I pull my hands back. "Don't."

"Kay, you want to start?" Franklin asks.

She nods. "I really must stress this point: Crosby wanted to tell you about your birth mother, but I felt it was best for both you and her to keep you apart. She knows you're here and wants to meet you. It is my opinion that neither of you is ready to deal with the emotional turbulence that a meeting would bring at this time. You've only been here a few months, and despite what you think, it is in your best interest to steer clear of her for the time being. Telling you about her would only have complicated matters."

"Because they're so simple now."

She ignores my snipe. "Crosby has some things he'd like to say, and I would appreciate it if you would keep in mind what we've just discussed. Please let him speak without interruption, and then you'll have a chance to say whatever you'd like. Are we in agreement?"

A scoff is the only answer she's getting from me.

Crosby looks at me, but I avoid his eyes. "Dez, I'm so sorry. I hate that you found out like this, and I wish you could know how awful I feel for hurting you." His voice is sad, his words strained. "You've been through a lot—"

"You have no idea."

"No interrupting," Franklin says. "Remember?"

I stare at the table, my eyes locked on the wood grain pattern as Crosby continues.

"We can work this out if you just give me a chance. Talk to me. Ask me anything you want and I'll tell you the truth, because I want to fix this."

I speak through clenched teeth. "Fine. How long have you known?"

"That she's here, and she's your birth mother?" He takes a deep breath. "Since I looked you up in our system that first time on the day you arrived. Our network shows familial relationships. Any relatives—birth or adoptive—who are at Atman at the same time are linked."

My hands clench into tight fists in my lap. My nails dig into my palms. "Why have you been meeting with her?"

Crosby and Kay exchange a look. She nods her approval and he continues. "Between her guilt about putting you in danger and her unresolved grief over the loss of her husband, she's had a lot to deal with. She was very close to being able to move on when she learned you were here and that you both died under similar circumstances. She backslid. As you and I formed a bond, I was instructed to meet with her on a semi-regular basis to discuss…" He rubs his face with his hands. "To discuss you. How you're doing, that sort of thing."

"What does semi-regular mean?"

"Every two weeks."

I do a quick calculation in my head. "Since I've been here, you've met with her seven times and haven't bothered to mention it to me?"

Crosby nods. Silence envelops the room.

"So Friday when I was pouring my heart out to you, and you said you had a meeting to get to, you meant you were heading to the city to see my birth mother?"

Crosby hunches down in his seat, silent, his shoulders slumped.

"Well?"

"Yes," he admits.

"What's the point, Kay?" I ask, my gaze fixed on Crosby.

"The point of this meeting? Or keeping you from your birth mother?"

"Any of it. If you're trying to fix things between Crosby and me, don't bother."

"It is interesting to note your open hostility toward Crosby yet your seeming indifference toward me, when it was my decision to keep the information from you. I think we should explore the feelings behind the compartmentalization of your anger."

"That's easy. I expect it from you."

Kay is scribbling notes in my file folder, but my words stop her pen's progress across the page. "Care to elaborate?"

I throw my hands up. "Sure, why not?" My palms come down hard against the table.

"Dez," Franklin warns.

"It's okay," Kay says. "Go ahead."

"Well, for starters, we've never been friends. You have a very clear role in my afterlife. You make clinical decisions based on getting me the hell out of here, so I don't expect anything more. I'm just one of a million kids—or a billion, for all I know—who've come through here, just another thread in this tapestry of yours, and I get that. Crosby, on the other hand…" The truth freezes me and pulls my gaze back to the table.

Franklin puts a hand on my shoulder. I shrug it off and spin in my chair to face him.

"Don't. Nice Franklin doesn't work on me, remember? So don't think you're going to step up as some sort of Crosby substitute."

He pulls his hand back in surrender. "I wasn't trying to—"

"Take it easy," Kay says, raising her hands in a mediating gesture. "Let's try to keep those ground rules in mind, shall we? Why don't we get back to what you were saying, because I think you're hitting on something very important. What were you about to say about Crosby?"

"I thought I mattered." My voice quakes.

Crosby gives me a pleading look. "Let me explain."

"You protected me; you got me through all the times I fell apart. And now it's over. What am I supposed to do?" I stagger to my feet.

Franklin stands, his hand on my arm. "It's going to be okay."

"No, it's not." I pull against him, but he holds on. "Let go of me."

"Dez, sit down," Kay commands, pointing to my chair.

I've never heard her raise her voice before.

"I know you've only been here a few months," she says, "and you're just learning to swim, but drastic times call for drastic measures, so I'm tossing you in the ocean."

I fall back into my chair.

She throws a frustrated glare from Crosby to me. "Franklin and I are going to leave the two of you here, and neither of you is to leave this room until you've sorted out your differences. Do I make myself clear?"

Franklin meets my alarmed look with a shrug. "Better do what she says. Eternity is a long time."

Kay flips the file shut and strides out of the room.

Franklin walks over to Crosby and gives his shoulders a reassuring squeeze. With a final pat on the back, he walks out and shuts the door behind him.

Crosby reaches across the table again, his hand stretching toward mine. "We can fix this."

"Don't." I pull my hand back. "I have nothing else to say to you." Tears begin to trickle down my cheeks, little droplets of treachery putting my emotions on public display.

"I wanted to tell you, I really did."

"You're always trying to fix me, Crosby, but you can't fix your lies. It's over. We're over." I push back from the table.

"You can't leave. Not until we work this out."

"Why? What are they going to do to me—make me stay longer than forever?"

He reaches for my arm as I brush by, but I jerk away and push through the door.

I don't look back as I head into the waiting area and pick up speed. I hit the final door at a run.

Bobby stands as I burst into the hallway outside Kay's office. His smile fades. "What happened?"

"I've made a decision." I wipe away my tears like I'm swatting a fly. "I want to find my birth mother. Feel like going M.I.A.?"

CHAPTER TWELVE

Bobby and I meet on an isolated bench at the edge Jhana Park to plan our trip.

"You got everything you need?" I ask.

He pats the messenger bag sitting next to him. "I never go to the city without supplies." Already wearing his own hoodie, he hands me one to put on. Sleeves more than three-quarter length are forbidden for tower residents, as we are required to have our identification bracelets visible at all times. The long sleeves of Bobby's black market sweatshirts help us blend in during city visits.

I pull on the too-big hoodie. "Did you see Franklin?"

"I saw no sign of him, although I can't be certain of his whereabouts, as I was quick to retrieve what I needed from my room."

"He's probably still with Kay and Crosby, figuring out what to do about me."

Soft light filters through the trees, casting us in a warm, sleepy glow in stark contrast to my jangling nerves.

"We'll have to be exceedingly cautious if you wish to travel in daylight," he says.

"The city can't be more dangerous in the daytime, can it?"

"No, but we will be without cover of darkness to mask our movements, thus greatly increasing the probability of an eagle-eyed staff member catching us as we make our way there."

This trip is a shot of adrenaline setting me ablaze with anticipation. The city perpetually beckons, and this time I'm giving in. I'm an addict about to get her fix. My fingers twist at my braids as Bobby plots our course. My mind shoves back the creeping doubt and nagging fear. Excitement takes their place, having tied up Sensible Dez and shoved her in a corner somewhere.

"Are you sure you want to go with me? There's no way we're not going to get in trouble for this. I'm sure I'm already in deep for leaving like I did. This definitely won't help."

"The city is an old friend of mine, but it is dangerous, especially for the inexperienced. I would be quite concerned about your safety should you go alone. You've already suffered one close call."

"Is it crazy that I want to find her? The city is gigantic."

"Yet the one thing of which we have an endless supply is time, is it not?"

"Where do we even start?"

"I know just the place." He stands and holds out his hand. "Shall we?"

We head deep into the woods with Bobby making frequent

checks over his shoulder to be sure we aren't being followed. The familiar rush of the journey surges through me as we pass through the dense brush at the edge of the park and approach the well-worn path leading up to the awaiting city.

Bobby stops. "Once we are on the path, we will have to make haste but not run. We want to avoid detection without standing out."

I bounce on the balls of my feet, ready to go. "Makes sense."

"This is where we will be most exposed." He squeezes my hand. "Ready?"

"Let's do this."

It's a quick trip up the hill and across the tracks, and we arrive at the outer limits of the city without incident. We mingle with the foot traffic on the same cobblestone street Bobby led me to on my first visit.

"Wow," is all I can manage as I stop to take in the sight of the varied architecture climbing up the hill before us. It's been months since I've been here, and the view is overwhelming.

"It is particularly lovely, is it not?"

"Do you ever get used to it?"

"It is difficult to quantify visceral reactions, especially in an indeterminate time frame, but in my own experience, I have yet to lose my appreciation for its beauty."

"I never thought I'd see the city again up close."

I gawk at the sites, the hodgepodge of stunning buildings with no apparent pattern or semblance of order, the strange array of people crowding the street. Souls from decades and even centuries past still cling to the habits and garb of their era, unfazed by the passage of time.

A woman in a corset and bustle with her hair in ringlets marches primly down the street beside a man in a black suit and top hat. They're in the middle of a heated argument and seem not to notice anyone else. The man's shoulder connects with mine as he passes, which causes me to stagger back a step.

He tips his hat. "I beg your pardon, Miss."

"Don't speak to street urchins!" the woman hisses.

His cheeks bloom in a vivid shade of red. "I shall not abide such a tone from the likes of you."

Bobby takes my hand and guides me away from the bickering couple. "We should keep moving."

We make our way toward Club Bromios, a nightclub that, for the moment, is deserted. I follow Bobby like a child. His hand pulls me down the street and I stumble along, staring at the buildings. A 1950s diner we once visited, a Victorian house, and a medieval inn stand side by side in the strangest business district I've ever seen.

Just before we reach the inn, he turns down a narrow, winding alley. I stop, hit with a sinking feeling about our destination.

"Bobby, no. We can't."

"This is our best chance."

"But, Crosby." I lean back against a grimy wall, afraid my legs will give out. "I can't do that again."

"I imagine Crosby is rather busy dealing with his own troubles. Nero's Fiddle will be the last thing on his mind."

"He always knows." Panic blossoms and makes me second-guess my hasty decision to venture to Atman City.

"You wish to find her, do you not?"

I scuffle my foot on the alley's bare ground. The toe of my

shoe drags through the hard-packed earth. "I'm not exactly good at breaking the rules."

"Fortunately for you, I excel at it." He slips a finger under my chin and lifts my gaze to his. A smile spreads across his face.

My face goes hot. "I like this side of you, Bobby."

I follow him down the zigzagging alley, my mind abuzz with a million thoughts.

Despite Bobby's newfound confidence, a twinge of anxiety hits me when we reach Nero's Fiddle, a rundown tavern where I ran headlong into Crosby's unholy wrath on my second visit to the city. The blowback led to an angry exchange with the owner when I dared to show my face at Nero's again a few nights later.

Bobby knocks on the heavy wooden door.

"I don't think he's going to be too happy to see me," I say.

"Nero is swift of temper, indeed. But he dispenses forgiveness in equally quick measure. He will have long since forgotten the incident."

An iron bar in the door slides open, and a pair of beady eyes stares out at Bobby. The bar slides shut and the door opens.

"Bobby, to what do I owe the pleasure?" Nero's round belly leads the way as he steps out. His face, more grimace than smile, falls into a frown as he catches sight of me. "Oh, no. Not her." His robust frame blocks the entrance.

"What was that you were saying?" I ask Bobby, my jaw set.

"You are a reasonable man, Nero. You cannot possibly hold Dez solely responsible for the unfortunate occurrence in this fine establishment. It was I who brought her here, and Crosby whose angry reaction led to these harsh feelings you harbor. If you are to hold a grudge against anyone, it would be most reasonable to place blame upon Crosby or me."

Nero scowls as he considers Bobby's words. "What is it you two want?"

"We need your expertise, and I can think of no one else in all of Atman with the sorts of connections we need to utilize. You are singularly qualified for the task at hand."

Nero takes a cautious look down the alley. His head swivels on his beefy neck as he checks all directions. "Enough with the buttering-up. This isn't exactly the best timing, but come on." He lumbers back into the tavern and holds the door for us. As I cross the threshold, he narrows his gaze and points an accusing finger at me. "But I expect no trouble from you, girlie. Are we clear?" He swings the door shut and rams the bolt into its locked position.

I nod, afraid if I say a word we'll be kicked back out into the alley.

He huffs and puffs his way across the room and steps behind the bar, where he grabs a rag that's about a month past clean and sets to work on a grimy mug. His gaze locks on two men seated at a small table in the corner farthest from the door.

They speak in hushed voices, punctuated by occasional laughter. Both are hard, harsh-featured men whose very presence makes the hairs on the back of my neck stand up. Sensing our focused attention on them, they turn in our direction.

A dizzying rush of energy hits me as my eyes lock with the raven-haired man on the left. His hazel eyes gleam, and he flashes a frightening smile.

"Hello, pretty," he says, his voice a low and silken growl.

His coppery-haired companion leans in and whispers

something. This sets off a short, heated discussion before they turn their attention back to us.

Their hard stares send pinpricks up my spine. I take a step back toward Bobby.

The two men return to their conversation, and Nero turns his attention back to us. "You kids gonna stay here all day, or are you gonna tell me what you want?"

Bobby takes a seat on one of the rickety barstools. I stand next to him and cling to his arm. "We are trying to locate someone," he says.

Nero pauses to inspect the glass he's cleaning. "Best of luck to you. This's a big city."

"It certainly is, which is why we would be most appreciative of your assistance. We are looking for a woman who resides in the adult, non-criminal housing."

"If you think I can track down a single, law-abiding woman, you've drastically overestimated my abilities. If she had some sort of reputation, maybe I could help you out."

Bobby holds up the index finger of his free hand. "We aren't asking you to locate her for us, we are simply asking you steer us in the proper direction to begin the search on our own. It is my presumption you know where the adult housing is located within this fair city. Am I correct?"

"You are."

"And I would imagine a man with your experience and connections might have a working knowledge of the housing assignment process."

Nero crosses his arms across his barrel chest. "I do."

"And with an approximate date of arrival, you could narrow

down the search area within the mass of existing housing to feasible search parameters, could you not?"

"I could, I suppose," he admits with a frown.

"Why do you know so much about housing?" I ask.

Nero glowers. "I thought I said I don't want trouble from you."

"Nero is a virtual encyclopedia of information on the city and its workings," Bobby tells me.

"Sorry, I didn't mean to pry."

Bobby smiles. "You are simply curious, a trait I'm certain he won't hold against you. Isn't that right?"

Nero grunts. "We'll see."

"As to the woman we seek"—Bobby turns to me—"how long has she been here?"

The memory of a found newspaper article in a forgotten box in the basement pushes into my mind.

SINGLE CAR ROLLOVER KILLS MOTHER; CHILD UNHARMED

"Seventeen years, almost to the day. She died on the Fourth of July."

"Seventeen years, eh?" Nero scratches the stubble on his chin while he considers my answer. "All right, follow me."

He leads us through a door behind the bar into a narrow, dusty hallway. "Now don't be getting any ideas." He points to a door at the end of the hall. "That is forever off limits to you, girlie. You too, Bobby, at least for today." He throws a wary glance back over his shoulder toward the bar.

I know all too well the temptation waiting behind that door: sleek, onyx communication pods, which allow contact with the living world. It was in one of the pods where I heard a conversation between my grieving parents before Crosby dragged me out and unleashed the full brunt of his fury. It caused trouble for Nero as well, the extent of which I never learned. When I returned some nights later seeking help, he made it clear I was no longer welcome in his establishment.

"Don't worry," I say. "Lesson learned." Curiosity still tugs at me, the pods' purpose a mystery, but I let it go.

He leads us through the first door on the left and into a large storeroom. A single, bare bulb hangs from the ceiling, illuminating the space in a harsh light. Rickety wooden shelves line the walls, stacked high with a dusty, disorganized mess of books, binders, and maps.

Nero walks to a shelf on the wall opposite the door and begins riffling through stacks of books and piles of loose papers, many of which cascade to the floor. After a brief search and a good deal of cursing, he locates a large tome and pushes aside a stack of binders to make room on the shelf.

He flips through the book and taps his index finger on a page at its midpoint. "There you are."

The rummaging and cursing begins again at another shelf, where he digs through a pile of scrolls and grabs the document he's looking for.

Bobby and I follow him out of the room and back to the bar.

Nero unrolls the large scroll on the bar top, revealing a detailed street map. "There's good news, and there's bad news."

"I think we would like to begin with the good news," Bobby says. "It's best to remain upbeat."

"The good news is, in a city with a population well north of a quarter billion, I've narrowed your search down to twelve city blocks."

"And the bad news?" I ask.

"You have to search twelve city blocks. Gonna take you a while, I'd imagine, but this map will at least show you the way."

Nero gives Bobby rapid-fire instructions. He shows him where we are on the map and warns us to stick to the given route.

"It's plenty dangerous if you go wandering or try to find yourselves a shortcut, so don't go off course. Stick to what I told you, and you should be fine." He gives a wary look in the direction of the two men in the corner. "All right, Bobby. You two best be on your way."

CHAPTER THIRTEEN

My hands bounce against my thighs as we stand alone on a platform, waiting. "Have you been on the city trains before?"

"I have, many times. There is no need for concern."

"It's just, the last one I was on…"

Bobby puts his hand on my shoulder. "I wouldn't take you if it was not a safe way to travel."

A sleek train slides up, silent and smooth. The doors hiss open and an elderly woman steps off, dressed in an immaculate purple suit with matching pillbox hat and snowy white gloves.

"Take care now, dears," she says as she passes.

"What was that?"

"She was simply being conversational," Bobby says. "Shall we?"

I step aboard and push back the instinctive feeling of dread creeping into my mind. We have the car to ourselves, but I squeeze up close to Bobby when we sit and draw bravery from his calm.

The view becomes a blur. "Do you need to check the map again?"

Bobby pats the side of his messenger bag. "I have committed the route to memory. We have four stops before ours."

The light outside begins to fade, and the interior lights of the train come up.

"It's getting dark already?"

Bobby glances out the window. "It was inevitable, was it not? How does this sound? Tonight, we will simply find the location where we are to begin our search and return tomorrow at first light. It will be a much improved trip, as we will be able to travel directly to our search area, saving us a great deal of time."

"Fine, so long as I'm not on house arrest by morning."

"I greatly doubt their ability to restrict your movements entirely. I am confident we shall have no difficulty slipping from the watchful eye of Franklin."

I lean against Bobby's shoulder. The doors whoosh open at our first stop, and several passengers board the train and spread out through the car. No one speaks or even makes eye contact as we make the next three stops before our destination.

We step off the train onto a platform awash in a yellow glow from a nearby lamppost. We've arrived in a residential neighborhood, where block upon block of condominiums rise from the well-lit streets. The vastness of our search grid becomes painfully clear as we make our way up the first block Nero designated a possibility.

My heart sinks. "How are we ever going to find her?"

"We will scour one building at a time. I would imagine

we will find a receptionist in each lobby, which could serve to significantly cut our search time."

"If they're willing to help us. This could take forever."

"Well, it is a good thing we have it."

"What about the City Guard?" I scan the streets, warily searching.

"We will have to be alert and aware, but from what Nero told me, they tend to focus their patrols on the newer arrivals. This housing is for residents who've been here nearly as long as I, and they need far less supervision."

We meander up and down streets for nearly an hour, content to enjoy each other's company while getting the lay of the land. The condos seem largely the same—gleaming white buildings with darkened windows. Two per gigantic block at opposite corners with matching courtyards give us twenty-four buildings to visit.

And not a member of the City Guard in sight. *Thank god.*

We crane our necks back, trying to get an idea of how high the buildings soar, but they disappear into the impenetrable blackness of the Atman night.

"We could check with the flashlight," Bobby offers.

"What's the point? They're tall. Crazy tall. A hundred floors or a thousand, it's going to be a ridiculous task to track down one person."

"We shall find her together."

The few people we encounter are striking in their normal appearance, odd by what I've seen of Atman City. No exotic faces, no lurkers in the shadows, just average people waiting on their shot at getting out of here. Tired faces of weary souls pass by, heading to their condos to face the DSR grind. Their numbers dwindle until, at last, we're alone.

"Is it weird that it's this deserted?" I ask.

"Not especially. This is merely a residential area. I see little reason for large crowds to be wandering the streets."

"Yeah, I guess. You don't see too many people out around the dorms after dark. Same thing here, I suppose."

"Precisely. Shall we head back to the train? We are a significant distance from the city's outskirts through which we entered, which leaves us a great deal of ground to cover."

"Sure. Not like we're going to find her tonight."

"A nighttime search for her would most likely prove fruitless, if not inconvenient. I believe our chances significantly improve with the assistance of daylight."

"We'll have to be extra careful tomorrow. I have a feeling it's not going to be so easy to sneak off again."

"You may be right, but let's leave our worries until tomorrow."

I squeeze Bobby's hand. "Deal."

"I must admit, from what we've observed thus far, I find myself preferring our accommodations to these."

"Yeah, it's kind of boring here, huh?"

"Indeed, although I should reserve judgment until a more exhaustive comparison can be made."

We reach the final block before the platform and decide to cut diagonally across the last courtyard. While small in comparison to Jhana Park, it's still beautiful. Stately willow trees run the perimeter of the manicured grounds. Intricate patterns laid out in flowers carpet the courtyard in a riot of color. We slow our pace, taking time to absorb the beauty and the quiet.

At the center of the courtyard is a large, tiered fountain. Its soft glow bathes the surrounding area in a soothing light. I stop to let the water cascade over my fingers, and Bobby steps behind me.

"This is nice," I say. "Makes me not want to go back."

"You make a compelling argument. At this moment, it is difficult to recall my reasons to return to the dorm."

"Let's stay a while. Who knows what's waiting back there."

He runs his slow, hesitant hands up and down the length of my arms. "I am certain it will not be as bad as you expect."

Something in his touch makes me brave enough to give voice to a nagging fear that's been chattering in the back of my mind since we left Jhana Park.

"What if she doesn't like me?"

Bobby's hands stop. "What do you mean?"

"My birth mother. What if she doesn't like who I've turned out to be?"

"Impossible. She will be nothing less than delighted to meet you and proud of who you have become."

"It's just…"

Bobby's hands move up to my shoulders, a gentle, steadying force. "You can tell me anything, you know."

"I've thought about her my whole life, who she was, what she was like, but never in a million years did I think I'd get to meet her. And now, if we find her, I will."

"*When* we find her. Your anxiety is understandable, but I hope it provides you with some measure of comfort to know you will not be alone."

"I can't imagine searching for her without you." I lean back against him. "I hope I haven't made things weird between us."

"Not in the least. I…" His voice falters and he goes silent.

"What is it?" I turn around to face him, but he's staring down at the ground. "Bobby?"

"I have done a great deal of thinking over these past twenty-four hours."

I smile. "That's no different from any other day."

His cheeks flush with color. "I am not certain I possess the courage for this."

"Bobby, it's me."

"Precisely."

I take his hands in mine, which brings their trembling to a stop.

His voice quavers, picking up where his hands left off. "Words, once spoken, can never be taken back."

"It's okay." My stomach does somersaults. "Whatever it is, you can tell me."

Our eyes meet. He stands up straight and squares his shoulders. "I think…" He takes a deep breath. "I think I'm falling in love with you, Dez."

I take a step back, reeling. "Bobby, I—"

"You don't have to say anything."

But it's Bobby. My friend. How can he—

"Well isn't that sweet."

Bobby moves close in a protective stance, and his arms tighten around me as two figures materialize out of the shadows. A split-second is all it takes to register the menacing faces of the men from Nero's Tavern.

A sense of impending doom immobilizes me and roots my feet to the ground.

"Hello again, pretty." The man with the hazel eyes stops inches from me, his breath hot on my face. His fingers curl around one of my braids, and he leans into me, inhaling deeply. "Mmm. Nothing so sweet as a new soul."

A strangled whimper escapes my lips.

"It's all right," Bobby says. He steps in front of me as I scramble back a step. "We were just leaving," he tells the men, his shaking voice betraying his brave front.

The man with the copper hair rocks back on his heels and laughs, deep and booming. "You hear that, Raum? They were just leaving." He grabs Bobby and pulls him away from me like a rag doll. "There's been a change of plans."

Raum flashes a dangerous smile and grabs a handful of my hair. "You picked a bad night to venture out, pretty."

"Please just let us go."

He lets out a throaty growl. His gaze burns into my flesh. "What do you think, Moloch?"

Moloch is like a cruel child burning ants with a magnifying glass. He watches Bobby struggle as he considers Raum's question. "I think they should have stayed in their cozy little dorm, in their cozy little afterlife. But since they didn't…" His eyes glimmer. "Seems like they were looking for trouble."

"And you've found it," Raum whispers, his lips pressed against my ear.

I pull hard against his tight grip. My mind races, searching for a way out. "Don't," I say with as much force as I can muster, but my demand comes out as a plea.

Bobby wrenches free from Moloch, all signs of his placid self gone. "Leave her alone," he shouts. "Don't touch her!"

Raum throws an irritated look over his shoulder. "Do you mind?"

Moloch bows. "My apologies. I'll take my toy elsewhere." With a single, vicious blow, he subdues Bobby and drags him into the dark.

"Bobby!" I pull against Raum and struggle to free myself from his iron grip, my fear replaced by fury.

"I do enjoy a girl with spirit." He grabs me in a chokehold as he half pushes, half carries me back toward the tree line.

My fists fly, punching at his chest, his arms, slapping at his face, but my blows are useless, a minor irritation—a fly buzzing around him.

His grip tightens. "That's enough. Now it's my turn." He throws me to the ground at the foot of a willow tree. The incredible force of his strength knocks the wind from me. My vision darkens, bursting with stars.

I scramble backward until I collide with the trunk of the willow.

Raum closes in on me with unnatural speed, a hunter after his prey. "You're not going anywhere. We have work to do." He grabs my foot and drags me a few feet away from the tree.

I kick with my free leg and scream. My sweatshirt catches on an exposed rock in the hard ground surrounding the willow. A rip of fabric is followed by searing pain as both cotton and flesh are torn.

"First, I need to see as you do." He straddles me, pinning my hips to the ground. "I'm not going to lie. This is going to hurt."

My already torn sweatshirt is reduced to tatters as I continue to fight, but the battle is short-lived. Raum shifts his weight and moves his knees across my wrists, holding them firm at my sides. Wearing a proud, twisted grin, he pulls a dagger from his belt. He wields it with expertise, an extension of his hand that slashes through the air with frightening precision. The steel glimmers in the faint light as he slices off the end of one of my braids.

"Why are you doing this?" I wail.

"A totem," he says. He holds the braid in his fist and runs his knuckles down my cheek. His voice is suddenly soft, gentle, the diametric opposite of the evil that radiates from his being. "Open your thoughts to me."

"Please, please, stop."

"In time, you'll learn to love me, to worship me."

A renewed sense of strength surges through me. I may not be able to move from the waist up, but I still have my legs, so I kick and twist in a desperate bid to escape.

Raum's tone sharpens to a razor's edge. "If you fight me, it will only serve to increase your suffering."

My every sense rushes into overdrive as this nightmare becomes vivid reality. I take in my surroundings in fragments and flashes.

His rough hands, like iron sandpaper on my skin.

The smell of him, a mixture of fresh-turned earth and pungent spice.

The cold ground beneath me, hard and unforgiving.

I have nowhere to go, no ability to fight against his otherworldly strength.

Tears well in my eyes with the painful awareness of how isolated we are, and how far I am from the dorms. My hope for escape evaporates into the night.

I have no Crosby to shelter me.

No Franklin to bring order to the chaos.

No Charlie to forgive me.

Nothing but this man and the horrors he'll unleash.

A months-old warning, stern and terrifying, pushes into my mind—the cautionary tale of another girl who ventured into the city and was brutally attacked. Crosby took her under his wing in his first year volunteering at Atman Station, and just like me, she ignored his warnings about the city and the evil lurking in its streets.

"You can't die twice, so she survived each vicious blow and every hideous moment."

It was that night, scared straight, that I promised never to return to Atman City.

A promise I've now broken twice.

Raum presses the tip of the dagger under my chin, shocking me back to the present. "Oh, no. You're not going anywhere. Mind, body, spirit, you're all mine." He wipes away my tears and runs his hand down my face. "*Baqash.*"

The consequence of his utterance is sudden and severe. It's as though the entirety of the collected experiences my ancestors bear down on me at once. My thoughts splinter—visions of lives I've never lived, of people I've never known, come at me rapid-fire. Flashes of life, death, joy, and agony flow through me like a river.

A woman does her wash in a stream, beating clothes against the rocks as she softly sings a hymn. Tears stream down her face, and I know her sorrow as though it is my own.

Her life has been little more than suffering, having lost two babies in the cradle and her oldest to a cholera outbreak five years past. Now her only son is dead, taken by men who strung him from a tree for a crime he didn't commit.

Her heartache is immobilizing, her burden too great for a single mind to bear.

The pain combines with the collected suffering of thousands and becomes my own.

"Stop," I beg.

"You are the sum of the lives lived before you," Raum says. "In order to possess your spirit, I must own not only your thoughts but those of your predecessors."

"I can't. I can't do this!" I wail.

"Let the pain cleanse your soul," he whispers. "There is beauty in suffering."

"Get off the girl," a man's voice booms out of the darkness, breaking through the echo of history.

Raum sits up. Irritation spreads across his face. "This doesn't concern you," he calls out over his shoulder. "Move along before I lose my temper."

"Now," the stranger commands.

Raum sighs and grabs me under my chin. His grip tightens until I cry out. "I apologize for the interruption, pretty. We still have much to do. If you move, or even think of trying to run from me, I will hurt you in ways that won't heal. There is nowhere you can go, nowhere you can hide from me. You belong to me, now. Do you understand?"

I whimper, and shake from head to toe.

"Good girl."

"This is your last warning," the stranger says. "Get up and step away from her." What sounds like the rip of Velcro is followed by a metallic click and a high-pitched squeal.

Alarm flashes in Raum's eyes. He stands and turns with the slow, controlled movements of a snake about to strike. "You're not authorized to use that."

I drag myself back to the base of the willow, pull my knees up to my chest, and wrap my arms around my legs.

A tall, well-muscled man steps out of the shadows. He's dressed in black fatigues and is pointing some sort of gun at Raum. "You really want to test that theory?"

"This isn't going to end well for you, friend." Raum takes a few cautious steps toward him.

"Bold words for a guy on the business end of a Departer."

"You'd better watch where you point that thing. Do you know who I am?"

"Doesn't matter."

"That"—Raum motions over his shoulder toward me—"is mine. You move along, and I'm willing to forgive this little breach of etiquette. Otherwise, we're going to have a problem."

"You're not calling the shots here. You have two choices right now: leave or cease to exist. Makes no difference to me, but you have five seconds to decide."

"You have no idea what you're starting."

"Four."

Raum steps away. "This isn't over," he warns before disappearing into the shadows.

"Come find me anytime." He keeps the gun trained on Raum, a watchful eye on him as he leaves the courtyard.

Finally satisfied he's gone, the man holsters his weapon and blows out a deep breath. He runs a quick hand through his dark hair and turns to me. "Dez?"

An earthquake erupts in my body and shakes me from head to toe. "No, please," I whisper.

He raises his hands in front of his chest, palms out, and takes a careful step forward. "I'm not going to hurt you."

I shake my head.

He comes closer and crouches down a few feet away. "My name is Mack. Crosby sent me."

"Crosby?"

"He was worried you might be in trouble."

"What about Bobby?"

"Bobby?"

"He's my—Moloch took him."

"Moloch?" He stares down at the ground. "Shit."

I try to cover myself with what remains of my sweatshirt, but my hands shake too much to be of any use.

"Right now we need to get you out of here." He glances over his shoulder. "Can you walk?"

"I—I don't know."

"It's okay. I can help you."

"No."

"I won't hurt you."

"I don't believe you," I say, shrill and unhinged. "Where's Bobby?"

"I promise I will do everything I can to find him, but first we need to take care of you." He sits cross-legged on the ground, his hands on his knees. "We've met before, Dez. Do you remember?"

The shack.

"When Crosby caught me in the city. You—you took Charlie—"

"Back to the dorms. That's right." His eyes are kind and strong. He holds his hand out to me again.

My trembling fingers reach toward him.

"That's a girl. Let's get you out of here."

CHAPTER FOURTEEN

My quaking arms push through the sleeves of a windbreaker much too big for me.

Every sound is an assault on my senses, every motion an attack.

Mack drifts in and out of my vision.

We're on the move.

It's dark.

Cold.

"Almost there," he says.

Buildings pass by.

Time is fragmented, sliding.

Am I walking?

Is he carrying me?

The room is too bright—the harsh overhead lights hurt my eyes. The cold metal chair makes me shiver. The walls are closing in on me, and it's all I can do not to jump out of my skin.

Mack crouches beside me, next to a small table. "You're safe, now, Dez. I need to go out in the hallway for a minute, but I'll be right back."

I grab his arm. "No."

"I promise I'll be right back. It's only for a minute."

I shake my head. "He said if I ran—"

"He can't hurt you anymore."

He sounds so sure.

"He said he'd find me, that there was nowhere I could go." *That I am his.*

"He won't come here. Nobody is going to hurt you."

"We have to find Bobby. Please, we have to go now." I struggle to stand, but Mack's stops me.

"Dez, calm down."

"What are they doing to him? We have to get him back." I'm hysterical, my mind haunted with possibilities.

He taps his ear and turns his face away from me. "I'm going to need Clara in here."

This is my fault.

My grip tightens on Mack's arm.

He puts a hand on mine. "We have teams out looking for Bobby right now. We'll find him."

The door opens, and in walks a petite woman with dark hair pulled back in a ponytail. She's dressed in the same black fatigues as Mack and carries a neatly folded stack of clothes and a towel. Two bottles of water are tucked under her arm.

"Dez, honey, I'm Clara."

Mack disentangles from my grip, taking great care as he frees himself. "I just need to take care of a few things. Clara is going to stay with you until I get back, okay?"

He steps into the hallway, and Clara pulls up a chair next to me. The sound of the legs dragging across the floor makes me jump.

Clara carefully places the clothes and towel on the table next to the bottles of water. "I'm so sorry about what happened to you tonight."

"I was so stupid. I never should have—"

"Don't do that to yourself. This wasn't your fault."

"Raum made me see things. What he did to me…" I close my eyes.

"You don't have to be scared anymore."

"But they took Bobby."

"We'll find him." She puts a hand on my knee. "Why don't we get you cleaned up and changed into some new clothes?"

My gaze darts to the door.

"Nobody's coming in here until I give the all-clear."

"Okay." I sniffle.

"There's no rush." She opens the bottle of water and wets a washcloth. "Let's start with getting you out of that jacket. Mack's stuff's a little big on you, huh?"

I shrug out of his windbreaker. Embarrassment and shame hit me as my tattered sweatshirt is exposed. The night comes crashing back.

His hands.

His voice.

His eyes.

The visions.

Clara begins to wipe the grime from me. She starts with my face and works her way down my neck, dabbing at the cuts and scrapes peppering my arms. "If this is upsetting you, tell me, and I'll stop."

I try in vain to push Raum from my mind as Clara works to clean away the evidence he left behind.

She checks the cut on my back. "This isn't so bad. Probably hurts like crazy, though."

I shrug, too numb to feel anything.

Her every move is restrained as she pats me dry with a towel. "How about some clean clothes?" She holds up a shirt. "I think it's going to be a little big, but we'll make do."

Clara tosses my shredded hoodie into a nearby trashcan. She hands me a blue t-shirt emblazoned with the letters ACEA in a bright yellow block text on the back. It's a bit baggy on me, but it beats what I had.

"What is this place?" I ask.

"You are in precinct seventy-three's central station of the Atman Council Enforcement Agency. As the name suggests, we enforce the Atman Council laws and provide crisis intervention and tactical support."

"Atman Council?"

"It's the governing body of Atman City, the station, and surrounding environs."

"So you're the City Guard?"

"Not exactly. If the City Guard is the local police department, we're a combination SWAT team and FBI."

Clara offers me the unopened bottle of water, which I accept. It's a struggle to take a drink; my shaking hands get more water on the table than in my mouth.

"Thanks for the shirt," I murmur.

"You're welcome. Do you want to get out of those jeans?"

They're dirty and one knee is torn, but the thought of taking them off makes me queasy. I shake my head.

"That's fine." She leans closer and wipes a last bit of stubborn dirt from my cheek.

I throw my trembling arms around her.

She pats my back and strokes my hair. "Oh, honey," she says. "You're going to be okay."

"But Bobby. We have to find him." I whimper into her shoulder.

"We will."

There is a sudden commotion at the door. Muffled voices argue, and a loud thud shakes the wall.

I cry out and pull back from Clara.

"Dez, it's okay." She puts an arm around me to keep me from scrambling out of the chair. "I'm going to go deal with whoever's out there—and I'm pretty sure I know exactly who it is."

She moves across the small room and slips into the hallway, leaving the door slightly ajar.

"Clara, move."

It's Crosby.

Overwhelmed to the point of near-shutdown, I have nothing left for a reaction to his arrival.

Clara lowers her voice. "I have a severely traumatized girl in there, and you are going to calm yourself down, because you are not helping. You get me?"

"Please."

"She's shaken up, but she'll be okay," Mack says.

"I need to see for myself."

"Then you're going to have to get ahold of yourself," Clara says. "Mack? Can you deal with this?"

"Go ahead and get back to her. Just give us a minute."

Clara comes back in the room and returns to the seat next to me. "As I'm sure you heard, Crosby is here, and he wants to see you. If you're not up to it, I will make him leave."

"I don't think he's going to just go away because you tell him to."

"Don't bet on it. I'll drag him out by his ear if need be."

A harsh, choking laugh escapes me. "I'd like to see that."

She smiles. "And I'd be happy to oblige."

"I'll have to see him eventually, right?"

"It doesn't have to be now. Not if you aren't ready."

"He can come in, I guess."

"You sure?"

I nod.

She pats my knee and stands. "I'll let him know."

She walks back into the hallway and shuts the door behind her. The conversation picks up again in low, muffled tones.

The door opens, and a frantic Crosby follows Mack into the room. I can feel him watching me, but I stay focused on Mack.

"Goddamn it, Mack. Why'd you let him go?" Crosby moves to step around him, but Mack catches his arm. Crosby spins to face him. "What's the matter with you? You had him, and you just let him leave?"

"Take it easy. She doesn't need you scaring her, too." Crosby tries to jerk free, but Mack pulls him into a tight embrace and holds him close. "Just calm down," he says softly. He whispers something into Crosby's ear, and then tells him, "She needs you right now. The you you've been for her from the start."

Crosby looks down and slumps, his forehead resting on Mack's shoulder. "I'm sorry."

Mack tilts his head against Crosby's. "We're fine." He turns to me. "I'm going to give you two some time alone, but then if you're up for it, I have some questions I need to ask you about tonight."

"You don't have to leave," I say.

"I have to go prep for the interview. I'll be back in a few." He turns his attention back to Crosby. "Go. She's waiting." His free hand brushes against Crosby's jaw before he turns to leave.

The door closes behind Mack and the silence that follows is deafening.

Crosby crosses the room and sits in Clara's empty chair. He reaches for my hand.

I pull away and cringe.

"Dez?"

"Don't. Don't say it."

"What do you mean?"

"I can't do this right now."

He puts his hand on my shoulder. I pull my arms in tight against my chest.

Crosby leans in close and tries to get me to look at him. "It's me, sweetie. Let me help you."

"I know what you're going to say."

"What do you mean?"

"After what happened today, everything I said, all the times you told me not to go to the city. You told me about that girl, the one you were helping when you first came here, how she was captured and—"

Raped.

Over and over.

"And now…" I shake my head. Hysteria grips me, twisting and wrenching what's left of my sanity.

"No. This is not your fault." He pulls me into his arms, and I don't fight him. "Do you hear me?"

Tears stream down my face. "Bobby was there because of me. He was trying to help—"

"Shh, it's okay."

"They came out of nowhere."

"It's over. Nobody's going to hurt you now."

"But what about Bobby? Where did they take him?"

"You let Mack worry about that."

"He was trying to protect me from them, but Moloch was too strong." I close my eyes as the memory assaults me again. "If you hadn't sent Mack; if he hadn't found me—"

"But he did."

"It all happened so fast. We were heading back to the train, and we cut across the courtyard by the condos." I stop, the memory too painful.

"Do you want to tell me about it?"

"No." I cling to him, my rage and sense of betrayal replaced by desperation and fear. The familiar comfort of Crosby is powerful, and he's all I have left. "I just wanted to meet her, Crosby."

"I know."

"It was stupid to go. I know that, but I was so mad. I spent my whole life wishing I could talk to her just once. Bobby knows the city really well, and I thought we'd be fine."

"I'm sorry we didn't tell you about her."

We sit in silence as I try to pull myself together, neither of us sure what to say. I take a deep, shuddering breath. "Charlie broke up with me."

"What?"

"I don't blame him." I run the back of my hand across my eyes, wiping away fresh tears. "He said he doesn't matter to me the way you do. That I don't tell him the important stuff. Pretty much everything you and I talked about."

"You want me to talk to him?"

"No. He's right. He deserves better than that."

"I'm sorry."

"Death sucks."

"Not always."

I sit up. "Yeah, when you have a guy like Mack, I suppose it's pretty great, huh?"

He turns away as he tries to hide the hint of a smile on his face. "Sorry."

"Don't be. He'd make me smile, too. Why haven't you ever told me about him?"

"Because we're supposed to talk about you, not me. And I did not foresee a situation in which you'd be meeting him."

"But I already did meet him, remember? You had him take Charlie back to the dorms when I…" I stop, not wanting to relive that night Crosby caught me at Nero's. Tonight is enough to deal with.

"Well, I was a little busy at the time."

There is a soft knock at the door, and it opens. Mack walks in, followed by Clara. They pull up chairs and sit across the table from Crosby and me.

I instinctively lean my head on Crosby's shoulder and close my eyes.

"How's she doing?" Mack asks.

I feel Crosby shrug. "About as well as she can be, right, kiddo?"

"I guess."

"Well, I'm not so sure either one of you is going to like this," Mack says.

I open my eyes.

Mack and Clara exchange a look, and he continues. "We've discussed it and feel it will be best for everyone if you wait outside, Crosby, while I conduct the interview."

"Not happening," Crosby says.

I grab his arm. "But—"

Mack holds up his hand to stop our protests. "I know. This isn't easy for anyone, but it's going to be more upsetting for both of you if Crosby stays." He gives me a sympathetic look, but it's clear he's made up his mind and is pulling rank. "Dez, I know you're scared, and you've been through a lot tonight, but Clara is going to sit with you, okay?"

Crosby pushes back from the table with an angry sigh and offers his seat to Clara.

"It's for the best, Cros," Mack says.

Crosby leaves without another word, and Clara slips into his seat.

Mack turns his attention to me. "First of all, I want to apologize for conducting this interview myself. Normally, we would have a ranking female agent handle this sort of situation, but we have all hands on deck, so to speak, out looking for Bobby. I'm the only senior officer on site."

A tremble runs through me. Clara takes my hand.

"Let's get the formalities out of the way first," he says. He puts a small, silver object the size of a credit card on the table. A tiny blue light comes on when he taps the card. "Victim interview to be conducted by Agent Paul Macklin at the central station of precinct seventy-three. Witnessing agent Clara Perkins." He glances up at the clock on the wall. "The time is twenty-three forty-nine."

Mack begins the interview, and I fill in all the blanks, from storming out of the conference room to his arrival in the courtyard. I fall into a trance of sorts and spill all the details with detached proficiency, simply pressing ahead and getting it over with, too numb to feel anything else.

Time slips into a void. Awareness eludes me.

A conversation goes on around me, but the words are lost.

Once again, Mack is crouched before me. I try to shake off the feelings of confusion and disorientation as I stare uncomprehending at him. He's been talking for a while, it seems, but I haven't taken in his words.

"You did great, Dez. Let's go get Crosby and get you back to the dorms."

CHAPTER FIFTEEN

Crosby and Mack stand to either side of me in the same protective formation we've been in since leaving the ACEA station. The elevator doors close swiftly behind us, almost as though they're aware of my urgent need to retreat to the shelter of my room.

"It's going to be fine, kiddo," Crosby says. "Abbey's back in her old room for tonight helping out the two new girls, so you won't have to see her."

"What about everybody else?"

"It's the middle of the night. Everyone's in their rooms in DSR."

In theory, he's right.

"They're going to be waiting for us," I say, knowing the rumor mill trumps DSR every time.

"They won't be."

"But—"

"If they are, they'll have to deal with me," Mack interjects.

"And I'm wearing my ass kicking boots tonight." He smiles and pats me on the back.

I flinch. "I just want to find Bobby."

"You let me worry about that. You've been through enough."

"He was only there because of me. We never should have gone."

"You're right, you shouldn't have," Crosby says. "But that does not make what happened your fault. You are not to blame."

The elevator doors slide open. Mack puts his hand on my shoulder. "We're right here with you."

It's quiet, the lights are dimmed to their night setting, and there's no one in sight. I let out a sigh of relief as we make our way across the common room toward the suites.

Passing through the game area, I catch Crosby out of the corner of my eye as he locks in on something. I turn to follow his gaze and spot Charlie making a beeline for us, a panicked look in his eyes.

I take a step back behind Crosby, who holds up a hand to stop him. "This isn't a good time, Charlie."

Charlie's posture is stiff and defensive. "Crosby, move."

Crosby puts his hand on Charlie's chest. "Just give her some time."

Charlie looks past him to me. "Dez? Whatever happened before, I…" His pleading eyes turn back to Crosby. "I just want to talk to her."

"Not right now. Why don't you go back to your room, and we can talk about this in the morning."

"You might get away with ordering her around, but it's not going to work on me." Resentment flashes in his eyes. He pushes at Crosby's hand, trying to get free.

Mack steps closer to me, and I cower against him. "You're okay," he says.

Crosby's hand stays firm, holding Charlie back. "All you're doing right now is upsetting her."

"It's always about you, isn't it? You afraid somebody might step up and take your place, Mister Fix-It?" Charlie's voice gets louder; his building anger amplifies his words. "You're the reason we had problems in the first place."

"I know you're upset, Charlie, but you need to control yourself. She doesn't need this right now."

"Why are you always the expert on what she needs?"

"I never said I was an expert, but I do know you're not helping."

"Oh, so I'm the problem?"

"At the moment? Yes."

"This is bullshit. Just let me talk to her."

Crosby turns to Mack, his voice tight but even. "Get her to her room. It's number six."

Mack steers me away from the escalating fight and stays between Charlie and me as we pass. "It's all right. He's just worried about you."

He wastes no time getting to my room, ushering me inside and closing the door behind us, which muffles the argument raging outside. He leads me over to the couch, and I crumble. Too overcome to be embarrassed about crying in front of a near-stranger and unable to hold back the crushing tide of the day, I finally come completely unglued.

He sits, and I lean against him, sobbing and helpless.

"It's over now, you're safe."

Every inch of me burns with fear and sorrow, desperate to get this night back from the evil that took it. I can't stand the feeling of my own skin, crawling with terror. Flashes from the courtyard lash out at me, snapping and snarling with fresh pain.

"I never meant for this to happen," I say.

"Of course you didn't."

"You don't even know me, and now you're stuck here and…" I can't slow down my words, my mind. There's no escape.

"Take a deep breath."

"Raum said he was going to come after you. They already have Bobby, and if they—"

"Don't you worry about me."

"He's going to find me. He said—"

"Dez, you listen to me." Mack holds onto my shoulders, his gaze steady and calm. "You are safe. He will never hurt you again."

Bobby.

I can't stop thinking about him, imagining what they've done, where they've taken him.

I have to do something.

There's a soft knock at the door. "It's just me," Crosby calls out as he enters the room.

Mack moves to a chair, and Crosby takes his place on the couch. "It's going to be okay. We're going to find Bobby."

"Why, Crosby? Why don't I listen?"

"It's not going to do you or Bobby any good to go down this road."

"But—"

"You skipped out on DSR last night, didn't you?"

I nod.

"You need the recovery time. You're drained. You're not thinking clearly right now."

"Raum's going to find me."

"He won't. He can't come here."

Mack brings me a box of tissues. "If you were in any danger, I would have an entire team parked outside your door. But he won't set foot anywhere near here."

"How do you know?"

"We'll talk about that tomorrow," Crosby says. "For now, you need a breather. You need DSR."

"Don't go, please."

"We can stay a little while longer, but then you need to rest."

I loosen my iron grip on Crosby and lean back on the couch, exhausted. "Is Charlie okay?"

"He'll be fine. He's with Franklin right now."

"Don't be mad at him."

"I'm not. He's just upset."

"I've never seen him like that."

"Whatever happened between you, he still cares. You know that, right?"

There's another knock at the door.

I curl up on the couch. "I don't want to see anybody else."

Mack moves to the door. "I'll take care of it."

I rub the back of my hand over my eyes in a futile effort to fight the pull of DSR.

"You really need to get some rest," Crosby says.

My tired eyes follow Mack to the door. "I can't, Crosby. Not until we find Bobby."

"I'm going to try and be as kind as I can when I say this." He takes a quick, sharp breath. "I need you to look at me."

Too tired to argue, I oblige and pull my attention away from Mack and whoever is on the other side of the door.

"You are to have nothing to do with the search for Bobby, got it?"

"Crosby—"

We're interrupted by the visitor at the door. "All right, boys, time to clear out. The last thing she needs is you two hovering all night." Clara steps around Mack, inviting herself in.

"We're right in the middle of something." Crosby glares at her.

"Whatever it is, it'll keep until tomorrow. You should get home." She shoos him off the couch and sits down. "How are you feeling?"

"She's exhausted," Crosby says.

"She can answer for herself, Mama Bear."

He frowns.

"Go on, now, both of you." She waves a dismissive hand at Crosby. "We'll be fine."

"It's best to just do what she says," Mack tells him.

"But you're her boss."

"You think she cares?" He takes Crosby's hand.

Crosby gives in and allows himself to be lead to the door. "I'll be back bright and early, I promise."

Mack drags him through the door, and it closes behind them.

"You didn't have to come all the way here," I tell Clara.

"It's no trouble."

"It must be some sort of record." I dab at my eyes with a tissue.

"What do you mean?"

"The number of staff members it takes to deal with me and all my chaos."

"Pfft." She waves a dismissive hand and smiles. "We don't even bat an eye until you hit a baker's dozen."

"Would you…?" I look away, embarrassed.

She curls up her legs on the couch and turns to face me. "What is it?"

"Never mind."

"It's okay, honey, you can ask me anything."

"I just—Crosby said I need to do DSR, but, I don't want to be alone."

"You want me to stay until you wake up?"

I wipe away a rogue tear that didn't get the memo that I'm cried out. "Please."

"Of course I will."

"Thanks."

"Why don't you go get cleaned up and ready for bed, and I'll go grab a book."

"O-okay," I stammer.

"I'll only be a few minutes, I promise. I can even have Franklin stand guard outside your door while I'm gone, if you'd like."

"That's too much."

"No, it isn't." She stands. "He won't mind, and it will make you feel better."

"I don't want to see him. Not right now."

"I'll have him wait outside."

I stand and hug her. "Thank you. For everything."

"Don't even mention it." She gives me a big squeeze. "I'll be back in a few."

I grab some pajamas from my closet and get changed, fold up the loaner ACEA shirt and leave it on the couch before I stumble across the room and collapse into bed.

A few seconds is all it takes for DSR to grab hold of me and draw me into its mystical embrace.

The visions start immediately, with no introduction or lecture from my formerly linked staff member. It stuns me to realize I miss her. Tonight, of all nights, her presence would be welcome.

I'm just a baby, cooing away on the lap of Gwendolyn Jackson. We're in a small, cramped office, sitting before a middle aged, stone-faced woman.

"I'm sorry, ma'am. As I've told you time and again, we've done everything we can. But with so little to go on, I am afraid there is no additional benefit your husband would gain from continued hospitalization at this time." She pushes a form across the desk. "I'm going to need you to sign these discharge papers."

"And what if I don't?"

"Refusal to sign the requisite paperwork may result in a delay in benefits, and I'm afraid we'll still have to discharge Sergeant Jackson. We need the bed."

"So, you can send him halfway around the world to some godforsaken desert to chase a dictator back to Baghdad, but when he comes home after being exposed to god-knows-what, he's on his own?"

"We will continue to monitor his symptoms, and if his condition worsens, we will reevaluate."

"What about our little girl?" she asks, holding my squirmy body tighter. "What if that poison got passed on to her?"

"Studies have found no concrete link between the types of symptoms your husband is experiencing and birth defects or other health complications passed on to children."

"No concrete link? Is that supposed to make me feel better?"

"I'm certain your daughter will have a happy, healthy life."

"Can you say the same for her father? It's been over five years, now, and you people won't even tell us what he was exposed to over there. Do you realize there are twenty-seven other members of his company who are sick? How many will it take before you'll do something?"

"I understand your concern. We're doing everything we can."

"Sure you are."

I start to fuss—a little whimper that quickly morphs into a squall. She lays me on her shoulder and rubs my back. "Shh, it's okay. Mama's just getting sick of the runaround, that's all."

"Ma'am, your husband is waiting in the lobby, and I'm sure he's eager to get home. Let's get this paperwork taken care of so we can all continue on with our day."

CHAPTER SIXTEEN

I wake from DSR with a jolt.

Finally, I got a glimpse of my birth mother, a snapshot of the life she had before her crash, before I was adopted by my mom and dad.

I look just like her.

I rub my eyes, roll over, and am shocked by the glowing red numbers on the clock next to my bed.

08:56

The numbers slam me back to reality. The night comes back with a crash.

I sit bolt upright. "Nine o'clock?" I kick my legs over the side of the bed.

A fresh batch of fear hits me when I realize I'm alone. Clara has left her post on the couch, but there's a note stuck to the wall. I cross the room and grab the message.

Hi Dez,

I have to get back to work, and I didn't want to wake you. Crosby is waiting outside your room, so no worries.

I will see you soon.

Clara

The feeling of dread and urgency picks right up where it left off.

My legs move as though propelled by their own will and hustle me to the closet where I dress on the move: I pull on a shirt and hop on alternating feet as I shimmy into a pair of jeans. A quick once-over in the bathroom mirror, and I'm on my way.

I open the exterior door just enough to peek out into the common area.

"Crosby," I call out in an urgent whisper before I retreat back into my room and pace in front of the couch, unsure if he heard me or not.

In a matter of seconds, the door opens. "Hey, kiddo, how are you feeling?"

"Why didn't you wake me?"

"You needed the rest. DSR knows what it's doing. We figured you wouldn't mind missing this morning's sessions." He sits on the couch. "Come sit down. I need to talk to you."

"But I have to help Bobby. We've got to do something."

"Just sit, please?" He pats the seat next to him. "We have a lot to talk about."

"Can't it wait?"

"No."

My fingers drum on my thighs as I pace. "Do we have to do this here?"

Crosby watches me from the couch as I ping-pong back and

forth before him. "Well, at least you're not tired anymore."

"I can't stay in this room another second, Crosby."

"I understand, but there's something you need to do first."

"What?"

"You need to talk to Charlie."

I collapse onto the couch, grab a throw pillow, and hold it tight in my arms. "Not right now."

"You've made your choice, and now I've made mine. It's over."

His angry words invade my already crowded thoughts and stir up fresh sorrow. After last night's terror, I have no more tears to shed and no more space in my heart for extra pain.

"I've been fending him off for hours," Crosby says. "He's frantic."

I fold up around the pillow. Flashes of Raum push into my mind.

His iron grip.

The weight of the suffering of thousands.

His dark eyes gleaming with perverse delight.

"I can't do this. I can't face Charlie right now. Don't make me." The stifling horror reaches forward from last night, grabs me, and gives me a shake. The absolute certainty that no one was going to stop Raum and nothing would save me from his savage assault possesses me once again. The fear is relentless, paralyzing, a lighting storm setting me ablaze.

Crosby pulls his hand back as I shrink away, pressed against the arm of the couch.

"Okay, kiddo, okay." He slides down the couch and gives me some space. "I'll go talk to him."

"I just can't right now."

"I'm sorry I brought it up." Crosby sighs. "Really."

I fall silent.

He's just trying to help, but for once, he's out of his depth.

"Are you going to be okay for a few minutes by yourself?"

I curl up on the couch. "I want to get out of here, Crosby."

He raises a hand to pat my arm, but stops. "I'll be back as quick as I can."

The door closes behind him, and I'm pummeled by waves of guilt and anxiety. I think again of Bobby, his gentle soul facing untold horror at the hands of Moloch and Raum. The image of the vicious blow he suffered plays on a merciless, unending loop. I struggle to grasp what he's facing now, alone.

My skin crawls. Acid burns at the back of my throat.

Unable to sit idle another second, I force myself off the couch and back into the bathroom.

I flick on the light and face the mirror. My terrified reflection stares back at me, but I straighten from a slouch and plaster determination on my face.

"Stop it," I hiss. "You don't get to fall apart. There's no more time for the luxury of freaking out, and you don't deserve it. Not with Bobby out there. They took him because of you." I square my shoulders. "Get it together and help him."

I storm out of the bathroom, stride across the suite to the floor-to-ceiling windows at the far end of the room, and kneel on the bench seat. My palms lie flat against the glass as I stare out into the city's hodgepodge of architecture that climbs up stepped foothills to the base of a mountain.

"Please don't give up. Don't let them take away who you are."

Eyes closed, I lean against the glass. Its cool, smooth touch soothes my forehead. "I still don't know if there's a god, but please, whoever or whatever is pulling all the strings, please help Bobby. I will do whatever it takes. Just give him back. He doesn't deserve this. He's kind, and brilliant, and he was only there because of me. He was just trying to help. He doesn't deserve to be punished for my mistakes. Please—"

I cut my prayer short at the sound of the opening door and turn to face Crosby as he enters.

"Ready to go?" he asks. "I know just the place."

Although he's supposed to be leading the way, I drag him through the common room to the elevator.

He tries to slow our pace. "Take it easy."

"I can't deal with anyone else right now, and we have to get moving. We're wasting time." I pull at his arm, urging him to move faster.

"You don't even know where we're going."

"We're in a tower, on a floor with one exit." I slap my hand against the elevator's call button.

"Good point."

✦✦✦

Crosby leads me down the marble staircase and into the main terminal of the train station. I cling to his arm as we wade through the endless flood of new arrivals on their way to the ticket windows to learn their fates. We're salmon swimming upstream, pressing ahead through the waiting area where the elbow room increases in the eerie quiet. Footfalls echo off the marble floors as an ocean of humanity passes through the vast hall.

So many people making so little noise. It bothers me nearly as much today as it did the day I arrived.

Hundreds upon hundreds of wooden benches spread out before us, occupied by the stoic souls who've gotten their tickets. From the very old to the very young, each expression is unique, but they all share one quality plainly written on their faces: acceptance. They're ready for whatever's next.

Despite everything that's happened in the past forty-eight hours, a twinge of jealousy stings me as we pass. I look away, my gaze drawn to the soaring glass ceiling that highlights the sky's swirling array of blues, and I nearly collide with a massive marble column.

"Easy, kiddo." Crosby catches my wrist at the last second and steers me clear. "That view will get you every time."

"Are you going to tell me where we're going?"

"Don't need to. We're almost there."

"You tend to have a rather loose definition of words like 'almost.'"

"There's my cranky charge." He smiles. "Good to see a bit of you coming back, even if that bit is grumpy."

He leads me toward the surging crowd at the station's main entrance, where seven enormous revolving doors in perpetual motion direct the steady stream of lemmings off the cliff of life and into the frigid sea of limbo.

We make our way to a side door on the adjacent wall, which leads to a narrow, windowless corridor. The walls and floor are dark and polished, reflecting our images back at us from all directions as we pass. A single door awaits us at the end of the hall. Crosby steps ahead and swings it open.

He ushers me through with his free hand. "I promise it was worth the trip."

My breath catches in my throat when I take in the room, a small but stunning space. "I've seen this before," I say in quiet reverence.

Three large stained glass windows separated by square pillars bathe the darkened room in deep blue. Each window is divided into twelve panels, each panel depicting a different art form. The parquet floor glows in reflection, illuminating a small wooden bench set before the middle window.

Crosby sits on the bench and pats the space next to him. "Tell me about it."

I sit next to him. My eyes never leave the windows. "It was the summer I turned eight. My dad used his flight privileges and took Aaron and me to Chicago for a day trip. It's only like an hour flight, so we left in the early morning and were back by dinner time.

"Dad said the day was up to us. We could do whatever Aaron and I picked. Aaron wanted to go to a Cubs game, and I wanted to go to Marshall Field's for an ice cream sundae. He wanted to go to Shedd Aquarium, and I wanted to go to Navy Pier. Of all the things the city had to offer, we couldn't agree on one. We must have fought about it for half an hour."

Crosby chuckles. "You?"

I let slip a little smile. "I know you're shocked. Aaron was my best friend, but he could push my buttons like nobody else. Until recently, that is." I bump my knee against Crosby's.

"Anyway, we were fighting like cats and dogs," I continue.

"I said baseball was stupid, and he said ice cream was stupid. I said fish were dumb, and he said Ferris wheels were dumb. There we were on Michigan Avenue, yelling at each other—these two little kids having a knock-down, drag-out war of words. My dad finally lost it and said, 'That's it. We're going to go do something I want.' He marched us to the Art Institute with a warning that if he heard one more peep out of either one of us, the only place we'd be going was back to O'Hare.

"Aaron and I sulked for a good long time, but neither one of us dared to say a word. We just exchanged these angry looks, both of us refusing to have fun or take in any of the amazing art around us. Not until we walked into this room." I point to the windows, one by one. "They changed everything. They were the most beautiful thing I'd ever seen. We just stood there, staring at them. It must have been ten full minutes of silence, when Aaron finally said, 'I'm glad we came here,' and I said 'me, too.' My dad just smiled.

"I put the 'I love Chicago' mug I got from the gift shop into Aaron's casket."

I heave out a long sigh. In my life, Aaron was the only boy I ever truly loved, and his loss still weighs heavily on me, made worse by the recent DSR visions.

"You'll get to see him again, kiddo."

"You promise?"

"I do."

I lean my head against Crosby and hold tight to the memory of that day in Chicago.

"I'm glad this spot means something to you. I had no idea—I just wanted to bring you somewhere peaceful and healing. I wasn't around to see these windows in life, but it's easy to feel what they mean here."

"Thanks. This really does help."

"You feel up to talking? There's a lot I need to tell you."

"Whatever will help get Bobby back." I sit up straight.

Crosby pivots to face me on the bench. "First things first. You need to know who we're dealing with. Hopefully the knowledge alone will dissuade you from any further talk of helping search for Bobby."

I shake my head. "No. It's my fault he's out there, and—"

Crosby's jaw sets and his expression turns to granite. "Stop it. I won't put up with any more of that talk from you. You are not to blame."

I hang my head. My cheeks and ears burn, and my eyes sting with the threat of more tears.

"I just want you to listen." His voice and expression soften.

I don't move or make a sound.

"First of all, this information is far beyond the scope of anything you should ever know about this place, but the situation is what it is. And you'd best keep my previous warnings in mind. Got it?" His voice is a mix of stern and worried. With my growing list of antics over these past months, it's a tone I've become all too familiar with.

"Okay." My skin crawls with anticipation of what's to come.

"Deep in the city—and don't bother asking me where— there's a gate. A portal, really. Remember when I told you about Maggie?"

"She's the one who was…"

Raped.

Beaten.

Held captive.

I fixate on the blue cast of the windows reflecting on my hands. "She's the one you told me about, to keep me out of the city. And I still didn't listen. And now Bobby—"

Crosby puts a hand on my shoulder to stop me before I ramp all the way back up to hysterical. "Remember how I said the man who attacked her was sent to Hell?"

"You said that only happens to a few. The ones who can't be redeemed."

"Well, the Atman Council, which is our governing body, has a millennia-old truce with the Grigori—"

"Who are they?"

Crosby drums his fingers on his knees, irritated with my interruption, but pondering my question. "That's a long story which we can get into later, but for this discussion's sake, think of them like Hell's equivalent of the Atman Council. When a soul is condemned to damnation—which requires a majority vote from the Council—they must be transferred from Atman custody to Hell. That's where the gate comes in. Just as the train station is a transfer point between life and the afterlife, this gate is the transfer point between Atman and Hell."

"If there's a transfer point, a gate, isn't it vulnerable? I mean, what's to stop them from overrunning the city, the towers, all of it? They don't care about right and wrong. All that matters to them is their own interests, right?"

"That's where Mack and the Enforcement Agency come in. Their primary mission is to maintain the truce and handle any breaches. There are a few carrots in the agreement hashed out between the Council and the Grigori, but the Agency is the stick."

"Is that why he had that gun?"

Crosby nods.

"What was that thing, anyway? It sure made Raum nervous."

"As well it should. Mack is one of seven agents entrusted with a Departer, and it does just what its name implies. It eliminates a soul's energy, forever banishing the Departer's target from existence."

I shudder. "Raum said he wasn't authorized to use it."

"Well, generally speaking, he's right. It's a weapon reserved for the most dire infractions and emergencies, and Raum is a particular sort of being who is cut an extraordinary amount of slack. But it's hard to argue semantics when you no longer exist."

"Would Mack really have used it? I mean, for me?"

Crosby holds up his hands. "I guess we'll never know, and it's a good thing we didn't have to find out."

"So last night, was that a breach? Is that how they got through the gate?"

"No. Part of the truce is that a select few of Hell's highest-ranking demons are free to explore the non-housing sectors of the city and partake of all the debauchery they wish, so long as no harm comes to any transitional souls. Raum and Moloch are two of Hell's royalty and can come and go as they please. But when they went after you and Bobby, they broke the treaty. It isn't the first time, and unfortunately, it won't be the last, but it's raised tensions on both sides. The Council is furious over the attack, and the Grigori are making quite a lot of noise over Mack drawing his Departer on Raum. The Atman Council will be convening later today to have a hearing on the matter."

I bury my face in my hands. "What have I started?"

"If it hadn't been you, it would have been someone else. Moloch and Raum were out for trouble last night. You were just a convenient target."

"Why'd they take Bobby? What do they want with him?"

"I don't know. I wish I did. But we'll find him."

I dig the heels of my palms into my face as I try to process everything Crosby has told me.

"There's one more thing," he says. "And I don't want you to freak out, because it isn't as bad as it sounds."

I slump, knowing that whatever it is, it will be at least as bad as it sounds, maybe worse.

"You've been summoned to appear before the Council."

CHAPTER SEVENTEEN

I'm a heap of nerves spun out on the bench seats set into the floor-to-ceiling windows in my room, trying my best to ignore the myriad emotions at war in my head. My back is to the wall, both literally and figuratively. The recessed window is cold against my skin, the fear icy in my mind. I clutch a pillow from my bed, hoping my tight grip will help me hold on to what little is left of my sanity.

Half an hour.

That's all I have before Crosby is coming back for me. It's all the time that remains before I'll leave for the city—for the first time with permission—to stand before the Atman Council.

What could they possibly want from me?

Can they evict me from Limbo? Is there somewhere worse? Some afterlife penal colony for the perpetually uncooperative who put not only themselves, but their dear friends, in danger?

I stare out the window as I search for some sign of Bobby

and plead with the universe for a clue to his whereabouts. The city looks the same as it always has, vast and stunning. There's no hint of what went terribly wrong last night, no oppressive fog hanging over the landscape, no flashing lights or alarms. Just business as usual.

Bobby's been taken, and the city shrugged it off like it was nothing.

The sound of the door opening snaps me out of my thoughts, on full alert.

"Dez?" Abbey calls out. "Is it okay if I come in?"

I let out a breath I didn't know I was holding and lean my head back against the wall. I close my eyes. "It's your room, too. You don't need my permission."

"After everything you've been through, asking is the least I can do." Her voice gets closer. "Stupid question, I know, but how are you doing?"

I open my eyes. "Charlie send you?"

The cushion shifts as she sits down on the opposite end of the window seat.

"He did, but he's not the only reason I'm here. I'm worried about you, Dez. We all are."

"Sure. Worried," I scoff. "The idiot who never learns, the reason Bobby was taken, the helpless loser who needs babysitters, the constant source of drama. I can see why."

Abbey stares down at her hands. "Nobody thinks that."

"Right."

She looks up, her face set with determination. "Bobby goes to the city all the time, and it's always dangerous. Something was bound to happen to him sooner or later."

Guilt burns at the back of my throat. "But he was only there because of me."

"This time. But Dez, he's a risk taker. He doesn't believe any of this is real, so he's careless. You can't blame yourself for what happened."

I brush away the tears springing from my eyes, my hand an impatient and rough extension of my mind. "I keep hearing that, but we were only there because I wanted to find my birth mom, because I was mad nobody told me about her. And you know what? I had the best parents I could have asked for. Why was I chasing around after a woman I never knew?"

"She's still a big part of who you are."

"We have eternity. I'd have met her eventually, but no. I had to let my pride and hurt feelings get in the way. I had to risk everything because I was impatient…it was so stupid."

Abbey scoots closer. "It was brave." She hands me a tissue. "I'd never have the guts to do the things you've done."

"Crosby and everyone else told me enough times to stay away, and I didn't listen, even after what happened last time. And now Bobby's gone."

"What good is it going to do to beat yourself up over it?"

"Somebody should. Everyone keeps saying it isn't my fault, but we all know it is."

Abbey leans closer. Her elbows rest on her knees. "Okay, for a moment, let's just say you're right, that somehow this is all your fault."

The words, even spoken as a hypothetical, sting like nettles.

"Even if it's true," Abbey continues, "what difference does it make? Does it bring Bobby back? Does it change what happened to you? Does it make a single bit of difference?"

I toss aside the pillow and cross my arms, refusing to accept the out she's giving me. "Why are you being so nice?"

"Because death's too long to hold grudges. You need a friend, and so do I."

"Being my friend is pretty hazardous."

"I think I'll be fine." She stands. "Come on, let's get you out of here. You shouldn't be sitting around all alone, finding reasons to be mad at yourself."

I glance toward the door, and a jolt of fear hits me. "I really don't feel like going anywhere."

"Which is exactly why you should."

"Crosby's going to be coming back for me."

"Now?"

"In a half-hour."

"Well then, we have just enough time. You need to do this, Dez."

I drop my legs over the side of the bench seat and lean forward, trying to muster the will to stand. "You're pushy."

"And you're not?"

"Not today."

She smiles. "Well, you need it. And you'll thank me later." She grabs my arm and pulls me to my feet. "Come on." She leads me to the door, and I follow like a shy child on her first day of school.

"If there's a crowd out there—"

"There isn't. Everyone is worried, but they all know you need space."

She guides me out of our room and into the deserted common

area. My shoulders drop in relief.

Until she leads me to Charlie's door.

I freeze. "Abbey, I can't."

"Yes, you can, and you need to."

"He broke up with me." My voice shakes and I begin to backpedal, but she holds on to my hand.

"I know he did, but that's not what matters right now. You need Charlie, and he needs to see you. He needs to know you're okay."

"But what if I'm not?"

"You will be, and he can help you. I'm just here to give you the push you need to get moving in the right direction."

She raps her knuckles in quick succession on his door and opens it without waiting for a response. She nudges me across the threshold and closes the door behind me, leaving me alone to face Charlie.

Trembling and queasy, I move to the couch.

Charlie springs up from the window seat, the burden of worry heavy on his face. "Dez?" With soft, swift footfalls, he crosses to sit beside me and places a gentle hand on my back, but it's Raum's rough hands I feel.

I recoil, and turn my face away.

"I'm not going to hurt you. You're safe, now."

I close my eyes and Raum is there, his eyes gleaming with menace, his solid, unmovable weight pinning me down, his cloying breath hot against my face.

"I'd never hurt you," Charlie whispers. He reaches for me, but I shrink away. "What did they do to you?"

I shake my head. My heart wants to pour itself out, to let

Charlie bear witness to the horror of last night, but fear is holding me captive.

"You don't have to go through this alone."

"They…" My breath comes in short gasps.

"Please tell me."

"He's everywhere, and I don't know how to make him leave."

"It's okay now."

My fingers wrap around his, and the panic begins to ebb. I want nothing more than to vanish into the safety and comfort of his waiting arms, but I can't give in. If I do, I might never let him go.

"I can't talk about it again. Not right now."

"Promise me you'll tell me when you're ready?"

I squeeze his hand and hope he'll accept the gesture as an answer.

His lips brush against the back of my hand. "I'm sorry about our fight. I never should have said those things to you."

"Don't. This doesn't change anything."

"It does. You mean everything to me, Dez, and last night was a reminder of how uncertain every minute is. Getting wrapped up in what it all means and where it's leading is stupid."

"But you broke up with me. It's over."

"It doesn't have to be. I'm so sorry I hurt you." He runs the back of his fingers down my jaw.

I reach for him with my free hand and push aside the dark hair hanging over his eyes. "You don't have to apologize for being honest."

"All I want is right now. That should be enough for me."

My last happy confusing moments with Bobby before

everything went so terribly wrong play in my head, drowning out Charlie's kindness and the comfort he offers.

"I think I'm falling in love with you."

"Charlie, I don't deserve your help."

He shifts closer and leans his head against mine. "I didn't mean to scare you last night."

"It's okay."

"No, it's not. I didn't mean what I said."

I squeeze his hand. "You don't have to be perfect all the time."

"Maybe, but I picked a hell of a time to be an ass."

I lean my head against his chest, no longer able to fight the lure of his comfort and strength.

He wraps his arms around me, at last making me feel safe.

"I wanted to find her," I whisper.

"Who?"

I sit up. "You didn't hear?"

"Hear what?"

"After that first fight we had, I ran off to be alone, and when I came back, I stopped at Crosby's office. Long story short, I snooped where I shouldn't have and found out my birth mom is here. In the city. And nobody told me."

"Oh, god." The color drains from his face. "That's what you were trying to tell me, isn't it? And that's why you went to the city?"

"Franklin and Kay made me go to a meeting with Crosby yesterday morning, and I flipped out. Shocking, huh? I decided right then and there that I wanted to go find her."

Charlie gives me a weak smile. He leans in and kisses my forehead, his lips soft, his kiss tender. He takes a sharp, pained breath and pulls me back into his arms.

"There's so much more, Charlie. Things happened, and…" I shake my head.

"Whatever they did to you, you can tell me. You need to tell someone, and it should be somebody who loves you."

He still loves me.

A phantom hand grips my heart. "It's not just what they did. Things happened with—" *Bobby.* I can't force out the explanation Charlie deserves.

Silence and shame coil around us like a snake and squeeze the courage from me.

Charlie shifts positions and gently pushes me back as he tries to make eye contact. "Dez?"

I close my eyes against the swirling confusion, my mind and emotions pulled in opposite directions. "I have to go back to the city with Crosby in a few minutes. There's so much happening." My arms tighten around him, and I hold on, seeking shelter from the relentless fear.

"It's going to be okay." He holds me close, his arms strong and solid, but not threatening.

I breathe him in, absorbing his presence and drawing strength from his certainty. "You're better than I deserve, Charlie Weimann."

"Don't start that. You are not that girl." He tilts my chin up. His blue eyes pierce my defenses.

"I don't know who I am anymore."

CHAPTER EIGHTEEN

The gentle swaying of the commuter line does little to calm my frayed nerves. My head is on a swivel. I search the car for threats, on constant alert as the train speeds deep into the city.

"Two more stops," Crosby says. He's calm, but his voice carries a hint of strain.

"And then what?"

There's so much he isn't telling me, I know, but I'm not sure I want to hear it.

"An agent will be waiting at our station stop to escort us the rest of the way. It's another couple of miles to the Council complex."

I sink low in my seat. "They're going to parade me through the city?"

"We're going to keep as low a profile as possible. It'll be an unmarked car with a driver and a single agent, both in street clothes."

"Mack?"

Crosby shakes his head. "He's out on the hunt."

Although I'd welcome the security of Mack's presence, it's actually a relief. Tracking Raum and Moloch, and in turn rescuing Bobby, is Mack's sole mission. The thought gives me little comfort, though. Finding a needle in a haystack is simple by comparison. Mack is searching for a needle in a stack of needles more than a quarter of a billion deep.

Crosby and I elicit many odd looks from passersby making their way on and off the train. My bracelet is on display this time, giving away my status as an underage soul. The hard stares from Crosby keep the gawkers moving, though. None dare to linger too long; their eyes may stick with us, but their feet stay in motion.

The train, at last, glides into the station, our arrival announced by a ding from the overhead PA system. The doors open with a hiss.

My knees wobble as I rise to my feet. I grab a handrail to steady myself and lean forward as a rush of energy pummels me from head to toe.

"You okay?" Crosby asks.

"No, but what difference does it make?"

Crosby helps me off the train and through the small crowd gathered at the doors waiting to board. I stick close to his side, his sturdy calm my shield against this strange place and the fear of what's to come.

We break from the crowd and step off the platform into a plaza bordered by a wide street where six lanes of traffic move in each direction. To our left, a dazzling pastel blue high-rise corkscrews skyward. To the right is a narrow, towering building in the shape of a dancing flame lapping at the sky.

The glassy surface of the obsidian street at the edge of the plaza mirrors the dense traffic. The bumper-to-bumper traffic moves along like a swift school of fish. Sleek vehicles speed by, all of them nearly identical models in black or dark shades of blue. Each dark sedan is a make and model I can't identify that I'm sure I've never seen before.

Crosby gives me a gentle nudge. "We're right on schedule, but there's no time to spare."

We pick up the pace and move through the bustling plaza toward the street.

A black sedan with tinted windows rolls up to the curb as we approach, and a familiar agent steps from the passenger side of the vehicle.

Clara. *Thank god.*

The tightness in my chest eases.

Once she's hustled Crosby and me into the back of the car, she checks over her shoulder, jumps back into the passenger seat, and we are in motion, sliding into the throng of cars.

The driver, a man with sharp, dark features, checks us in the rearview mirror.

Clara pivots so she's looking over the back of the car's bench seat at us.

"Thanks for coming," I say.

She smiles. "You think I'd let anybody else handle your security detail?"

"Does that mean I'm in danger?"

"It's just a precaution."

Even if she's not being entirely truthful, there's nothing I can do about it, so I change the subject. "You still haven't told me what the Council wants with me," I tell Crosby.

"They want to question you about what happened in order to try and get some sense of what Raum's intentions were. Most importantly, they are going to want to construct a timeline of the events leading up to Bobby's—" He stops abruptly when I flinch.

"But Mack already interviewed me. He recorded it, right?"

Clara nods. "He did, but the Council wants to hear directly from you. They have their own questions." Her left arm dangles over the back of the seat, and she bumps her hand against my knee. "Think of it like you're a witness testifying in court."

"Great."

"It won't be so bad, really." Her reassuring smile isn't doing its job.

A small, scared voice in the back of my mind urges me to open the door and jump, to flee to some far-flung corner of the city where no one will find me. Instead, I stare out the window and take in nothing, for the first time disinterested in the sights passing by. Icy fear trickles down my spine.

"I don't want to go over it again."

"I know, sweetie," Crosby says. "But your testimony might reveal clues they can use to find Bobby."

The car slows, and Clara faces forward. "We're here." She glances over her shoulder at me, her casual demeanor gone. "Stay here with Crosby. I'll be right back."

She hops out of the car while it's still rolling to a stop. Her head pivots as she takes in the surroundings. Satisfied, she opens Crosby's door.

He steps out into the busy plaza and offers me a hand.

My stomach lurches. I slide across the seat and am whisked from the car, flanked by Crosby and Clara. The driver pulls away the moment the door shuts behind me, and the car's cocoon of security disappears into the dense traffic.

We move across the plaza toward a vast, sprawling complex that shines like silver in the light. Its front is a series of columns and arches with a balustrade running its length. A massive dome rises at its center that easily dwarfs the Capitol Building I saw up close during a tenth grade class trip to Washington, D.C.

The cherry blossoms were in bloom.

I take a deep breath and recall the sweetly scented air of the Tidal Basin on that warm April morning. The memory washes me in a brief but needed sense of calm.

We climb the stone steps to an entrance at the center of the building. A whoosh of air sounds our arrival as Clara pulls open a steel and glass door and leads us into a marble foyer. At its center is a large, circular desk manned by a dozen men and women dressed in the familiar sky blue uniforms worn by many of Atman's staff.

We approach the desk, and a painful sense of déjà vu hits me. My gaze is drawn to the floor, just as it was when I first stumbled off the train and into Atman Station. I grapple with the same sense of disbelief and shock I felt on that fateful morning, but this time, my fear is not just for myself.

A tall, bronzed man with blond hair looks up from a screen built into the desk. His name badge says he's Oliver.

"Welcome to the GCAP. How may I help you?" His smile reveals gleaming white teeth. Between his tan, his uniform, and his pearly whites, he practically glows.

"*Gee-cap?*" I ask.

"Government Center of Atman Proper," he says, like he's about to break into a sales pitch.

Clara steps up to the desk. "Clara Perkins and Crosby Ebble—" She stops mid-sentence as Crosby shoots her a poisonous look.

"Perkins and…?" Oliver's eyebrows dart up. His index finger slides across the screen on his desk. "I need your full names in order to register you."

"Ebblewhite," Crosby mutters, scowling.

Clara smirks at him before turning her attention back to Oliver. "We're escorting Desiree Donnelly." She rattles off my ID number and tower assignment.

Oliver's fingers fly across the screen. "You may proceed up the north staircase directly behind me." He raises his arm and points behind his back. "Follow the hallway all the way to the end. You'll be in the Grand Chambers."

Clara leads the way to the stairs. I trail a few steps behind, fixated on Crosby's back. "Crosby Ebblewhite?" I savor the words as they roll off my tongue. For a moment, everything else is pushed aside. All I can think of is the delicious bit of news I now possess.

Crosby spins around to face me and walks backward toward the staircase. "Quiet."

"I didn't even know you had a last name. Ebblewhite, huh?"

He turns back around and waggles a finger in the air. "Not smart, troublemaker. I know where you sleep."

"It's *Dream-State Reflection*, not sleep." I take a few quick steps to catch up and give him a friendly elbow. "Does Crosby

Ebblewhite have a middle name?"

"You want to be on kitchen detail forever? I could arrange that."

"So sensitive." I smile, and it's a relief. My steps a bit lighter, I press ahead, up the stairs and down the hall with Crosby and Clara by my side.

We arrive at an enormous set of oaken doors manned by a guard in Atman Blue fatigues. Without a word, he pulls open the door on the left and motions for us to enter.

Clara turns to me. "You ready?"

My heart sinks, the moment of lighthearted fun at Crosby's expense forgotten.

No, I'm not.

CHAPTER NINETEEN

We enter the upper level of the Grand Chambers, which certainly lives up to its name. A viewing gallery set up like a stadium cascades out before us with seating for several thousand. A set of stairs leads down to the main level and a towering judges' bench. A few hundred observers are scattered throughout the gallery. Their gazes focus on us as we descend the stairs.

At the bottom is a small desk, where an elegant, older woman with silver hair sits, sorting through a stack of paperwork. Clara speaks to her in a low voice. "Desiree Donnelly, called to appear before the Council."

The woman heaves open a huge appointment book. She runs her finger down a page and searches for my name. "Very well, you may be seated. You will be called shortly." She points to a row of seats in front with a sign marked RESERVED and turns her attention back to her work.

My hands start to shake. I press them against my thighs and

try to calm the tremor before it takes over the rest of me. Crosby offers me his arm and leads me to the seats. "It's going to be okay, sweetie."

He and Clara sit on either side of me, anchoring me with their strength. Clara points to the witness box near the judges' bench. "The Council members will take turns asking you questions. Answer truthfully, and don't be afraid."

"Just stay focused on us," Crosby says. "We'll be right here the whole time."

I count fifteen chairs behind the judges' bench. Fifteen people questioning me.

I can't do this.

"You're here for Bobby," Crosby reminds me. "Don't forget that."

I'm bolstered by the memory of the harsh lecture I gave myself in the mirror. My spine stiffens. "Mack's going to get him back, right?"

Crosby looks down at his hands and takes his time before answering. His response is slow and deliberate. "He will do everything in his power to find him."

A shiver tracks up my back. Crosby has never avoided my gaze, even at our worst moments. "What does that mean?"

Clara gives me a squeeze. "Let's just get you through this, and we'll talk about it later."

I fall silent, haunted by the implications of Crosby's words and his crumbling confidence. Atman City is a big place—well over two hundred and fifty million souls, if Nero is to be believed. How can Mack possibly find one missing resident? No matter how good of an agent he is, numbers are numbers, and a quarter-billion is a big one.

Time creeps by until a white haired man dressed in Atman Blue robes steps from behind a door to the left of the bench and announces, "The venerable Atman Council, the singular authority, is now in session. Stand as is due. Today's emergency hearing will now come to order."

We stand. The Grand Chambers begins to fill with observers, and the Council members enter single-file. There are eight women and seven men, all wearing judge's robes, all looking grim as they take their seats behind the bench. A woman with dark hair and olive skin sits in the middle on a chair that is raised a foot or two above the others.

She folds her hands in front of her on the bench and addresses the courtroom. "You may be seated." She waits while we all do as instructed. "We have called this special session today due to a yet-unfolding event which began last evening, involving two of our underage tower residents on an unauthorized visit within the city limits. It is my understanding that one of the residents"— she pauses to consult a legal pad on the bench before her—"a Robert Jeffrey Hammond, was abducted. The other resident, a Miss Desiree Anne Donnelly, has been called here today as our only witness to the incident.

"Let the record show the Council held an in-chamber session this morning in order to record testimony from Agent Paul Macklin regarding his role in last night's events. He will not appear in today's session as he is otherwise engaged in pursuit of the two suspects in this unwarranted attack."

She turns her attention to the white haired man who called the session to order. "Steward Darach, our witness, please."

"The Atman Council calls Desiree Donnelly," the man announces. "Miss Donnelly, please step forward and be heard."

My legs shake, making it almost impossible to stand.

Clara squeezes my hand. "You'll do fine. Just tell the truth."

I take a few unsteady steps toward the witness box. The steward meets me halfway and takes my elbow in an uncomfortably tight grip. He leads me the rest of the way.

His rough hand sparks a fire in me, sudden and wild. "I've been grabbed by enough men, thanks." I pull my arm free, careful to steady the tremble in my tone.

Steward Darach narrows his gaze. His steel gray eyes bore into mine.

Regret freezes me in my tracks.

Too far, Dez. Not smart.

We're a single stride from the witness box, locked in a moment of…what? I glance back at Crosby. He's wearing that patented look of his—the "you've really done it this time" one I've grown all too familiar with.

The steward clears his throat, jolting my attention back to the confrontation at hand. "Bold girl," he mutters, a hint of respect mixed into his voice. He holds out his hand—the one previously clamped down on my elbow—and ushers me into the witness box.

I scurry into my seat while he returns to his post.

The presiding councilwoman looks down from her perch at the center of the bench. Her gaze makes me feel ill. The magnitude of the situation is a physical burden weighing heavily on me.

This is for Bobby, I remind myself.

"Thank you for joining us today, Miss Donnelly."

My words evaporate in my throat, and I can only squeak an unintelligible reply.

"We shall begin with a few demographic questions and move forward from there. Please state for the record your full name, age at death, date of arrival, housing assignment, and level."

"My name is Desiree Anne Donnelly, but I go by Dez." There is no microphone to speak into, but my shaky voice is nonetheless amplified throughout the chambers as I rattle off my post-life demographics.

The judge looks to the council member sitting to her left, a dour man with silver hair and a face like a basset hound. He clears his throat. "We'd like to begin with your visit to Nero's Tavern, which to our understanding is where events began to unfold. Tell us about your arrival."

"Bobby and I were…" I pause, trying to collect my thoughts.

"It's all right," he says, already irritated with my sputtering. "You are not on trial. You make speak freely without fear of repercussion."

His annoyance fuels my own. "Bobby took me to Nero's," I say, finding my voice. "And once Nero decided to let us in—"

"This was an issue?"

"Well, yeah. Bobby goes there all the time, but Nero—I got him in trouble when I visited before, so he wasn't too eager to let me back in."

"Explain what you mean."

I steal a glance at Clara. She gives me an encouraging smile. *Tell the truth.*

"When I first got here, Bobby and I got to be good friends right away." I pause in an effort to scoop up the courage that's leaking from me like a sieve. "Bobby took me to the city. A couple of times. Nero's Fiddle is his favorite place to go, so he took me one night. I went in one of the pods. Bobby told me not to, but I wanted to tell my parents I was okay. And then…"

"And then?" Basset Hound Face prods.

"Crosby caught us. He dragged me out of the pod, and I guess there was a lot of fallout for Nero. There's probably even more now, huh?"

"You needn't concern yourself with Nero," the lead councilwoman says. The others on the bench nod in agreement, breaking ever so slightly from their roles thus far as silent observers.

"Describe the scene when you entered the tavern yesterday," Basset Hound Face instructs, his words prodding and impatient.

I press on, doing my best to ignore his tone. "The place was empty except for these two men sitting at a table in the corner, who we later found out were Raum and Moloch."

"That was your first contact?"

"We didn't talk to them or anything." I'm jolted by a memory. "Raum did say something, though. There was this moment when he looked at me and said, 'Hello, pretty.' Our eyes locked and there was this surge, like I was hit with a pulse of energy. It was almost like when I had a link-burst when I first got here, but not as strong."

On my second day at Atman, I was overcome by a surge of energy that knocked me flat. I learned it was a link-burst, the result of my overwhelmed parents' grief traveling across a thread of energy that still linked us together in the immediate aftermath of my death. I saw them, witnessed the suffering that resulted from the careless mistake that cost me my life.

"Does that mean something?" I ask.

"It might," the lead councilwoman says. "But we won't know without additional information."

Basset Hound Face jumps back in. "Did you have further contact with these men while at the tavern?"

"No. Nero took us in a back room, gave us a map, and sent us on our way. He seemed like he was in a rush to get us out of there."

The questions begin to come at me rapid-fire, each member of the Council taking a turn peppering me, searching for details. Once again, I explain every excruciating moment, from the terrifying to the embarrassing, until they're finally satisfied. It seems to drag on for the better part of the day, but my constant checks of my bracelet show a mere hour has passed when all is said and done.

"The last thing Raum said to me was, 'You belong to me, now.'"

A murmur runs across the bench. The Council members turn to each other and break into conversation. They carry on for several long moments, speaking in hushed tones. I can only pick up random words, none of them enough to piece together what's being discussed.

The stalled questioning gets the best of me. "What did he mean by that? What did he do to me?"

A woman at the opposite end of the bench from where I sit speaks up. "Based on the sum of your interactions, from the surge of energy to the ritualistic nature of his behavior in the courtyard, it would seem you have been bound to him."

"What does that mean?" My voice is little more than a squeak.

The lead councilwoman plasters a phony smile on her face. "It's no cause for alarm. The effects are temporary, a few hours at most."

The woman at the other end of the bench shakes her head and speaks up. "That's true for lesser demons, but realm lords such as Raum have the power to affect their target for days, even weeks. And if the bonding was complete—"

Basset Hound Face interrupts. "There is no need for this discussion. It is *not* germane to the conversation we are here to have with this witness."

Realm lord? Bound? My stomach churns, and I begin to shake.

The lead councilwoman sends an angry look down the bench to her peer. "You are needlessly frightening our witness, Anaitis."

"Lying to the child serves no purpose, Liadan," Anaitis shoots back, losing some of her decorum. "She is already frightened. She gave us her honest testimony. The least we can do is be frank in our responses."

Liadan looks down at me from her high seat. "Desiree, it is most likely Raum has, by now, crossed out of this plane and back into his own realm, thus severing the binding you experienced. We will provide further information to your staff escort, which will help answer any remaining questions you may have.

"The Council thanks you for your honesty, Desiree," Liadan says. "We know you've been through a great ordeal, so you are now released back to the care of your escort staff and may return to your tower. Rest and recuperation are in order. You needn't worry yourself further with this matter."

Steward Darach steps forward. "All rise as is due. This session of the venerable Atman Council is now in recess."

Everyone stands and waits as the Council members file out of the chambers. When the room begins to clear, I step down from the witness box and into Clara's awaiting hug, thoroughly shaken by the bomb of information that was just dropped on me.

"Good job," she says.

"You did great," Crosby agrees.

"Can we go? I need to get out of here." The gallery has cleared out, and I want to follow suit.

"You bet, kiddo." Crosby points to his ear. "We have places to be. I just heard from Mack, and he wants to meet and update us on the day."

"I want to come with," I insist, ready for the inevitable argument, hands planted firmly on my hips. My world may be spiraling out of control, but I'm still going to fight.

"Easy cowgirl." Crosby rolls his eyes. "He wants you there, too."

CHAPTER TWENTY

We're back on the train, gliding toward the city's outskirts. Crosby and I are alone, Clara having left us at our station stop with a promise to see me again soon. It's been a silent ride as we both struggle to absorb the overload of information and events of the past day.

"I thought we were going to see Mack," I say, finally speaking up after the stop that would, if my hazy memory serves me correctly, have taken us back to the ACEA station.

Crosby pulls his gaze from the nearby window. "What's that?"

"You said we were going to go see Mack."

"I said he wants to meet with us. He's coming to the tower tonight. We'll be meeting in Franklin's suite after Evening Reflection." He rubs his hands across his weary face.

I've never seen Crosby so un-Crosby-like. He's always been attentive and upbeat, so assured in all he does. This change in his demeanor only serves to fuel my uneasiness.

"There's so much you're not telling me." I lean against the seat, but its hard, plastic surface provides no comfort.

"One thing at a time, kiddo. You have enough on your plate."

I scoot across the bench seat, closer to him. "And you have too much on yours. Ever since the day I got here, you've shielded me from the worst, but you can't this time." My mind is swimming. "Will you at least tell me what being bound to Raum means?"

Crosby's muscles tense. He looks around the train car, searching, before his gaze falls back on me. "I don't want to have this discussion here."

"There's never going to be a good place or time. It's all varying degrees of bad. At this point, I'm not sure things can get much worse, and I really need to know what's going on. Please?"

Crosby gives the deserted train car one last appraisal. "Okay." He pivots on the seat to face me. "First, there are some things you need to know about Raum." He lets out a tired breath.

"Just tell me."

"He is what's known as a Great Earl of Hell."

"What? What does that mean? It sounds like something out of a movie."

"Well it isn't. This is real, and it's serious."

The train slides into the next station, and the PA system dings to announce our arrival. Only when we're back in motion with no new passengers does Crosby continue. "As a Great Earl, Raum rules thirty legions of demons.

"He is ancient and powerful. Normally, the truce is enough to keep him from using his powers outside of Hell, but he's clearly operating well outside the accepted bounds. One of his many powers is his ability to bond with another soul, which is what the

Council thinks happened to you."

"What's that mean? Am I still bound to him?" My stomach ties in knots, but I do my best not to show how scared the conversation is making me, for fear Crosby will end it.

He runs a hand through his hair, stalling. "It's not likely. The odds are that he's crossed back through the gate into his own realm. If he did that, the bond is broken."

"And if he hasn't?" I tuck my hands into the front pockets at the bottom of my shirt so Crosby won't see how badly they're shaking.

"I'm positive he has. There's too much of a risk for him if he stays. Too many agents out looking for him and Moloch."

"Oh, god." I moan, hit with sudden realization. "Does that mean Moloch's taken Bobby—"

"No. It doesn't mean anything."

"But what if they took Bobby with them?" I begin to hyperventilate. "What are they going to do with him? There's nobody to keep him safe. Who is going to protect him from them?"

Crosby puts a hand on my arm. "Sweetie, this isn't helping you or Bobby."

"It's my fault, Crosby. None of this would have happened if it wasn't for me. He's gone because I wanted to find my birth mom, and god only knows what they're doing to him."

I feel like I'm going to throw up. The sickening lurch of my stomach is almost too much to take as yet another idea, too horrible to consider, pops into my head. "If they're so powerful, do they have something in Hell like Mack's Departer? Can they make Bobby vanish from existence?"

"We're going to get him back. You've got to calm down."

Crosby's words roll off me with no impact. The train arrives at the next station, and I lurch to my feet.

He grabs my hand, and his voice takes on the soothing tone he saves for when I'm about to plunge over the edge of sanity. "Dez, sit down. We'll be back to the dorms soon, and we can discuss this with Mack. It's going to be okay."

"No, it's not!" I pull free and bolt through the doors as they hiss open.

"Dez," Crosby yells. He jumps to his feet and chases after me.

I pelt down the platform steps and onto the sidewalk, where I pause for an instant to weigh my options.

To my left and a block down is the perimeter of a small park, its boundaries marked by a waist high hedgerow. It's neatly defined with little cover.

No good.

To the right is an architectural jumble that spreads out for endless blocks. I opt for the chaos of buildings.

I steal a glance over my shoulder and see Crosby is right on my heels. I pick up the pace as I weave down the crowded sidewalk.

Why are you running? Running away is stupid and ultimately pointless, but once you make such a bold decision, it's hard to take it back.

Crosby falls a few paces behind me as he shouts out commands via his earpiece, giving me a tenuous lead. "She's heading north on Barrington toward Myria's Flight. Use utmost care, do you understand me?"

I duck down an alley, not unlike the one leading to Nero's.

It's a zigzagging labyrinth, perfect for getting lost. I slow to a jog, weaving a random path down twisting, narrow passageways and losing all sense of place and direction. When I'm sure I've lost him, I stop to listen and hear no footsteps or voices. Panting, I lean against a wall and slide to the ground, alone with the unthinkable anguish dancing around my mind.

Exile. It's what I deserve. If Bobby isn't safe, I shouldn't be, either.

CHAPTER TWENTY-ONE

"Southwest corridor, clear," a woman calls out from the other side of the alley wall.

I curse under my breath and spring to my feet. A quick glance to my bracelet shows I've only been here twenty minutes.

They're closing in.

Making my steps as light and klutz-free as I can manage, I move down the alley, away from the voices. At every junction I turn left, hoping the tactic will help me work my way back to the street undetected. I rub my bracelet and curse my lack of long sleeves. It won't be dark for hours.

I'm so vulnerable.

Twenty-six left turns later, I've nearly given up hope of finding my way out. As luck would have it, turn number twenty-seven proves to be the key. I peek around the corner into a residential street, free at last from the maze. I step out of the shelter of the narrow alleyway, and pray I'm in a non-criminal sector of the city.

This is insane.

I try to mingle in the light foot traffic.

The neighborhood seems nice, the buildings neat and tidy with manicured grounds and ample shade trees. Storefronts line the left side of the street, and small apartment buildings take up the right.

A shop named *Atman Adventures* catches my interest. With the urgent sense I need to get off the street and out of sight, I hurry inside.

A bell chimes as I enter the small store. The walls are covered in maps, and against the back wall is a table with a rack of brochures. The store is empty, so I step over to the display and begin to browse: *The Canyon of the Sun: a Study in Serenity*; *The Blossoms of Saint's View Mountain; Hiking the Rustic Falls.*

A woman with curly red hair steps out from the back room. "Why hello, dear, how may I help you today?" She glances down at my bracelet but looks back up, smiling, unfazed by my unauthorized presence.

"I—I'm not sure. I'm just…" I stare at her, helpless.

"Browsing?"

"Um, yeah."

"Well, we offer a wide variety of day-trip options, from a lovely countryside excursion to the serenity of a Buddhist temple tour. You'll find it all, from A to Z, at Atman Adventures," she recites like a commercial. "Is there something special you had in mind?"

I opt for throwing caution to the wind.

In for a penny, in for a pound.

"Yes, actually. Exile. Do you do exile?"

The smile falls from her face. "I'm sorry, dear, did you say… exile?"

"That's right. What if a person doesn't want to wait for whoever's in charge to decide they can leave? What if I want to go off somewhere and be on my own?"

She gives me a blank stare. "I'm not sure what you mean."

"This has got to be more than a coincidence, right? I mean, of all the places for me to stumble upon, it just happens to be this—what exactly is it? An afterlife travel agency?" I grab a chair from against the wall and sit. "What would happen if I went to the edge of the city and just kept walking into the wilderness? Where would I end up?"

"If you just walked?" She shakes her head, confused. "For how long?"

"You tell me. Days? Weeks? Months? What's out there?"

"I'm afraid I won't be able to help you with that." She stares down at my bracelet again, but this time, she's nervous. "I think perhaps you should talk to your advisor. You do have those in your towers, right?"

A sizeable map on the wall displays vast areas surrounding the city in intricate detail. I try again. "What's beyond the map's borders?"

The woman stares at the map a long moment before responding. "Maybe I have a brochure in the back. Stay right here and I'll check." She hurries out of sight.

I lean back in the chair, exhausted, content to lounge while I wait.

She returns after a few minutes, the smile back on her face. "I couldn't find anything, but if you want to wait a few minutes, my associate will be in shortly. He's much more knowledgeable about our more...*exotic* locales."

I shrug. "Sure, why not?"

She looks out the window behind me and smiles. "Why, here he comes now."

I look over my shoulder, and my months-dead heart seizes in my chest. A woman and a man, both dressed in Atman Blue fatigues, are entering the store. On their belts, they wear handcuffs and nightsticks, as well as several other items I can't identify, and I'm not sure I want to.

The store owner slips out the front door.

I jump from the chair but have nowhere to go in the close confines of the store. The female officer is the first through the door. She holds up her hands, palms out at shoulder level, a gesture familiar to me from my growing list of tense encounters with Atman staff.

The "I come in peace" stance.

"It's okay, Dez," she says. "I'm Officer Beckworth, and this is Officer Freeman. Nobody's going to hurt you. We just want to get you back where you're safe."

I take a step back. "Safe? It's a little late for that." My breath comes in short gasps. Dark spots distort my vision.

"Take it easy," Officer Freeman says. "Come with us, and we'll get you back to Crosby. We're here to help you." His voice is too kind and too calm.

"So, you're the City Guard, huh?" I take another step back, keeping myself beyond arm's length. "Could have used your help last night. Now? Not so much."

Maybe the back room has an exit.

I take slow, deliberate steps and retreat toward my last hope of escape. The officers creep after me in a bizarre dance that none of us want any part of.

"Nobody's going to hurt you, Dez," Beckworth repeats, like that's going to help.

I shake my head. "I know what happens next. I may have only just crossed the hundred-day mark, but I'm not stupid. I go with you, and you drag me off to the psych ward."

The two officers exchange a wary look.

"RPS? Yeah, I know all about it. I've been manhandled enough for one afterlife, thanks."

Unwanted memories of my frightening first day at Atman flood my brain. My freak-out at Crosby upon arrival ended with a Resident Protective Services staff member chasing me down and rendering me unconscious with a debilitating orb when I refused to cooperate. I was briefly placed in protective custody until I was no longer considered a threat to myself or others.

And I am not *going back. Especially not with Bobby missing.*

Officer Beckworth looks over my shoulder. "There's nothing back there but a storage room filled with boxes. No way out."

My knees start to shake. "See, that's where you screwed up. You're supposed to say something reassuring like, 'RPS? No way. We'd never send you there.' But you didn't, so I guess I know where this is headed."

"There's a chair right behind you, about two paces," Officer Freeman says gently. "If you sit down and let us bring in someone to talk to you, I give you my word we won't drag you out of here kicking and screaming."

I keep shuffling back until my heel hits the chair's leg.

Breathing hard, I drop into the seat and hold out a shaking hand. "Stay back," I plead. "Just give me a minute, okay?"

Beckworth turns her back to me and taps her ear. "We've got her. We're Code Four at Atman Adventures in sector thirty-three."

"It's déjà vu all over again," I say, choking on the words.

Officer Freeman crouches down, but stays a respectful distance back. "Nobody is here to make things worse. As a sworn officer of the City Guard, it's my job to protect you."

"Then where the hell were you last night?"

"I can only imagine how you must be feeling, and I'm sorry we weren't there for you last night. But we're here now, and I want to help."

"Where's Crosby?" I look past Freeman and see Beckworth exiting the store. "Is she going to get him?"

He pulls up a chair and sits, facing me, about five feet away. "We're going to have somebody else talk to you first."

"Clara? From ACEA?"

He shakes his head. "We need to have a member of the crisis team do an assessment to assure you're in an appropriate state to be returned to Crosby's custody. We want to make sure everyone stays safe."

"Just let me go away somewhere, and I promise I won't bother anyone again."

He leans forward, elbows on his knees. "We wouldn't be doing our jobs if we let you run off to some solitary existence in a perpetual state of limbo. I know you've had a terrible go of things lately, but you're going to be okay, Dez."

"I doubt it." I scuff my shoe on the carpet. "Where is this

assessment person?"

Freeman glances back over his shoulder at the door. "They're bringing someone in from Admin to talk to you. They were dispatched right when you…"

"Went crazy and ran? It's okay to say it."

He smiles, reluctant. "Okay, when you went crazy and ran. They should be here any minute."

"Someone from Admin?" *Kay, I'm sure. Great.*

Freeman pauses for a moment, listening. He taps his ear and says, "Okay, I'll let her know. She was just asking." He looks at me and smiles. "He's here."

"He?"

The door opens, and in walks my fate.

CHAPTER TWENTY-TWO

"No," I whisper.

Gideon.

There is a blur of activity. Beckworth follows Gideon into the store, Freeman offers up his seat, and Gideon tells the two officers to wait outside.

Of all the people in the afterlife, why does it have to be him?

My eyes lock on the floor, and I wish in vain to simply vanish from this existence. Each time I think I've hit the absolute bottom, whoever or whatever is in charge laughs in my face and offers up more. This time, the karmic slap comes in the form of the man who took me into custody on my first day, in my first hours off the train.

And here we sit, together again. The location may be different, but the scene is the same. He has me cornered. I've run as far and as fast as I can, but it's ended just the same as it did that first day.

I have no tears left, so I just stare at the dingy carpet. "I'm tired, Gideon."

The legs of his chair drag across the floor as he moves closer. His shoes come into my field of vision, but I have no energy left to so much as sit up.

He bumps his foot against mine. "This would be a lot easier if I could talk to you and not the top of your head."

I twist a braid between my fingers and remember Raum slicing off the end of one.

"You want to tell me what's going on, Dez?"

"Not really."

His dark eyes send a chill up my spine when I meet his gaze.

"What are you doing here?" I ask.

"I'm deciding whether you're coming with me back to RPS, or if I can hand you over to Crosby. He's worried about you."

"Well, I'm worried about Bobby, so I guess that makes us even."

Gideon leans back in his chair. "And you think this is helping him?"

My throat burns. The words come out like acid. "It isn't hurting him. Moloch and Raum are doing that."

"Using up all these resources? Taking all the personnel required to track you down who could otherwise be looking for Bobby; you think that's not hurting him?"

"I…" My words dry up in my throat as gravity of his words press down on me.

All the time I've wasted.

All the agents.

"I wasn't thinking."

"That you weren't," Gideon agrees. "And let's not forget,

you're hurting yourself."

"Maybe I deserve some hurt."

He watches me like he's reading a book. "When Mack gets him back, Bobby is going to need you, which means you're going to have to pull yourself together and be there for him. You can't run away from what Raum did to you last night any more than you can punish yourself for whatever it is they're doing to Bobby."

"What do you want from me?"

"I want you to get on your feet and walk with me out of this store and down to the deli on the corner."

"What for? We both know how this is going to end."

"When's the last time you ate something?"

I know what he's getting at. Even though we're dead and no longer need food, maintaining habits like eating can calm irrational souls. Eating is a comfort measure, one of the stronger remnants of life we cling to. Food is a placebo.

"A couple of days, maybe?" I answer, loath to share even that much.

Gideon stands and offers me his hand. "Come on. Just you and me. No tricks and no orbs. You have my word. But we need to give this lady her store back."

He's letting me off easy. Reluctant, I take his hand, and he pulls me to my feet.

✦✦✦

The deli is tiny, with only four small booths and a counter with six stools. We have the place to ourselves. Gideon picks a booth by the window and without bothering to look at the menu, orders pastrami on rye and a Coke.

The waitress sets the order down on the table a few minutes later, and my stomach begins to growl. Gideon slides the Coke and the plate across the table and hands me the straw. "Eat something."

I peel the paper off the straw and take a long pull off the soda before I dig into the enormous sandwich, inhaling half of it in just a few bites.

Gideon grabs the pickle off my plate and takes a bite. "Better?"

I nod. "Thanks." My ears and cheeks burn with embarrassment as the foolishness of my flight begins to sink in.

Gideon drums his fingers on the tabletop. The muscles of his forearms ripple to the rhythm as he studies me with his dark eyes. "What am I going to do with you?"

"I just panicked, and before I knew it…don't drag me back to RPS." My words begin to race as fast as my mind. "We never should have come here last night, and now I'm screwing things up left and right."

"Take it easy." He keeps watching me while he finishes the pickle. "If you promise me you are not going to pull any more stunts, I will release you back to Crosby just as soon as you finish that sandwich."

"I swear."

"If I have to come after you again—"

"You won't." My voice is tiny. Defeated.

He leans forward and extends his hand across the table. "Deal?"

"Deal." We shake on it.

Gideon taps his ear. "Come on in."

My back is to the entrance, but I seize up when the jingling bell signals the opening of the door.

Gideon stands and offers his seat to Crosby, who I can't bring myself to look at.

"I'll let you two hash things out," Gideon says. "Remember what we talked about, Dez." He claps Crosby on the shoulder and leaves.

Crosby slides into the booth across from me. "You all right?"

The waitress stops at our table to see if he wants anything, but he waves her off.

"Not really." I struggle to find the words I owe him. "I'm sorry," is the best I can manage.

"I'm just glad you're safe."

"I'm sure it would have been a lot worse if you hadn't told the City Guard to go easy on me."

"Nobody is trying to hurt you, not the staff, not the Guard, not Gideon. You don't have to run from us."

"I don't know what to do, Crosby. I want to help, but I don't even know how to not make things worse."

Crosby slides out of the booth. Whether he's more angry or worried, I can't tell. "We can talk about it later. Right now I want to get you back to the towers."

CHAPTER TWENTY-THREE

We arrive back on floor ninety-five as the evening's scheduled free time is coming to a close. Franklin is parked outside the elevator where he's pulled up a chair to wait for us, thus assuring his is the first face we see when the doors open. He sits with his arms crossed, the embodiment of impatience.

"You're just in time for Evening Reflection," he says, dispensing with any pleasantries.

My shoulders slump. "This hasn't exactly been a great day, Franklin."

His expression is flat. "I know you've had a very difficult time." His tone borders on disinterest.

"I can't handle being around everyone right now." The tinge of whining in my voice is cloying, but I can't be bothered to care. "Can I take a pass for tonight?"

His face gives me his answer before the words pass his lips. "Absolutely not. You've missed enough sessions as it is."

I turn to Crosby, but there's no sympathy to be had. "You heard the man."

"But—"

Crosby's hand drops onto my shoulder. "You've been through a lot. We all get that. But you have nobody but yourself to blame for what happened after we left the Council." He points toward the common room with his free hand, his other still clamped on my shoulder. "Let's go."

"I've ruined enough of your day." I pull free of his grasp. "I think I can handle the thirty second walk without you. See you tomorrow, I guess."

Franklin and Crosby exchange a wary look. "May as well tell her now," Franklin says.

I plant my hands on my hips. "Tell me what?"

Crosby takes a step closer to Franklin. "We'll meet you at Reflection in a minute." He pulls me over to a nearby couch.

I yank my arm free. "What now?"

He sits and motions for me to do the same. "Your status has changed."

I drop into the seat next to him. "What are you talking about?"

"Look at your bracelet."

It flashes red.

RESTRICTED

Try as I might to scroll through the menu, I can't access any other information aside from the time—level, ID number, tower assignment; they're all gone, replaced by a single word.

"What the hell?"

"You have temporarily been placed on restricted status."

"What does that mean?" My knees begin to bounce up and

down. The jump-from-your-skin feeling crawls across me as my mind cycles through numerous possibilities, none of them good.

"It means, for the time being, you will have an escort whenever you leave the floor, and when you are in-residence, you will be monitored by staff. We have a meeting with Kay tomorrow morning at eight forty-five to discuss it further."

"So, all that 'you're not being punished' crap was just a line you were feeding me so I'd cooperate?"

"This is not a punishment."

"Really? You people sure have a funny way of not punishing me."

"This is a direct result of you going on the run this afternoon. It was the decision of senior staff members that you're a danger to yourself right now, and we need to take appropriate measures to protect you." He stands. "And we have no more time to talk about this. Evening Reflection is starting. Let's go." He walks away, leaving me to choose between cooperation and whatever awaits an uncooperative, restricted resident.

I jump up and hurry after him.

✦✦✦

"There you are, Dez," Franklin says, front and center in the common room. Next to him sits Mack, the sight of whom both comforts and scares me.

Is there any news on Bobby?

Is he here because he's mad at me for taking away resources this afternoon?

I'm too frazzled, and perhaps too paranoid, to get any sort of read on his expression. My female floormates, however, read like an open book, practically drooling as they stare at this hot stranger in our midst. It's almost enough to make me laugh, but I have no space in my heart or mind for humor.

Franklin points to the empty chair beside Mack. "I'd like you to join us up here."

Crosby sits off to the side, a silent observer.

The last few stragglers find seats among the chairs and couches spread throughout the common room. The group falls silent, all eyes trained on me.

I trudge to the front to join Mack and Franklin for whatever is planned in my first post-attack, post-world-imploding appearance among my peers.

Mack leans in close as I take my seat. "You and I need to talk after this," he whispers.

Abbey offers me an encouraging smile from where she sits, bookended by Erin and Jenna. The two new girls still wear the same twin looks of fear and disbelief, feelings I can relate to now more than ever.

I scan the group and find Charlie. My desire for the comfort of his arms is a physical ache almost too much to bear. It's as though a magnetic pull is drawing me to him, but I don't dare move for fear of bringing down the full brunt of Franklin's wrath. He's relentless in his rules and their enforcement, and so long as I sit on the razor's edge of peril, he holds all the cards.

Charlie and I have to settle for a silent exchange of long looks. His eyes are deep pools of worry. It takes all my remaining strength not to go to him.

"Okay, everyone," Franklin begins, "normally we reserve Evening Reflection for a review of the day and what we've learned—you know the drill. Given what has transpired these past twenty-four-plus hours, I feel it's important we process the events as a group."

Franklin motions to Mack. "This is Senior Agent Macklin. He is heading up the search for Bobby and has agreed to join us tonight to help answer any questions you may have. I am going to open the floor, and you can ask anything you want, but please be thoughtful and respectful in both your questions and actions. Are we clear?"

The group stares back at us and nods as one, silent.

Franklin turns to me. "Is there anything you want to say first?"

I shake my head. I couldn't get a word out even if I wanted to, which I definitely do not.

"Well, feel free to jump in at any time, Dez." He scans the group, searching for volunteers. "Who wants to ask the first question?"

A tan, bleach-blond boy on the couch closest to us raises his hand. He's Bobby's roommate Shawn, and I shudder to think how much he must hate me right now. Shawn's a level nine, which means he'll be getting his ticket soon. I can only imagine how leaving without any kind of closure on Bobby would go over with him.

Like a lead balloon.

"Is there any word on where Bobby is?" he asks. His expression is pained, the diametric opposite of his normal, surfer-guy calm.

"I have to be careful in what I say regarding an active investigation, but—"

"I never meant for this to happen, Shawn," I blurt out, choking on my feeble apology. "Bobby shouldn't have been there...I never should have asked him to go. He was only trying to help me. I'm so sorry."

"You should be," Shawn snaps, his hands in tight fists.

I've never before heard an angry sentiment cross his lips. His words are a punch in the gut, a bucket of ice water dumped on me. I recoil and turn my face away as if he actually hit me.

Charlie jumps to his feet. "What the hell is your problem? Do you have any idea what she's been through?"

"You think I give a crap? Bobby never once had a problem in the city until she came along."

Charlie strides toward him, and Shawn jumps to his feet, shoulders squared, ready to fight.

"Enough," Franklin bellows, but it's too late.

Charlie hits Shawn square in the chest with a hard shove, which sends Shawn stumbling back a step. He comes back swinging and catches Charlie on the cheek with a glancing blow.

Mack and Crosby leap from their seats. They pull them apart as Charlie takes a wild swing that just misses Crosby.

Crosby holds Shawn back, his size a significant advantage over the lanky teen. "Sit down right now, Shawn, or you're out of here."

Shawn pushes his long hair back out of his face, which blooms in an angry shade of crimson. "She's the one who did this." Fury burns up his blue eyes. He points a shaky finger at me. "This is on you. All of it."

"I know," I murmur, but no one hears me amidst the bedlam. Charlie makes another lunge at Shawn, but Mack pushes him back into a corner. He pins him against the wall with his powerful forearm.

"This ends now," Mack commands.

"Get off me." Charlie seethes as he struggles to free himself.

Mack leans against him, and it's clear Charlie is seriously outmatched. Compared to tangling with a Great Earl of Hell, this must be child's play for Mack. "Not until you get control of yourself," he says. "If you can't do that, I'm sure you know how fast I can have RPS here."

"Fine." Charlie stares daggers at Shawn but stops fighting.

"You understand me?"

"I said fine."

"We good?" Mack calls over his shoulder, his gaze still locked on Charlie.

"We're good." Crosby says, in the midst of his own stare-down with Shawn.

Once everyone has returned to their seats, Franklin stands. His face is beet red. "One more outburst from anyone will result in consequences for everyone. Are we clear?"

Erin and Jenna huddle close to Abbey. Nobody dares to speak, and the silence is deafening.

Franklin lets out a slow breath and turns to Mack. "You were going to give us an update."

Mack pauses to collect his thoughts. "As I was saying before we were interrupted, I'm not at liberty to divulge a great deal of information on an ongoing criminal investigation. But I want you all to rest assured that we are doing everything in our power to locate Bobby. We have our best and brightest working at recovering him and apprehending the two suspects."

Abbey raises her hand. "These two guys are on the loose? Aren't they super dangerous?"

"They are extremely dangerous, but you don't need to worry. They pose no threat to tower residents. Their powers do not grant them the ability to travel outside of the city's boundaries."

Kira, another floormate, speaks up. "They're in the city?"

"Well, that's where things get a bit complicated," Mack says. "Without divulging too much, I can tell you these two suspects are beings who possess the ability to travel outside of this realm. Because of these abilities, we can't say with certainty where they are. Not right now. But we're working on it."

"What are you going to do when you catch them?" Kira asks.

"That will be up to the Atman Council to decide. Attacks on transitional souls, especially underage, are not taken lightly."

Keenan, another boy on our floor, clears his throat and raises his hand. "Is there anything we can do to help?"

Mack shakes his head. "Your willingness to help your floormates is admirable, but I cannot stress enough how important it is that each and every one of you stay well clear of this matter. Do not venture outside of authorized areas. Under no circumstances should you visit the city. This is a job for professionally trained agents."

More questions are raised, mostly repeats of what I've already heard and responded to more times than I care to count, so I let Mack handle it and tune out the conversation. My mind drifts to thoughts of Bobby. The image of Moloch subduing him and dragging him off into the night plays over and over in my mind on a sickening loop. I try to shake free of the painful memory, but it's no use.

Finally, the session comes to a close. Franklin scans the room, waiting for any lingering questions. "Does anyone else have anything to ask?"

The group stays quiet.

"If that's it," Franklin says, "you're all dismissed to your rooms for quiet time. Except you, Dez." He stands. "Shawn and Charlie, you can both expect a visit from me before DSR."

CHAPTER TWENTY-FOUR

We've gathered outside the door to Franklin's suite for the promised update on the search for Bobby, but Mack catches my arm as I'm about to follow Crosby inside.

"We'll be in in a few minutes," Mack says. "Dez and I need to talk."

"Isn't Crosby coming?" A silent prayer tags along with my words.

"Nope, just you and me."

The pleading look I give Crosby elicits only a shrug.

"Where's Clara?" I ask in a last ditch effort at delay.

"Working," Mack says. "Come on."

I trail after him toward the library. The comfort normally offered by the plethora of books has no effect on me this time. The power of unease is an overwhelming force that can't be trumped, even by literature.

Mack settles on a pair of chairs facing a picture window

looking out on a darkening Jhana Park. The city's lights twinkle in the distance. He pivots his chair to face the other, paying no mind to the amazing view of the skyline.

"Have a seat," he says.

"Can I go talk to Charlie first?"

"No, you may not. You need to focus on yourself right now."

I sit as far back in my chair as I can. "I know what you're going to say."

Mack's eyebrows dart up. "You do, huh?"

"Running from Crosby was stupid. I just…I really freaked out after the Council meeting. I begged Crosby to tell me more, to tell me about Raum, and when he did I flipped out and ran. The City Guard came after me, and I wound up having Gideon on my case, too." I shake my head. "And now I'm on this restricted status, which means there's no chance I can help find Bobby. I know Crosby's pissed at me, and I'm sure you are, too. I wasted time and personnel by acting crazy. I don't think I can screw up any more than I already have, so whatever it is you're going to say, it's nothing I don't already know." I try to keep myself from taking the plunge into pure panic yet again, but it might be too late.

Mack lets out a long breath while he considers my words. "I can't have you pull something like that again."

Our eyes lock, and I can't look away. "I won't, I swear."

"I know you and Gideon have a history, but you owe him big. He was well within his rights—not to mention protocol—to put you on a long-term RPS placement." He gives me a hard appraisal. "To be honest, I'm still not convinced he made the right choice."

My head swims.

"I'm not saying this just for you, Dez. I can't watch Crosby go through what he did with Maggie, not again." Mack drums his fingers on the arms of his chair. "But I'm going to trust you. This time. Don't make me regret it."

✦✦✦

Franklin has the fireplace lit when we arrive, but its warmth offers little comfort. The relentless assault of guilt and worry chill me to my core. Of all that's wrong, however, I realize there is one small weight I can shed.

I join Crosby on the couch facing the two chairs where Franklin and Mack sit and focus my energy on Franklin as I prepare to make my plea. "Don't punish Shawn. He has every right to be mad at me."

Franklin's mouth drops into a hard frown. "He's a level nine. At least, he was. The standard for our nines is very high."

"I know, but he's under a lot of stress. Stress I helped cause."

"He displayed extremely poor decision making tonight, regardless of the circumstances."

"But—"

Franklin holds up a hand. "His lack of empathy is unacceptable, and that outburst was completely out of bounds."

"He's just worried about Bobby."

"I don't know why you're defending him. If it's some sort of attempt at penance, it's not warranted. Let it go."

"When's the last time Shawn did anything wrong?"

"That's not the point, and it's not what we're here to discuss."

"What about Charlie? Why does everyone else have to suffer because I did something stupid?"

"Dez, that's enough."

Franklin is completely calm, all signs of irritation gone. New arrivals often fall into this trap he sets, seeing his sudden change in demeanor mid-argument as a positive sign, but I have no such delusions.

Serious consequences await.

Crosby knows it, too. He puts his hand on my shoulder and guides me into a less aggressive posture. "Let's get back on track. We're here for Bobby, remember?"

My fury boils over. "Remember? How in the hell could I possibly forget? Do you think that for one second since this happened that I've done anything but think about him? About what they've done? What they're still doing?"

"Dez," Crosby tries to put his hand on my arm, but I yank it away.

"Bobby believes this whole existence is a creation of his mind. Do you think that's helping him right now?"

"This isn't doing either one of you any good."

My hands clench. My fingernails dig deep into my palms. I lash out, and my fists crash against Crosby's chest. "Why don't we have him back? Why do those monsters get free run of the city?"

In the blink of an eye and the blur of my tears, Mack pulls me off him. Without a word, save my screams, he drags me into the hallway, ignoring Crosby's protests. With a tight grip on my upper arm, Mack half drags, half carries me to my own door and into my room.

Abbey, sprawled on our couch reading a book, bolts upright when we burst through the door, a sudden tangle of rage in her midst. Her eyes are like saucers, staring at the two of us struggling in the entryway—although to be honest, only one of us struggles. Mack has me entirely outmatched, both in size and strength, not to mention levelheadedness.

The door opens and shuts again. "We're going to need the room, Abbey," Crosby says from behind me.

She hesitates for an instant before hurrying to the door.

"I'll come find you in a bit," he calls after her.

Mack points to the couch. "Sit down," he commands through clenched teeth.

I rub my freed arm while I consider my next move. My whole body deflates when I realize I don't have one. The only real option I have is the couch, so I sit.

Mack turns to Crosby. "Dez and I need to have another little talk."

Crosby looks at me and then back to Mack. He takes his hand. "Go easy, okay?"

Mack brushes Crosby's cheek with his fingertips of his free hand. "Just wait outside."

Crosby hesitates, their fingers still twinned.

Mack's expression softens. "It was okay last night when I kicked you out of the room at HQ, and it will be okay this time, too."

Crosby leaves without further protest and without so much as another glance in my direction. The door closes behind him.

I pull my knees to my chest and hug my legs.

Mack towers over me, way too close for comfort. He tilts his gaze to the ceiling.

I stare at the deep gashes my fingernails left in the soft flesh of my palms. "I…"

Mack takes a step closer, focusing his anger on me. "What did we just talk about? Did you hear a word I said?" He points back toward the door. "Do you have any idea what this is doing to him?"

"I know."

"I don't think you do. You have been cut so much slack in the last twenty-four hours, given so many chances, yet you continue to walk all over those of us who are trying the hardest to help you."

"I'm sorry."

"That's not good enough; not anymore." He taps his ear and gives me a hard stare. "I'm going to need you after all. We're in her room. Number six." He pauses. "Yeah, just let yourself in."

"Who was that?" I say, not sure I really want the answer.

"You've given me no other choice, so you're getting my backup plan."

CHAPTER TWENTY-FIVE

My feet fall to the floor, and I lean back against the couch in surrender.

The door opens, and Gideon slips into the room, his catlike agility still a marvel to me despite the dread his presence brings. He sits next to me on the couch and leans forward, his elbows resting on his knees. "What did I say about having to come after you again?"

"Where's Crosby?" I ask weakly.

"This has nothing to do with him. Mine is the only vote that counts right now, and based on your actions today, I've made my decision."

"Please, I—I need to stay here on the floor. I won't cause any more trouble."

"It's too late for that. You are going to sit here and listen to what Mack has to say, you're going to answer any questions he has, and then you're going to come with me."

Mack sits across from us in Hannah's recliner chair.

None of this would be happening if she were still here.

"It won't be so bad," Mack says, his storm of anger dissipating. "It's just for tonight, right?"

Gideon nods. "It's up to Kay to decide tomorrow how we proceed. If you do what we say and don't give me any more trouble, she may be inclined to release you back to your floor after your meeting."

Crosby comes back in the room and takes a seat in the other recliner next to Mack. He looks almost as bad as I feel. "You take good care of her, Gideon."

"You know I will." He glances back at the door. "Is Franklin joining us?"

"No," Crosby says. "He has to deal with Shawn and Charlie, plus the two new girls are having another rough night. I told him we could handle things just fine in here."

"Before we went off the rails," Mack says, "I was going to give everyone an update on what we've learned today in our investigation. I decided to include you in the conversation, Dez, because you were directly involved in the attack. I will stick by that decision, so long as there are no further outbursts. Understood?"

I nod, not daring to say a word.

Mack pauses a moment before continuing, like he's testing the waters, waiting to see if I'll flip out again. "We all but turned the city upside down today, bringing in every available agent and most of the City Guard. Unfortunately, we found no sign of Raum, Moloch, or Bobby. This leaves us with one increasingly likely scenario."

"They crossed back through the gate," Crosby says.

"If they did, it was immediately after the attack. We had guards on the gate within an hour after getting Dez back to HQ. But there's still a lot of ground to cover, and we have to be sure before we take it to the next level."

"If they went back through the gate," I say, "what does that mean for getting Bobby back?"

"It would mean changing our investigation from one of search and recovery to a mission of negotiation. But it's too early to make that call."

"Could they have left Bobby somewhere?" I grasp at any straw I can, no matter how thin. "Maybe they got tired of him and dumped him off. Maybe he just hasn't found his way back, yet."

"Anything's possible, I suppose," Mack concedes, but not without a face full of doubt.

Gideon glances at the clock on the wall. "Is that it?"

"I wish I had better news, or at least more to tell you," Mack says. "What I really need tonight, though, is to ask you a few more questions."

I lay my head back against the couch and groan. "Seriously? Hasn't today been enough?" My eyelids are heavy with exhaustion.

"Are we going to have a problem?" Gideon asks. The question hangs heavy in the air.

Crosby opts for the gentler approach. "Anything for Bobby, right? That's what you said, and we really need you to stick to your word."

"It's important, Dez," Mack leans forward in Hannah's chair. "I'm doing everything in my power to catch Raum and Moloch and bring Bobby back. If you want to help, this is how you can do it."

"Okay." I sit up and draw from the shallow pool of my remaining strength to face this next round of questioning.

Mack wastes no time. "All the focus thus far has been on the attack in the courtyard, but I want to talk to you a bit more about Nero's."

"But nothing happened there. Raum said exactly two words to me, but aside from that, there was nothing."

"It's not what he said that I'm interested in. It's what you and Bobby may have seen."

"They were just sitting there at the table. I'm telling you, we didn't see anything. Why are you so sure we did? Is it because of what he did to me?" I swallow back nausea.

Mack leans over and whispers something in Crosby's ear.

Crosby nods at Mack and announces, "We're going to step outside for a minute."

"We'll be right here, waiting," Gideon says.

This just keeps getting better.

My level of discomfort climbs with each silent moment that passes.

At the five-minute mark, Gideon finally speaks. "You can bring a change of clothes. Nothing else."

"What?" My wheels spin as I try to comprehend the words he's chosen to break the silence.

"When we leave. That's what you can bring with you."

"Oh." I run my hand across my throbbing forehead. There's so much I want to get off my chest, but I'm not sure how to say it. "You want to know the truth?"

"I'm a big fan of the truth. Tends to clear the air."

I pull at a loose thread on the couch in an effort to avoid

his gaze. "You scare the hell out of me. RPS scares me almost as much."

Gideon nods. "We get that a lot. If you're seeing me, things probably aren't going great to begin with, and when you're backed into a corner, it tends to get scary for you."

My face burns from shame. "You have no idea what it means for me to admit that."

"Duly noted." He tilts his head, studying me. "But there's obviously more. What aren't you telling me?"

"You were one of the first people I met here."

"I remember. You were fresh off the train."

"And you saw me at my worst. Crosby did, too. But in that hallway, with you? That was by far my low point."

"It's nothing to be ashamed of. I told you about what happened to me."

"Yeah, you did."

In the first few days after my arrival at Atman, Gideon tried to help me by sharing his own story—a World War One veteran turned heroin addict who took nearly thirty years to earn his ticket out of here. He urged me to follow the rules and stay on the path of progress, but I was still too mad about our first encounter to hear any of it.

"You were trying to help, and I blew it off," I admit. "Listening might have saved everyone a lot of trouble."

"It happens."

"Crosby sees me every day, and most of the time I'm doing okay. But you—you only ever see Crazy Dez."

"It's my job."

"But I'm more than that, more than some out of control

lunatic. I know it doesn't change anything, and it doesn't change where we're going tonight, but…" I run out of words and energy. My well is dry.

"You want me to see you as more." His leans back on the couch, giving me a bit of space.

The door opens, and Mack and Crosby join us again.

Gideon holds up a finger. "To be continued."

"Okay." Mack returns to his seat. "Crosby and I were discussing how much we should share with you, Dez. Given the circumstances and what you already know, we feel the benefits outweigh the risk in this situation, but what we tell you cannot leave this room. Do you understand?"

"Not a word to Charlie or anyone else," Crosby says.

"Okay," I promise.

Mack gives Crosby one last look of doubt before proceeding. "For starters, we've had Nero in custody since last night."

"Oh, god." I blanch at the thought. "I've already caused that man enough trouble. Two times I go in his bar and two times he gets hell to pay for it. He's going to—"

"Be thankful he gets out of this at all," Mack says, leaving no room for argument. "He hasn't exactly been the most cooperative witness, but we have a strong hunch as to why Raum and Moloch were in his tavern, and it wasn't for the drinks."

"That's where you come in," Crosby says.

I remain completely puzzled. "But I told you, we didn't see anything. We went in to the bar, Raum and Moloch were at a table talking. Raum said two words to me: 'Hello pretty.' That's it."

"You didn't see them go anywhere? Didn't hear what they

were talking about?" Mack presses me, his tone urgent.

"No. Nero seemed unhappy about them being there, but he didn't say anything. He just looked a little uneasy and was kind of in a hurry to get us out of there. So, we told him we wanted to find my birth mom, he took us in the back to find a map, and—" I pause, my memory jogged by a tiny detail.

"What is it?" Crosby says.

"It's just something Nero said. When we were walking down the hallway in back, he scolded me about staying out of the pod room, which was no surprise. He said it was 'forever off limits' to me. But then what he said to Bobby, it was a little odd."

"What did he say?" Mack prompts.

I close my eyes and try to remember the exact words. "After he got on my case about it being off limits, he said, 'And you too, Bobby. At least for today.' Bobby never goes in the pods, but he's been in the pod room hundreds of times. He likes to observe the people who use them. And he still goes, even after what happened with you and me, Crosby, so it's weird Nero told him to stay out." I open my eyes, the memory now crystal clear. "Nero had this look in his eyes when he said it, like he was nervous, and he looked back over his shoulder toward the bar."

Mack slams a closed fist down on the arm of the chair. "I knew it."

"What does it mean?" I'm stretched too thin to wrap my brain around this big break of his.

"They were there to use the pods," Mack says.

"But why?"

"The pods let you communicate with anyone living. Think of the damage a couple of high-ranking demons could do with access to vulnerable, living beings. They can prey on the mentally ill, the insolated, the desperate, and unleash them on the living. That's why you were attacked."

"What?"

"They were out for more than just mayhem. They wanted to be sure you didn't let slip that you saw them there."

Crosby closes his eyes. "The mayhem was just an added bonus."

Mack stands and begins to pace. "They may have even recognized Bobby. You said he goes there a lot to watch people use the pods?"

"He even keeps journals."

Mack freezes in his tracks. "Show me."

CHAPTER TWENTY-SIX

We wait in the common room for the all-clear from Crosby, who has gone ahead to smooth the way with Shawn. His still-percolating anger is not something I want to deal with on top of everything else.

"This isn't right," I protest. "These are Bobby's private journals we're talking about."

As floor adviser, going through Bobby's things is ultimately Franklin's call, but he's fully onboard.

No surprise there.

"The privacy rights of our residents are something I take very seriously," he says. "But the benefit of what his journals might provide outweighs the ethical questions raised by reading them."

Even if I had a vote, I'm outnumbered. The thought of going through Bobby's things sickens me nearly as much as the thought of what might be happening to him at the hands of Raum and Moloch.

If he knew what we were about to do—what I am about to do…"Bobby wouldn't want us doing this, even under these circumstances."

Franklin ignores my protest. "If that's everything you need from me, Mack, I have a few more fires to put out tonight."

"We're good, thanks," Mack says.

"If anything changes, you know where to find me."

With that, we split up. Franklin heads for his first stop of the night—Erin and Jenna's room—while Mack leads the way to Shawn and Bobby's.

I make one last plea. "We can't do this, Mack. It isn't right."

"His journals are potential evidence. They might contain clues that could help us find him."

My stomach clenches. "I don't want a whole team of strangers reading his private thoughts."

"You have my word his journals will not leave my sight, and I will involve a minimum of personnel in examining them."

"They mean the world to him." I grab Mack's arm. "You have to promise."

"I will be as respectful of his privacy as is possible."

I lean against the wall outside their door. "He doesn't let just anyone see his journals, and to riffle through what might end up being his last work—"

"Don't talk like that. We will find him and get him back here where he belongs."

I meet his gaze. "He's never belonged here."

Shawn storms out of the room and slams the door with Crosby close on his heels.

"I guess we're clear," Mack says, unfazed by Shawn's fury.

"Come on. We've wasted too much time already."

He leads me into the room, and I make my way to the tidy stacks of journals piled high on both sides of Bobby's bed. His closet is filled to overflowing with even more research.

"That's his more recent stuff." I point to the stacks on the floor. "His archived work is in the closet. He has a filing system, but he's never really explained it to me."

Mack stops to marvel at the sheer volume of it all. Bobby's always been fascinated by Atman, despite his belief that it's all a figment of his imagination. As a renowned scientist, it's how he's coped with this strange existence all these years.

Mack sets to work skimming the covers of each book in the first stack.

"That's not what you want," I say. "He keeps the pod journals in here. He always wants them close by." I open the drawer on his nightstand and carefully remove the three notebooks Mack is looking for. "The pods are special to him. He believes they're the nerve center of his unconscious mind."

"You've seen these before?"

I cradle Bobby's research like I'm holding a baby, reluctant to hand it over. "He finally let me see a few weeks ago."

"That's a lucky break." Mack smiles.

"There's no such thing as luck. Or if there is, it sure wants nothing to do with me."

Mack holds out his hand. "It's okay, I promise."

I hand him the journals.

Bobby will never forgive me for this.

Distracted by the fresh evidence now in his possession, Mack doesn't seem to notice me climb onto the bed and lie down. I wrap my arms around Bobby's pillow and breathe in the scent of him, desperate to reach across eternity and grab him back from the monsters who took him.

This might be the closest I ever get to Bobby again.

The grief is indistinguishable from blinding fear.

I don't know if I'll ever get up again.

Mack starts to leaf through the first notebook. "I'm going to need your help sorting through this." He looks up from a page he's attempting to decipher.

I can't speak, can't form any kind of coherent response.

Mack places the journals back on the nightstand and steps over to the bed. "Dez?" He leans over me.

I curl up in a ball, wrapped tight around Bobby's pillow.

"Come on, Dez," he says softly. "You've got to talk to me."

Leave me alone.

"I know you miss him, and I know your mind is running wild with all the horrible scenarios you can imagine, but you have to believe me when I tell you we're going to get him back."

"In what condition? Will he be the friend I've gotten to know and…"

Love. Just say it.

"Is he going to hate me as much as Shawn does?" I ask instead.

"He will get the best care available, and he could never hate you. Shawn doesn't either. He's just hurting right now."

"How can he possibly get through this, even if you do get him back? Ten minutes with Raum was more than I could take, and they've had him for twenty-four hours." My hysteria is rising again like a tide.

"I'm going to get Crosby. Just hang in there, Dez."

They won't let me help.

They won't let me run away.

What's left?

Mack hurries from the room and returns quickly with a worried Crosby in tow, but it's not soon enough.

"Come on, sweetie," Crosby says. The bed sinks as he sits down next to me. "You can't do this to yourself. Not again."

"Just leave me alone."

"Gideon is waiting outside, and I can't keep him at bay for long."

"If that stupid orb is the best he's got, I say bring it on. Unconscious would be a welcome relief compared to this."

"You don't mean that."

"The hell I don't. I can't take one more second inside my own brain." I sit up, and my feet drop to the floor with a thud. "In fact, forget unconscious." I turn to Mack. "You have your Departer with you? Because I've about had it."

Mack stares at me, stunned.

I hold my arms out at my sides. "I'm serious. Go for it."

Crosby hangs his head and covers his face with his hands. "Dez..."

Mack's hand moves in slow motion to his ear. "We need you in here. Right now."

CHAPTER TWENTY-SEVEN

Crosby, Mack, and Gideon stand in the entryway. They speak in low tones, trying to work out a game plan.

"Normally, I'd call for backup," Gideon says, "but we're going to see how this goes solo. If I call in anyone else, it could get ugly. You remember how her first brush with us went."

Crosby nods. "I appreciate that."

Gideon turns to Crosby. "I'm your friend, and that's why I'm here, but right now, I have to put that aside and tell you something as an RPS interventionist. You're not going to like it, but you both need to step outside. You can't be here for what comes next."

Crosby shakes his head. "I can help."

"I can't let you. In making the threat she did, we've crossed a threshold. Only RPS staff can have direct contact with her for the next twelve hours while we assess her condition."

I sit on Bobby's bed listening to the conversation with

complete detachment, as though they're talking about someone else, some other crazy girl.

The door closes behind Mack and Crosby. Gideon crosses the room in silence and crouches in front of me.

A glimmer of surprise breaks through my funk when I see genuine, anger-free concern on his face. He speaks softly, moves slowly, like the slightest disturbance might send me over the edge.

But it's too late.

"I need to ask you some questions, Dez. Is that okay?"

"I don't care. Do what you want."

"You said something to Crosby and Mack indicating a desire to do harm to yourself. Do you remember that?"

I grab one of my braids, the one shortened by Raum's dagger, and twist it between my fingers. "I asked Mack if he had his Departer with him."

"Why?"

I smooth Bobby's pillow and set it next to me on the bed. "Because I'm tired."

"Do you know what a Departer does?"

"It eliminates you from existence."

"Is that what you want? To cease to exist?"

"With this as the alternative, it doesn't sound so bad."

Gideon purses his lips, lost in thought for a moment. "We'll revisit that later." He stands. "There are a few more things we need to do, and then we'll go. So long as you cooperate and follow my instructions, there won't be any need for additional staff involvement. You ready?"

I nod, focused on Bobby's cast-off pillow.

"Okay Dez. Nice and slow, I want you to stand up."

I do as instructed, no longer in possession of the will or interest to fight.

"Do you have on your person any weapons you could use to harm yourself or others?"

I let out a weak laugh. "Does it matter? Isn't pain all in our heads?"

"Just answer the question, please."

"No, I don't have anything."

"Good. Do you feel capable of walking with me under your own power back to RPS? It's about a twenty minute walk from here."

"I think I can manage."

"We're going to take our time, and I want you to do your best to avoid any sudden movements. Do you understand?"

"Sure."

"I am going to hold onto your arm while we walk to reduce the risk of any potential incidents."

"Like I said, do what you want."

"When we walk to the elevators, I want you to avoid communication with anyone but me. If anything comes up, I will handle it. That includes Crosby and Mack."

"Fine."

He takes my arm in a gentle grip. "Let's go."

We step out of Shawn and Bobby's suite, and I spot Crosby on a couch at the edge of the common room. He sits huddled against Mack. The pain in his eyes punches through the numbness and distance that have infected me.

I falter, stumbling as my knees buckle.

Gideon slips his arm around me and holds me steady. "Easy, now. I've got you."

Somehow we make it into the elevator, and Gideon is kind enough to grant me the dignity of freedom, even if only for the duration of our descent. I lean against the wall and close my eyes, grateful for the few feet of space between us.

"Did you ever feel like this?" My voice is flat, almost unrecognizable.

"Every day for about a decade."

I open my eyes. "Is that why you work for RPS?"

Our eyes meet, and he nods.

"How did you get through it?"

"When I finally decided I wanted to get better, I did. But I couldn't do it by myself." He takes my arm again as the doors open.

We pass through the empty lobby into Jhana Park, where the familiar route along the winding path brings us to the Admin building. Somehow time passes, one shuffling step after another, until we arrive at the locked ward of Resident Protection Services.

Gideon's punches a code into a keypad, and the frosted glass doors swing open. He leads me past a reception desk to a nurse's station where a tall woman with dark skin and curly black hair is waiting. She smiles warmly. "You must be Desiree."

"It's Dez," I murmur, fixated on her Atman Blue scrubs.

"My name is Francesca." She turns to Gideon. "She'll be in room one ninety-two. Let me go grab her chart, and I'll take her down."

Gideon shakes his head. "You can meet us there. I'm staying with her until she's checked in."

Francesca steps into a small room behind the nurse's station, and Gideon leads me down the corridor to the right. It's identical to every other hospital I've seen, with polished linoleum floors and pastel, nondescript paintings on the walls. The room numbers climb into the one hundreds as we make our way to my assigned room at the end of the hall on the left.

The room is small and sparse, with only a bed, a chair, a small nightstand, and a poster on the wall that declares its message of propaganda in bold type. I've seen so many of these since arriving that I hardly notice them anymore, but this one is hard to miss, placed directly above the bed.

COURAGE IS LIKE LOVE. IT MUST HAVE HOPE FOR NOURISHMENT.

"Have a seat," Gideon says, pointing to the bed.

The first tendrils of fear snake through my fog of indifference. On shaky legs, I do as I'm told and sit at the edge of the bed.

My voice trembles. "What happens now?"

Gideon pulls the chair closer to the bed and sits. "Francesca will be here in just a minute to get you checked in. She'll be the one looking after you tonight. In a few minutes, a member of our intake staff will be in to ask you some questions and do an assessment of your condition." He leans forward in his chair. "I have to leave for a little while, but I'll be checking in on you again tonight and will be here in the morning for your evaluation."

"What about Clara? I want to see her."

"You can't have any visitors in your first twelve hours. Your only contact will be with RPS staff."

Francesca walks into the room, all smiles. "Okay, honey, we're going to get you settled in for the night. Won't take but a few minutes, and then you can get some rest, which is exactly what you need."

Gideon pauses in the doorway on his way out. "You're more than just a couple of bad days, Dez. Remember that."

Francesca smiles and watches him leave. "You're a lucky girl. He's a good man to have looking out for you."

I give her a noncommittal shrug. "I guess."

"Let's get you ready, shall we?" She hands me a neatly folded stack of clothes and sets a large zip-top bag on the nightstand. "Take everything off but your underwear, and put your clothes into the bag." She motions to a call button attached to the bed. "Push that button just as soon as you're changed, and I'll be back in a jiffy." She whisks out of the room and pulls the door shut behind her.

The door emits a soft beep, and I'm alone. Taking my time, I unfold the clothes she's given me—plain white scrubs. I take off my shirt and put it in the bag, but as I unbutton my jeans, I'm assaulted by terrifying memories.

I can see Raum.

Smell him.

Hear him.

"There is nowhere you can go, nowhere you can hide from me. You understand?"

Gripping the scrubs to my face, I fall to my knees. The well-worn top muffles my cries. Raum's attack plays again without mercy, the assault of memories that flooded my mind no easier to face now than it was the first time. I rock back and forth and try to shake the pain.

Charlie.

Think of Charlie.

His arms, his lips, his perfect blue eyes.

Get lost in them again.

My pulse begins to slow as I take deep, deliberate breaths. With one last calming inhalation, I open my eyes.

"Did you think you'd get away so easy?" Raum snarls.

I look up at the chair with a jolt, and he's there, right where Gideon sat not five minutes ago. His hazel eyes glimmer with malice. Dressed all in black, he stands and takes off a long coat. His muscles ripple under a tight-fitting t-shirt. He looks behind me and smiles. "At least we have a bed this time, pretty. Must be your lucky day."

I scramble backward and scream. My back hits the bedframe, its cold metal a shock against my bare skin.

Two strides and Raum is on me. He clucks his tongue. "What did I tell you about running away?" His dagger is out in a flash of steel. He kneels down before me and presses the cold tip of the blade against my cheek.

"No!" I wail.

He strokes my cheek with his free hand. "You're bound to me, sweet one. There is nowhere you can go that I can't find you."

He presses close and growls in my ear, the stubble on his cheek rough against my skin. "I am not to be trifled with, child." He looks over his shoulder, back toward the door. "We haven't much time, but I want you to see I mean what I say. I can find you anywhere. You should never have run from me." He grabs my arm and lifts me to my feet. "You belong to me, and I will not be denied what is mine."

The thunder of footsteps charging down the hallway is the sweetest sound I've ever heard. The door bursts open, and I fall to the bed, overwhelmed by the competing sensations of terror and relief.

Gideon rushes to my side. "Dez?"

Francesca sits next to me on the bed and tries in vain to calm me. "Honey, talk to me. What's going on?"

"Stop him," I wail.

Gideon's eyes scan the tiny room. "Who?"

"Raum!"

Francesca covers me with a blanket, but it does nothing to stop my shivering.

"Dez, there's nobody here," Gideon says.

Francesca moves the hair out of my face. "You've just had a very long day. I'm going to go get you something to eat, and you'll feel a lot better." She leans in closer, studying me. Her fingers brush across my cheek. "Gideon?"

He steps closer.

"She's bleeding," Francesca says. "Look at this gash on her cheek." She rubs my back. "Honey, did you do something to hurt yourself?"

"It was him," I moan.

Gideon leans in and points to my neck. "That looks like a hand print. A pretty big one. There's no way she did that to herself."

He moves to the doorway and taps his ear. "Mack, it's me. How fast can you get to RPS?"

CHAPTER TWENTY-EIGHT

Clara sits beside me at the edge of the bed. "We're going to fix this. I promise."

Crosby and Gideon are just outside the room having an urgent discussion while Mack gives instructions to the two ACEA agents he's posted at my door.

"I don't want to see anybody else," I insist.

"I know," Clara says, "but I'm not sure I can drag all three of them out of here by their ears. I'm good but not that good." She gives me a squeeze and coaxes a tiny smile out of me.

"My money's on you."

She turns her attention to Mack as he enters the room. "Make it quick, boss."

Mack holds his hands up. "Just wanted to let you know we'll be back in the morning to escort you to your session with Kay. By then, I hope we'll have an update on what exactly is going on. In the meantime, I have two of my best agents out there. I promise you'll be safe." He turns to Clara. "Do you mind staying here with her until she's settled and resting?"

She gives me another squeeze. "I wouldn't have it any other way."

Crosby walks away from the conversation still brewing in the hallway and steps into the room. He's a study in barely-contained rage. His jaw is set, his posture rigid.

Before he can say a word to us, Gideon steps in and puts a hand on his shoulder. "This is the safest place for her."

Crosby shakes his head. "Look what he did to her. You call that safe?"

"She's safe now."

"We need to move her to a more secure location."

Mack jumps into the conversation. "A locked ward with two agents outside her door is about as secure as it gets."

The look on Crosby's face makes it clear his input is not appreciated

"Raum's appearance doesn't change what happened in Bobby's room," Gideon says. "She needs to be here."

Crosby finally concedes with a sigh. He steps over to the bed. "If you need anything—and I mean anything—you push that call button and tell them to call me."

"I will."

"Okay, kiddo." He reaches for my hand but thinks better of it. "You get some rest."

Clara shoos the trio out of the room. "You gentlemen have a good night. I'll take it from here."

Gideon frowns. "You can't kick me out. I work here."

"Watch me." She smiles sweetly and gives him a last little

nudge into the hallway before closing the door.

"There's no way I'm going to get any rest." I lie back on the bed, but my nerves are a live wire. I can't keep still.

"You'd be surprised. As exhausted as you are, you'll be out in no time."

Every muscle in my body tenses. "He's going to come back."

"Not while we're watching you, he won't." Clara sits in the chair next to the bed and pats my knee. "He was just trying to scare you."

"Mission accomplished. I'm going to close my eyes, and he'll be there. And then I have to face DSR."

"Nope. No DSR for you, tonight. It's one of the perks of being here."

I scoff. "RPS has exactly zero perks."

"Okay, well, it's one of the less awful things."

I roll over to face Clara. "Thank you," I say. "For everything. For coming here, for staying with me. I—"

"Don't waste another word on it," she says, waving her hand. "You have entirely too many men in your orbit, and I have to do what I can to level things out."

"Did Mack tell you what I said?" My face burns with shame.

"He did. Did you mean it?"

My eyelids grow heavy, but I fight to stay alert. "I don't know."

"Yes, you do."

"Part of me wishes that when Mack pulled his Departer…"

"Come on, honey. You can tell me."

"I wish he'd have used it on Raum and me both."

Clara sits next to me on the bed. "You've been through hell these last twenty-four hours. But this is *not* how it's going to be for you. Not forever. We're going to get Bobby back, and Raum and Moloch are going to pay for what they did."

"I wish I could believe you."

She covers me with the blanket, and for the first time since we met last night, she looks sad. "Things will be better after you get some rest."

✦✦✦

The morning comes whether I'm ready or not. The bliss of dreamless rest was nothing more than a brief escape. The world comes crashing down, a solid, physical reality that descends on me the instant my eyes open.

I sit up with a start. My gaze goes immediately to the chair by the bed, but it's empty.

The door opens and Abbey enters, carrying a change of clothes in her arms. I rub my eyes, convinced I'm hallucinating.

"Abbey? What are you doing here?"

She pulls the door shut behind her.

"How did you get past the guards?"

She drops into the chair, which has now seated everyone from tower residents to Great Earls of Hell. "My job rotation this cycle. I do filing at the nurse's station, and I sweet-talked them into letting me bring you some clothes. They said no at first, but since you have a meeting with Kay this morning and didn't get to bring anything with you last night, they gave in." She smiles. "I can be persistent."

"Thanks," I say, stunned and at a loss for any sort of

meaningful interaction.

"They're only letting me stay a minute, though. And those guards out there?" Her eyes go wide. "Yikes." She hands me the clothes. "I hope what I picked out for you is okay."

I hold the jeans and t-shirt close, like precious cargo. "I really appreciate this, Abbey."

"I'd better go. Like I said, those agents are scary." She leans in close to my ear and whispers, "Check your jeans pockets. Don't let anyone see you, though."

She hurries from the room without another word.

Don't let anyone see me?

There's nowhere for me to go in this tiny room, so I slip the clothes under the blanket with me.

There's a knock at the door, and it opens a crack. One of Mack's agents peeks in. "Just got word that your escorts will be here in ten minutes."

I do my best to look offended. "Thanks, but may I have some privacy, please? I need to get dressed."

"Of course." He pulls the door shut in haste.

I slip into the t-shirt Abbey brought me and, with another cautious glance at the door, pull on my jeans and search the pockets. In the front right pocket are a folded piece of blank paper and a little stub of a pencil. Puzzled, I keep searching. In the back right pocket is another folded up piece of paper, but this one is a letter.

I open it with shaking hands. My breath catches in my throat when I recognize Charlie's handwriting.

Dez,

I heard what happened to you tonight, and I want you to know I love you. *Everything else aside,* I love you. *No matter what.*

You've been facing things I couldn't begin to imagine, but I do know how it feels to be at your absolute worst. Of all people, I understand what it's like to be so low that you'd do anything to make the pain stop. I know you're scared and you're hurting, but please don't give up.

It will get better, Dez, I promise.

Forget everything else that came before right now. This is your moment. This is the time when you fight.

They may have taken you from our floor, but you are not alone. I know you're still in there—the smart, funny, tough girl I fell in love with while she was busy laughing at Alice tumbling down the rabbit hole.

Please come back to me. There's nobody I'd rather spend my eternity with.

Love,

Charlie

I read the note over and over, absorbing his words and grappling with feelings of love, confusion, and guilt, piled on top of everything else.

The muffled voice of Gideon outside the door snaps me back to attention. With no time for a better plan, I shove the letter, blank page, and pencil under the mattress and position myself at the edge of the bed.

The door opens and Gideon leans in. "Ready to go?"

"Where's everybody else?"

"Crosby's waiting for us at the nurse's station, and Mack and Clara are going to meet us at Kay's office."

"What's he doing at the nurse's station?"

"Probably giving them hell for what happened last night."

"What for? It's not their fault."

"Doesn't matter. Crosby's on the warpath. He gave *me* hell well into the morning hours."

"But—"

Gideon waves off my concern. "Don't sweat it." He motions for me to follow him, and we set out down the hallway. The two ACEA agents fall into formation on either side of me.

I turn to the agent on my right, the same man who knocked on my door a few minutes ago. "You're coming with?"

"We go where you go until Mack tells us otherwise."

The woman on my left nods her agreement. "Raum's had enough shots at you. He's not getting another one."

When we reach the nurse's station, Crosby is waiting, his jaw set. Two nurses take quick advantage of the distraction and hustle away the moment his gaze turns my way.

Gideon steps over to him. "If you're done terrorizing the staff, we're ready to go."

CHAPTER TWENTY-NINE

My decidedly unwanted entourage and I are the last to arrive at my meeting with Kay. The two guards take positions outside the door, and Crosby, Gideon, and I file into the conference room. It's the same room I stormed out of two days ago, two days that now seem like a lifetime.

Kay looks up from a thick file, and Mack and Clara break from the conversation they're having.

"Saved you a spot." Clara smiles and pats the open seat next to her.

Crosby sits on the other side of Mack, and Gideon sits across the table from us, next to Kay. Once we finish our game of musical chairs, Kay clears her throat and begins.

"Thank you all for joining us this morning. I appreciate you taking the time to be here, especially in light of the ongoing developments in this case. I'm certain Dez shares my gratitude." She looks at me with raised eyebrows, daring me to say otherwise.

Wow. Not an inch of slack to be had.

Kay drums the tip of her pen against the file folder. "Franklin is unable to join us this morning, but I will fill him in this afternoon on what we cover. We have a lot to get through, so unless anyone has any questions, I say we get right to it."

No one speaks up, so she dives right into my nightmare. "First of all, Dez, I want you to know that I will do everything in my power to help you through the trauma you've experienced. The first step starts right now, which is why we're all here." She leans back in her chair and turns to Mack. "I think we should begin with last night's attack."

Mack nods. "I know it's difficult, but I want you to walk us through exactly what happened, and what Raum said to you."

I slip my arm through Clara's and the words spill out, every gruesome detail from getting undressed to the dagger. I hold back his final words, though. They're too terrifying to consider, much less repeat.

I pivot my chair to face Crosby. "If Gideon and Francesca hadn't gotten there when they did…" My stomach churns at the memory. "That's twice I've been saved from that monster. So don't take it out on them."

Crosby remains silent, his only response a frown.

Kay looks up from the notes she's taking. "We all appreciate your candor. As for the details of what happened to you and Bobby in the courtyard, we will save that for a private session at another time."

I struggle against the whirling chaos in my mind. "Thanks."

Kay turns her attention to Mack. "Have we come to any sort of conclusion as to what happened last night? Is there an update?"

"For starters, Raum never passed through the gate. We learned that with certainty last night when he showed up in Dez's room at RPS. This means she's still bound to him, so we have to be absolutely vigilant. Our only option now is twenty-four hour guards, in-room."

"So, I'll just never have a shred of privacy again?"

"The only compromise I can offer is two guards outside your door and a staff member in your room with you. At all times."

"That's fantastic." I roll my eyes.

Mack's expression hardens. "What happened to you last night was the alternative to that plan."

"Point taken," I concede, cowed by the simple statement of terrifying fact. "But how did he get in? You said he couldn't travel outside city limits."

Mack and Crosby exchange another look of debate and consideration.

I'm all for love, but this two peas in a pod mindset is starting to grate on my nerves.

"It's because you're bound to him," Mack says. "He has access to anywhere you are. Until we catch him, we have to assume you're still vulnerable."

My stomach twists in knots. "So there's nowhere I'm safe?"

"He won't show up so long as you have agents watching you."

"How does the bonding work? Can he read my thoughts?"

Mack shakes his head. "He can sense your presence and can tell who is in your immediate vicinity. He knows when you're unprotected."

"Do we have any idea why he didn't cross?" Crosby asks.

"I wish I knew. He's obviously sticking around for some

reason, but I have no idea why."

"I do." My rapid breathing is as loud as a hurricane in the quiet room.

Clara takes my hand. "Did he say something about it last night?"

My roiling stomach plays hell with my ability to speak. "He said I belong to him, and that he won't be denied what's his."

All eyes focus on me.

"Those were his exact words last night. 'You belong to me, and I will not be denied what is mine.' I'm sorry I didn't tell you, but I just couldn't." I shift in my seat, my skin crawling. "What does that even mean?"

Mack considers my question in a prolonged moment of agonizing silence. "I believe I may have interrupted his bonding process when I found you in the park. If that's the case, the bond is incomplete, and for whatever reason he's concocted in his twisted mind, he intends to finish it. He thinks that you, quite literally, belong to him, and that you are his for the taking." He holds on to Crosby's shoulder to keep him in his seat. "We are not going to let that happen." His words are directed as much at Crosby as they are at me.

"We've let too much happen already," Crosby says.

Kay takes the reins of the conversation in hand. "Let's all just settle down. Is there anything else we should know about the investigation?"

"That's about everything," Mack says. "I will keep you updated as we collect more information."

"Very well. I think we can all agree that Mack is fully capable of seeing to Dez's security, so further incidents will not be an issue. Let's move on." She skims several pages of my file and shifts gears. "The main purpose of this morning's meeting is to come to a consensus on the issue which cropped up last night in Bobby's room. Normally, I would not involve Mack and Clara in this conversation, but because you require around the clock protection, it's pertinent that they remain informed."

I scoff. "Any delusions I had about privacy rights went out the door on day one when I was on the receiving end of that orb Gideon flung at me."

With a nod from Kay, Gideon takes over the conversation, paying no mind to my jab as he recounts every embarrassing detail, from my flight in the city to bottoming out in Bobby's suite.

My thoughts drift back to the fountain in the city, to the sweet, confusing moments before everything went so wrong, but the reprieve is short lived. Raised voices jar me back to the conversation at hand.

"She attacked you," Gideon insists, tied in a stare down with Crosby.

"That's a complete exaggeration," Crosby snaps. "You weren't even there."

"So Mack's lying? Is that what you're saying?"

I squeeze the bridge of my nose between my fingers. *Who is this crazy person?*

Crosby's face reddens. "Dez has been pushed well beyond what any underage soul could possibly—"

I wave my hand to stop him. "You keep defending me, even when I don't deserve it. I've been too much. I just wish I knew how to be something else."

Crosby's shoulders slump as though he's deflating.

"This is what we're here for," Kay says. "To work through this and help you develop the tools you need to move forward." She takes another glance at her lengthy notes. "And we're to the elephant in the room. There's nothing to do but face it. Right, Dez?"

I shift closer to Clara.

Kay continues, unabated. "Perhaps it would be best to begin with Mack describing the incident that raised alarm."

Mack is slow and deliberate, retelling the whole ugly story with precision and painful accuracy while I huddle against Clara.

Get it together, I scold myself. *When did you become such a coward?*

"I meant it," I blurt out. "I knew what I was saying. But how the hell can you fix me, Kay? Can you teach me to escape my own mind? Can you make all of this stop?"

"I can teach you coping strategies."

"Bobby's gone because of me, and I can't stop thinking about what they might be doing to him. I told you what Raum said to me. There is no coping. Not with this."

"I know it feels that way right now."

"It's not how it feels; it's how it is. So forgive me for falling apart and looking for a way out."

"Do you understand what Mack's Departer does?"

I heave out a heavy sigh. "Yes, Kay. For the millionth time, yes. I get it. It wipes you out. You no longer exist." I lock eyes with Gideon. "And like I said, compared with this latest reality, it doesn't sound that bad."

Kay closes my file folder. "What you're saying is very serious, Dez."

"Then give me a purpose. Give me something to do, some way to help, some sense of hope, because I'm hanging on by a ratty thread." I try to slow my racing everything. Mind, heart, spirit, existence—it's all out of control, careening at breakneck speed.

CHAPTER THIRTY

Gideon closes the door behind us. After a mind-numbing marathon session with Kay, it was decided that I was in no condition to return to the dorm—not that I had any say in the matter. I remain a threat to myself, she said, so at least until RPS staff can evaluate me, this is where I'll stay.

"No offense, but I'm not exactly crazy about you being in here with me," I say.

"None taken." Gideon settles into the chair next to the bed. "Look, I know this is far from ideal, but we have to keep you safe."

"But why are you here? Couldn't they find a more suitable staff member to lord over me?"

"Clara will be here shortly."

I flop onto the bed in a huff.

"You need to get changed anyway," he says. "So I'll clear out."

I curl my lip and scrunch up my nose. "Into those scrubs? Yuck."

"It's not so bad. And you have zero choice in the matter. Why don't you get dressed, and I'll go find Clara."

The door clicks shut behind him, and I'm as alone as I can be for the foreseeable future. I strip out of my clothes, leaving them in a heap on the floor, and pull on the ugly white scrubs. In an obsessive attempt to assure myself Gideon's not coming back in, I do a slow count to ten—never mind that I just got undressed without thinking twice—and with a last glance at the door I shove my hand under the mattress. My fingers fumble around, searching for the clandestine communication tools Abbey delivered to me with Charlie's letter. The tip of the sharpened pencil jabs into my fingertip, but I pay the tiny needle of pain no mind.

With no time to waste, I grab the paper and pencil but leave Charlie's letter behind.

No time to read it again. Not right now.

Sitting in the chair where Raum was not twelve hours ago sends a chill through me. *He knows I'm here.* I shove the fear aside and bring calm to my shaking hands, my mission clear.

Charlie,

I wish I had the courage to say the things you need to hear, to speak the words aloud in your presence. You deserve that. You deserve so much more. But I've become a coward, forged in the hell that has been these last two days. And my actions last night mean I'm stuck here. For how long, I don't know.

I love you, Charlie. I couldn't bring myself to say it to your face, but I would give anything to have those hundreds of chances back, all those sweet moments when I could have told you, before everything went so wrong. I do love you. I was too scared to say it, too afraid of what would happen if I let myself be in love with you, when I know you'll someday be leaving Atman without me. I tried not to love you, but I do, and I need you.

But I may not deserve you.

There's something you need to know. I wanted to tell you yesterday, before I left to testify. You held me close and made some of this nightmare ebb away, and I got selfish. I wanted to be in your arms where the screaming world finally went quiet for a while. But I owe you an explanation.

Something happened in the city. Something other than the attack.

I gasp for breath and squeeze the tiny pencil so hard, I'm afraid it might snap, but Gideon could be back at any moment, so I press on.

It's Bobby. I know you suspected, but I hope you believe me when I tell you I didn't. The last thing he said before those monsters took him was, "I think I'm falling in love with you." I know now that it was building all day, spilling over from the night before, maybe even days before. His words echo in my mind every time I close my eyes. I had no time to react, no time to think before they took him. But I've had nothing but time since.

Am I in love with him? I don't know, Charlie. I love him as a dear friend, but I don't know if there's more. I wish I had a better answer; you certainly deserve one. In the day leading up to his confession, I knew something had changed, but I truly had no idea he felt this way.

Before you spend another moment of thought on me and where we stand, I wanted you to know the truth. I'm so sorry that this is the way I'm telling you.

I miss you, and I love you.

Dez

I fold the page back up and shove it under the mattress. The door swings open just as I'm settling back on the bed.

I scowl at Gideon. "Doesn't anybody knock?"

"Sorry," he says. "But it's time for group."

"Group? Dressed like this?"

"Everyone else is wearing the same thing. You'll fit right in. Come on."

He leads me down the hallway to RPS's version of our common room on floor ninety-five, with my guards following just a few feet behind. This common area is a smaller, gloomier space, with a pool table against one wall and an assortment of couches and chairs scattered throughout. The walls are a dull hue of what may have at some point been green and littered with posters.

BETTER TO LIGHT ONE SMALL CANDLE THAN TO CURSE THE DARKNESS.

A HERO IS ONE WHO KNOWS HOW TO HANG ON ONE MINUTE LONGER.

OPPORTUNITIES MULTIPLY AS THEY ARE SEIZED.

THE HARDER THE CONFLICT, THE MORE GLORIOUS THE TRIUMPH.

It's all I can do to keep myself from ripping the posters down, but even in this mental state, I realize it would be an exercise in disaster and self-destruction. I trudge to the center of the room, where someone has set up a dozen folding chairs in a large circle, and take a seat while my guards take positions at the far edge of the common area to keep watch.

Other residents begin to file into the room, some jumpy with anxiety, others barely coherent. None of them even bats an eye at the presence of the guards. A scrawny girl of about sixteen with mousy brown hair and deep-set green eyes walks in like she owns the place. She surveys the group before choosing the chair next to me.

The act of sitting seems to send her body into overdrive. Her knees bounce up and down, and her fingers do a little dance in front of her face like she's a cheerleader hopped up on a triple overdose of caffeine and crazy.

"You must be the new girl." She cocks her head to one side and leans in close. "I heard about you." She drags the fingers of her left hand through her hair while she chews on the nails of her right. She's so close that her jittery leg is bumping against mine.

Gideon steps up behind us. "Remember your boundaries, Bailey."

"Why you always gotta hassle me, Gideon?" she whines.

"Boundaries," he repeats in his not-messing-around tone.

Sulking, she slides back into her seat, kicks her legs out straight, and crosses her ankles. Her feet begin to bounce. "I was just being polite."

I glare at him, but he only shrugs. "I'll see you after group, Dez."

Bailey turns to watch him leave. Once he's out of sight, she scoots even closer and leans in so far that I can feel her breath on my cheek. "Is it true you stabbed a staff member?"

"What?" I slide my chair back.

"Yeah, you went on the run, and then when they caught you in some lady's store, you went crazy and buried a knife in a dude's chest." Her clenched fist slices an invisible weapon through the air, her face scrunched up in a grimace. "City Guard, I heard. Prolly had it coming, right? He try and grab you or something?" She puts her hands on her chest and squeezes in a pantomimed grope.

I stare up at the ceiling and try to stay calm. "No. Just…no."

"Yeah, that's why you got guards and all the extra staff around."

"Not even close."

A scowling boy across the circle from us who's been twisting his short blond hair with his fingertips snaps, "Damn, Bailey, don't you ever shut up?"

She sits up straight in her chair. "Nobody was talking to you, Jake."

His hand drops from his hair to his side. "And nobody's ever talking to you."

A short, stocky man with a head of salt and pepper hair takes a seat in the last open chair, and the group goes quiet. "Bailey and Jacob, it is far too early in the day for your squabbling. Let's find our center and focus our energy toward the positive."

Bailey slouches in her chair and resumes sulking.

"As you can all see, we have a new resident." The man looks at me and smiles. "Would you like to introduce yourself?"

He waits but gets nothing from me.

"Tell you what, I'll start. My name is Levi, and I am one of the group counselors here at RPS."

"I'm Dez," I say, reluctant. "I'm not going to be here long."

"Welcome, Dez," the group chimes as one. Even Bailey joins in.

Creepy.

"A positive attitude goes a long way," Levi says. "We're going to get started, so feel free to share as much as you are comfortable with. Let's begin with today's inspiration, which comes to us from Carl Schurz. Who can tell me who that is?"

Everyone zones out and stares at their feet or off into space. Each resident is slouched, detached, off in their own world.

"Anyone have a guess?"

"German revolutionary and Union Army General in the U.S. Civil War, among other things," I say.

Everyone stares at me in surprise, the group for the moment pulled from their otherworldly trance.

Levi nods. "Very good, Dez."

I hitch my shoulders. "I wrote a pretty extensive essay on Reconstruction my last quarter at school. It's just a coincidence."

"Are you so sure about that?"

"It better be. If this isn't all a matter of coincidence and chance, the universe has a lot of explaining to do."

A chuckle rolls through the group, and Levi holds up his hands to quiet the laughter. "Coincidence or not, Schurz is our source for today's quote. He said, 'Ideals are like stars; you will not succeed in touching them with your hands. But like the seafaring man on the desert of waters, you choose them as your guides, and, following them, you reach your destiny.' As we work through group today, I'd like you all to think of his words and decide what they mean to you."

Levi then instructs the residents to introduce themselves, but my complete lack of focus causes their names to pass right over me. Aside from Levi, Bailey, and Jake, I can't identify a single person here.

"Now, Dez, we won't press you too hard today, but as our newest resident, we do have one requirement. Since this is your first group session, you have to tell us something you've never told anyone else."

My mouth hangs open and my wheels spin. "You want me to…"

"Share something you've never told anyone else," Levi repeats, slower this time.

Hell no.

Bailey leans in and whispers, "Tell us about stabbing that guy."

"Come on," Levi says. "It doesn't have to be anything bad. Just something you've never told anyone."

An early childhood memory flashes in my mind.

We were at Ben Franklin—my little hometown's solitary craft-slash-hardware store—and my mom was getting a photograph framed. It was taking forever. She was debating between UV glass and regular, what kind of mat board to get, what color the frame should be…seriously, it was forever. *I asked her if I could get a treat in a tone that she always said was like driving a nail directly into her brain.*

"Please, Mommy, I've been good all day."

"It's only ten in the morning," she said. "That's hardly all day."

"But you're taking for-ev-er."

"Is that the behavior of a little girl who deserves a treat?"

She looked away from me to make her final decision on the frame, and I slipped from her watchful eye just long enough to get away with something.

"Fine," I concede. "When I was six, I stole a box of Milk

Duds, and I can tell you for sure, ill-gotten candy tastes even better than its legally acquired counterpart."

Everyone laughs, Levi included.

"Do you have any idea how hard it is to be sneaky with Milk Duds? They're really loud in that little cardboard box." A hint of a smile pulls at me, and I relax the tiniest bit.

Levi claps his hands together. "Excellent. Thank you, Dez. Let's get down to business, shall we?"

Well played, sir.

CHAPTER THIRTY-ONE

There's a knock at my door, and my male guard peeks in. "The book cart is here if you'd like to get something to read."

I drag myself from bed and check the time on my bracelet. Only two hours have passed since group, but with nothing to do but stare at the walls, and a non-communicative female guard as my only companion, time has ground to a crawl. It's a struggle just to move, and an even greater battle to care enough to do so.

Abbey walks in, pushing a metal cart piled high with books The room is small and the cart just big enough to make it uncomfortably crowded, so my female guard steps out into the hallway and joins her colleague at his post.

Abbey shuts the door, not bothering to ask the guards if it's okay. "Hey, Dez. Thought you might be getting bored," she says to the door more than me, a little too practiced and loud.

With my eyes locked on the closed door, I slip my hand under the mattress and grab my letter to Charlie, which I've folded up into a small rectangle. I offer her my hand with my letter tucked against my palm. "Thanks for coming."

She shakes my hand and slips the letter into her pocket. "No problem." She grabs a book off the cart and hands it to me. "I know this one's your favorite."

Alice's Adventures in Wonderland. My hands caress the cover and my heart aches. "Thank you, Abbey. I still don't know why you're being so nice to me, but thank you."

"For one, you need a friend. But it's more than that. I know what it's like to be in a place like this."

"You've never had an RPS placement, have you?"

She shakes her head. "That doesn't mean I don't understand. Believe me, I know what this is like."

"How?"

Abbey pushes the cart aside and sits at the edge of the bed, her gaze distant, focused on something not in this tiny room. "When you have anorexia, you literally can't see yourself the way other people do. All you see is fat and ugly. It's skinny, skinny, skinny. Get there, get there. One more pound, one more ounce. But it's never enough. I could never see the problem everyone else said I had, not even when I got down to seventy pounds."

"Oh, Abbey."

She nods. "That's what a ten year old should weigh. It sounds crazy, I know, but the idea of dying never even crossed my mind. Not really. I mean, people would tell me I was killing myself, but I didn't believe them. I thought it was just something they were saying to try to make me do what they wanted." She tucks a strand of her long blond hair behind her ear. "My parents may have lost me in the end, but it wasn't without a fight. So, yeah, I know what this is like."

"I had no idea. I didn't even know you were anorexic. I'm sorry."

She looks down at the book. "You have something worth fighting for, Dez."

A hard knock at the door jolts us from our conversation. "Wrap it up, ladies," the male guard says.

Abbey stands. "I'd better go before I get us both in trouble."

"Thanks again," I say, but my words are inadequate for the debt I owe her.

She waves off my thanks. "It's no biggie. I'll see you soon."

Abbey pulls the door shut tight behind her, and I hear her muffled voice thank the guards.

Alone again, at least for the moment, I leaf through the book's pages, searching for the passage I read on my first day at Atman when I met Charlie.

A slip of paper falls into my lap.

"Being deeply loved by someone gives you strength, while loving someone deeply gives you courage." I will be your strength, Dez, and I will wait as long as it takes for you to find your courage.

Charlie.

I shove the note under my pillow and jump to my feet.

What have I done?

I yank the door open just as my female guard is reaching for the doorknob to come back into the room.

"You have to stay in there," she says.

"I know, but is Abbey still here? I need to talk to her."

"She's gone back to the dorms," the male guard tells me. "This was her last stop before her shift ended. You'll have to wait until she comes back tomorrow."

"But—"

"Rules are rules," he says. "Back in your room, please."

"I *need* to talk to her."

He looks at me with precisely zero sympathy. "There's nothing we can do about it."

I'm like a forest fire that's been doused with water and forgotten. Just when the smoke clears, I flare up again. "As unhappy as you are to be stuck here with me, I assure you, I have it worse. There's nothing I'd rather do than be free of all of this and be rid of you two."

Lucky for me, the cavalry arrives right as I dive into the deep end of the trouble pool. Clara steps between the agents and me. "Looks like I'm just in time." She turns back to her two coworkers. "I've got this."

She steers me back into the room and closes the door. "What's up?"

"I made a huge mistake. Another one." I start to pace in the tiny room. "Every time I think I've hit rock bottom, this place redefines what rock bottom is. I can't do this anymore, Clara."

"Tell me what's going on."

"The walls are closing in. How is this supposed to help me? How's it supposed to help anybody? Oh, you're feeling desperate and miserable? How about we stick you in a little, tiny room, where time will grind to a halt, and the things that seemed horrible to begin with are magnified a million times."

"Dez, honey, slow down. I have an idea."

I stop and turn my desperate gaze her way. "What? What can possibly help me right now?"

"How about I step out long enough for you to get dressed, and then we get you out of here for a bit?"

✦✦✦

I don't know how she pulled it off, but Clara managed to talk Gideon into letting her take me to Shanti Park, which is nearest to the RPS wing where I'm being held. His one condition—aside from us not staying out more than a few hours—was that my guards had to come along. In another coup nearly as remarkable, she's convinced them to trail a few yards back so we could talk privately.

For the first time in days, I can stretch my arms out and not hit anyone. Even Clara is giving me space.

"What was going on back there?" she asks.

I pluck a bright pink and orange frangipani blossom from a small tree as we pass and inhale the tropical scent of the delicate flower, but it isn't the aromatic salve I was hoping for. "I don't really want to talk about it. Not right now."

"Might do you some good to get it out."

"Can I show you something, instead?" I ask.

"Of course."

"It's a bit of a hike, if I can even find it again."

"We have time," Clara says. "As long as we're back in two, three hours tops."

I do a quick calculation in my head. "Shouldn't be a problem."

Clara looks back over her shoulder at my two guards and tilts her head, signaling them to catch up to us.

We head down the park's main path, and I scan the dense foliage for a small, well-worn sign. "Should be right about here," I say, still searching.

I finally spot it.

PEACE COMES FROM WITHIN. DO NOT SEEK IT WITHOUT.

"You sure about this?" I ask. "Mack is not going to be happy with you if we go. It's way off the beaten path."

Clara smiles. "You think I'm scared of him?"

I am.

"It'll be fine," she says, stepping up to examine the sign. "Besides, this has me intrigued."

The journey up the narrow path to the clearing seems much shorter and more pleasant this time, perhaps because I'm not alone. Clara and I chat away as the path continues to narrow, but the guards remain silent and watchful as we trek single-file, deep into the jungle.

I stop when we reach the clearing and urge everyone to be silent.

"What are you looking for?" Clara whispers.

"There were deer here last time," I say. "I thought they might come back."

The male guard walks slowly around the perimeter, surveying the scene and making enough noise to ensure the deer won't be making a repeat appearance. "You dragged us all the way out here, kid? For what? Park's got plenty of trees."

Clara shoots him an irritated look.

"Lighten up," the other guard tells him. "I kind of like it. Beats foot patrol, right?"

"Don't see the point, is all," he says with a shrug. "Trees are trees, far as I'm concerned."

Clara examines the stone carving embedded in the earth at the center of the clearing. She runs her fingers over the black stone, just as I did during my first visit.

"Looks like a ship's wheel," I say. "Do you know what it is?"

She nods. "A Dharma wheel. Symbolizes the endless cycle of birth and rebirth in Buddhism."

"Should have known that." I frown. "This wasn't what I was bringing you to see, anyway," I say, more to the guard than Clara.

We press on, up the steep steps to the beautiful vista that pulls even harder at my heart this time and stops me in my tracks. As I take in the painfully familiar view, I'm hit with a flood of emotions. Homesickness competes fiercely with my need to feel the comfort of Charlie's arms, my desire to escape the pain of these recent, nightmare days, and the crushing ache of wanting Bobby back. The pain that sent me to RPS rears its ugly head again, but this time it's different.

I fall to my knees.

Clara rushes to my side. "Dez, honey? What's wrong?"

My fists ball up. I pound them against my thighs. "I can't."

"Can't what?"

"Can't say the words."

Clara kneels beside me and puts her hand on my shoulder. "Maybe that's why we're out here."

You don't get to fall apart. I force myself to stand and take some time to regroup before we continue on our trek.

"We're almost there," I say, still reeling as we approach the footbridge. I reach once again for Buddha and rub his belly as we pass, but it brings me no comfort, and I seriously doubt if any luck is in my future.

"How did you find this place?" Clara asks.

"I didn't, really. I was being a jerk to everyone and ran off. It kind of found me."

She laughs, and it's nice to hear. I take a deep, slow breath just as the temple and its exotic grounds appear.

CHAPTER THIRTY-TWO

The raised platform at the center of the temple's courtyard has only one occupant, save Buddha. The familiar monk sits with a contented look on his face, matching that of the statue beside him. It's almost as though he's been waiting in the same spot since I left a few days ago, before things went so terribly wrong.

"Come, child," he says, smiling as he motions for us to approach. "I am so glad you have returned."

"I'm not sure why I came back. I've…" I look at Clara, hoping she can piece my fragmented communication into something that makes sense.

"Dez has suffered a great deal of trauma in these past few days." She touches my hair with her fingertips and moves a few of my braids off my shoulder. "This seems the perfect place to seek comfort and healing."

"Indeed," the monk says. His hand pats gently on the platform. "Sit beside me."

Clara gives me a little nudge. "Go ahead, honey. It's okay."

The guards hang back at the courtyard's perimeter, out of earshot and too busy keeping a vigilant eye on our surroundings to be bothered with our conversation.

I climb up and sit next to the monk, feeling especially small. "I don't know what I'm supposed to say." My voice catches, and another surge of hurt threatens to bring fresh tears to my eyes.

Clara hops up on the platform and sits next to me. "Is this okay? Or do you want me to go wait with the guards?"

I lay my head on her shoulder, answering her question.

"Maybe you can start by telling him what happened on the way here," she says. "There was a lot going on in your head, wasn't there?"

A gentle breeze makes my shirtsleeve flutter, a focal point that gives me the distraction I need in order to detach enough from the present to speak to my pain. "All I've wanted since I got here is to go home. To have another chance. To have my life back. And when we looked down on the valley…"

I'm hit by sudden awareness. "I've made attachments here. I care about more than just the life I no longer have. There are people I love, and people who love me. There's so much to fix. People I wouldn't—I couldn't—just walk away from." Tears spill down my cheeks. "If I could go home right now, I don't know that I would, yet the last thing I want is to be here like this."

"Don't fear attachment," the monk tells me. "This source of fear and anxiety, these souls you care about, this is progress. You are traveling down the right path, child."

"But there's so much more."

"You are wounded," he says. "Give voice to your trouble."

"We were attacked in a park, and they took my friend. I've been bound to a monster." I gasp. "I'm unraveling, and I don't know what to do. I said I don't want to exist anymore, and I think I might mean it." It's as much as I can bring myself to say, a fact the monk seems to sense.

He straightens his spine and slowly raises his chin. "All conditioned things are impermanent—when one sees this with wisdom, one turns away from suffering."

I study his wizened face and soulful eyes. "I don't know what that means."

"The conditions of pain, the situations of fear and suffering, these things are temporary. Your torment will not be eternal. Our experiences are in constant motion. Do not fight against the current. Accept what is behind you and strive for peace and acceptance."

"I don't know how."

"Begin with the serenity that surrounds us. Close your eyes and breathe it in like air."

My body tenses. "If I close my eyes, he'll be there."

"The only power he has within the confines of your thoughts is that which you give him."

I inhale deeply and push aside my fright and despair.

The monk begins to chant, and my soul drifts away in the wind.

✦✦✦

We've returned safely to Shanti, and sit on the soft grass of the edge of the stream that winds through the park. Thanks to our visit to the temple, I'm feeling a much needed sense of relief.

"Tell me what had you so upset when I got to RPS," Clara says.

I frown, not wanting to dredge up thoughts of how badly I've screwed things up with Charlie. "I'm in deep enough already."

"Which is why you should tell me. How much more trouble do you think you're going to get in at this point?"

"Boy problems," I finally say.

She knits her brow. "I see."

"Please don't give me the 'no dating' lecture. I've heard it before."

"It's a dumb rule, anyway." She bumps my arm with her elbow. "What's the trouble?"

"I don't want to think about it right now." The drive to unburden myself is overwhelming, but it's comfort I don't deserve.

"What do you want to talk about?"

I check over my shoulder for the guards and find they are at least twenty feet back, leaning against a tree and having their own conversation.

Satisfied there's a decent measure of privacy, I ask, "What's it like when you leave here?"

Clara takes her time answering. "I'm really not supposed to tell you about it, but I will say this much. It's better than anything you could possibly imagine. There's no pain, no fear, no doubt."

"Then why are you here? Why would you leave that for this?"

"We're all here because it's our calling."

"I don't know. If all this called to me from paradise, I'd say it had the wrong number."

She smiles and wrinkles her nose. "Can you imagine Mack doing this without me?"

I can't help but smile. "Clara Perkins, the metaphysical glue holding the fabric of the universe together. No pressure or anything."

"All in a day's work." She laughs. "How are you holding up in RPS? Survived group okay, I see."

"Barely." I grab a small, smooth stone and hold it flat. My thumb and forefinger curl around its edge. With a practiced arm, I toss the stone at the stream and count as it skips four times before disappearing into the water.

Getting rusty.

"Four days ago, I had a routine," I continue. "I was getting a sense of normal, which a couple of months ago I wouldn't have believed was possible. But now?"

"Give yourself some time."

"I got stuck at Atman because I wasn't ready to die, and now I'm stuck in RPS because I said I don't want to exist. How's time going to fix that?"

"You've had—" Clara stops, interrupted by a hissing, creaking sound behind us, coming from the trees. "That's weird." She looks over her shoulder and jumps to her feet, on sudden, full alert. "Get behind me. Right now, Dez."

I scramble to my feet and spin toward the sound of guttural screams coming from my guards. The tree they were leaning against has come to life, its bark transformed to dozens of hands with razor sharp claws that dig and tear at the two agents. Bursts of light shoot from their gaping wounds as they writhe and scream in a desperate effort to escape.

I never even bothered to learn their names.

Clara grabs me by my shoulders. "Run. Now. Admin is closest. Don't look back, no matter what."

"But—"

She shakes me hard. "Do what I tell you!"

I look over her shoulder, distracted by the terrible screams, the nightmare made worse when Raum emerges from the trees, chanting in a language I can't understand. His eyes gleam with power. Light dances from his fingertips.

My breath catches in my throat.

"Run!" Clara screams, snapping me from my stunned immobility.

Every inch of me is alight with terror, but my feet do the thinking my brain can't.

CHAPTER THIRTY-THREE

The park is empty. There's not a soul to be found as I tear down the walking path, once again on the run, this time toward the safety of the Admin building. I can't allow myself to process the sounds coming from behind me—the screams, the sickening thuds, the hissing and cracking of the forest bending to Raum's will.

Just run.

The path takes a sharp left turn ahead, and I press on, leaving a trail of gasps and whimpers in my wake like the contrails of a jet.

I round the corner into the last half-mile that stands between me and the safety of Admin, and a tiny bit of hope begins to creep into my being.

Get help. For Clara. For the guards. Hurry.

I hit the straightaway at full-tilt, the massive complex looming large ahead. I press on with all I have. The wind whistles in my ears, the only sound I hear save my labored breath.

A shadowy figure slips out of the trees and into the path directly in front of me. My footsteps falter when I recognize Moloch.

I try to dodge his grasp, but he's too fast. His hand strikes like a cobra, clamping down on my wrist and pulling me off balance.

"You're right on time." His powerful arm snakes around my neck in a single fluid motion, paralyzing me in a chokehold. He drags me off the trail, through a thicket of ivy and into a nearby stand of birch trees.

I can't even scream. My feet drag along the ground, a useless extension of my limp, immobilized body.

Moloch slams me against a tree and presses his weight into the forearm he holds against my throat. "You are quite a bit of trouble. You know that?"

The trunk of the birch chills me through the thin cotton of my shirt. "You—you can't…" I gasp.

His eyes glimmer. "I can't leave the city? Yet here I am, breaking the precious Council's rules." He shakes his head, his lips pressed together in a tight frown. "Just when you thought it was safe to go out for a little stroll."

He lets me go, but I'm paralyzed. Immobile. "They said only Raum can go where I do."

"The lies told to frightened children to keep the monsters at bay." He smiles, a being in total, unquestioned control. "You'd think they'd know better."

"What are you doing here?"

He leans in close and taps my forehead with his fingertip. "You don't learn, do you? Raum's visit last night wasn't enough for you?"

"Where's Bobby?"

"You're about to find out." He clamps down on the back of my neck with an iron grip and takes me deeper into the woods where tall evergreens spread out in tidy rows, towering over us. His lips press against my ear as we walk. "You run again, you call out for help, you so much as make a sound at the wrong moment, and I will take it out on your precious Bobby. You understand?"

"Please."

His hand tightens on the back of my neck. "It's too late for please."

There is a thunder of hurried footfalls and shouts as a large group approaches on the trail. Someone barks out commands, dispatching the others to spread out and form a search grid.

Moloch pulls me behind a tree and puts his finger to my lips. "Not a sound," he whispers. "You speak, he pays."

"Dez," a voice shouts.

Crosby.

"Let her go, and we can end this without anyone else getting hurt." His demand is desperate and furious. "Send her toward the sound of my voice, right now."

"We can work it out," I whisper. "It's not too late to fix this."

Moloch chuckles and whispers back to me. "You think you have any control?"

He marches me deeper into the woods, away from Crosby, away from hope. The voices calling out my name grow faint and then disappear entirely as we descend into a deep ravine. Spindly pines climb toward the sky, casting long shadows over the snaking path.

Moloch pushes me in front of him but keeps me within his reach. "Keep moving."

The embankment to either side grows far too steep for me to have any chance at escape, even if I was willing to risk Bobby's safety. The ground is soft and covered in needles from the trees growing at sharp angles, scattered up the side of the ravine. It would be a slipping, dangerous escape, impossible against a captor with superhuman strength and speed.

"Where are you taking me?"

Moloch laughs, hard and menacing. "You'll see." He steps closer to me and leans in, his breath hot on my neck. "You're lucky Raum doesn't like to share his toys."

I pick up the pace and manage to get a few strides ahead.

"What's the rush?" he taunts. "Come on, I make excellent company. How often does one have the chance to spend quality time with a being such as myself, rich with history and culture?"

I spin around to face him, too exhausted, too stretched to feel the degree of fear I ought to. "You're a monster. And if you've hurt Bobby, I—"

"You'll what?" His eyes flare. "Make no mistake, this will not end well for you. Make me angry, and it will end worse."

He grabs my arm, his fingertips like blazing-hot iron against my skin.

I will not scream. "This is just a blip on the radar of eternity."

He throws me to the ground and towers over me.

I scramble to my feet. "Too bad you can't break Raum's toys, huh?"

"The branch of a young tree will bend quite far before it breaks."

I look over Moloch's shoulder. "Speaking of Raum, where is he?"

His eyes darken. "He will be with us soon."

"If he still exists. Mack will make sure he doesn't if you don't let me go. Bobby, too."

"You are brave, I'll grant you that much. But you're a fool in need of a lesson."

I take a defensive step back, but he grabs me and pulls me close. The index and middle fingers of his free hand trace down my forehead and stop between my eyes. "*Taw.*"

This time I scream.

The pain has weight, volume, gravity.

I gasp for air my dead lungs don't need. A thousand claws tear at my heart, rending flesh from bone, setting my veins alight, but it's the fear that hurts the most. Visions of Bobby, of all the horrible acts he's endured, flood my mind.

"This isn't real," he pleads. He's curled up, dripping wet and shivering on a rough-cut stone floor. His curls are plastered against his head, his hair matted with blood. His face is covered in welts and bruises; his bare feet are swollen and blackened. Chains bind his wrists and ankles.

A heavy wooden door creaks open, and Moloch enters. His eyes burn with malice and, worst of all, glee. He holds a short metal rod in his hand.

"This is all in my mind. I created you," Bobby screams. "You have to stop!" The chains go taut and pull him to a standing position, his arms and legs splayed. He wails, hovering on the brink of unconsciousness. His eyes flutter shut.

Moloch crosses the room and slaps Bobby hard across the face. "You're not getting away that easy."

"Please stop," Bobby begs.

"This will not stop, so long as you are still you." The metal rod

glows white, and he drives it deep into Bobby's chest.

Bobby's screams are inhuman. I scream along with him, but it's no help. He finally goes silent and hangs limp from the chains that bind him to the wall.

"Stop," I plead. I fall to my knees and grip my head between my hands. The pain is alarming, the fear and horror oppressive.

Moloch pulls me to my feet. "That was just a taste."

Adding insult and humiliation to injury, I have to lean against him for support as we continue down the path, each step bringing us closer to whatever nightmare awaits.

CHAPTER THIRTY-FOUR

We cross the tracks into a dingy, rundown sector of the city where ramshackle row houses in varying degrees of disrepair crowd both sides of the street. The stench of decay hangs heavy in the air. Everything is dangerous here, even the ground. Spindly weeds creep up through cavernous cracks in the sidewalk and make the footing treacherous.

Moloch's arm snakes around my waist, and he catches me before I even realize I've tripped.

He narrows his gaze as he watches me take in our surroundings. "Remember, you try to run, and I take it out on Bobby."

I haven't said a word in at least an hour—not since whatever that was he did to me. I simply trudge along beside him and nod. *If he can catch me before I even fall, what hope do I have of escape?*

We continue down countless blocks, deeper into the city's seedy underbelly. Menacing faces stare out at us from the shadowy alleys, but everyone we meet gives us a wide berth, most going so far as to cross the street to avoid us. One thing is certain: I will not be harmed on the journey to meet my doom. Moloch walks beside me with absolute authority, radiating a clear message to all we encounter.

"Why so quiet?" he taunts. "Nothing clever to say?"

Despite a complete lack of evidence to justify it, I cling to a sliver of hope. *This monster will not be the end of me.* "You're never going to get us through the gate."

"We aren't going to the gate, clever girl. Even if we were, do you really think a couple of agents could stop me?"

"Are you so sure Clara didn't stop Raum?" The thought of any other outcome is too much to bear. *She has to be okay.*

He laughs, deep and booming. "Cling to whatever fantasies you wish, child, but fantasies won't save you."

On the next block is a crumbling stone tavern with a steep-pitched thatch roof, its collapse seemingly eminent. An unmanaged hedge runs its perimeter, and a battered, weather-beaten sign in front reads "Gallus."

Weather-beaten? What weather? It's always perfect here.

Moloch leads me up the pathway.

I follow close behind, trying my best to sound unfazed. "You may want to rethink this plan. Crosby's not a fan of me going in bars. Never ends well for anybody."

"If you think your precious Crosby is any match for me, you really are living in a fantasy world."

Moloch walks into the tavern like he owns it. It's dim and dirty, with rickety barstools and grimy tables. Aside from the bartender and us, the place is empty. He strides up to the bar, not bothering to check if I'm following. I wouldn't run even if I could, not in this neighborhood. The known threat of Moloch, at least for the moment, beats the unknown threat of everyone else. *Better the devil you know...*

This bartender makes Nero the picture of integrity by comparison. His face is scarred and pockmarked, his eyes cloudy from cataracts. His teeth are brown and largely absent.

"Well, look what the cat dragged in," he slurs.

"Spare me the pleasantries." Moloch scans the room. "Is Raum here yet?"

The bartender hacks into a spittoon and shakes his head. "Haven't seen 'em."

"When he gets here, tell him I have the girl, and we'll meet him at the house. Are we clear?"

The bartender shrugs. "If he shows, I'll tell 'em."

Moloch spins around. "You've been so very helpful," he calls over his shoulder as he drags me back outside.

"Should have been here by now, huh?"

Moloch presses me against the wall of the tavern, his face inches from mine. "You have a weak sense of self-preservation."

His words and proximity scare me into silence. Satisfied, he directs me back to the street, and we continue on.

The minutes trudge by in a slow and agonizing march until we round the corner on the final block of our trek. Moloch leads me up the walkway of a large brownstone. Its brickwork is cracked and stained, and the front stoop is black with soot. Insects scatter at the sound of our footfalls and scurry up the steps.

He pulls open a set of arched oak and glass doors and bows grandly, holding out his arm. "After you."

I take a moment to collect myself. With steel in my spine, I step across the threshold.

I will not let him see me afraid. Not again.

The house has what was once a grand foyer that has fallen into disrepair. The ceiling soars thirty feet or more to a dome of stained glass depicting in gruesome detail a man and woman lying nude and cowering as their flesh is ripped from their bodies by a horde of demons. I can almost hear the couple's screams.

Moloch leans in close. "Breathtaking, isn't it?"

My skin crawls, but I don't react. *I won't give him the satisfaction.*

To the left is a winding staircase. To the right, the foyer opens into a parlor decorated in yellowed and peeling damask wallpaper. Large cracks run through the plaster beneath. The pale, hardwood floor is marred with dents and scratches. A deep gouge runs its length, giving the room the appearance that it's split in two.

An upright piano sits against the back wall in the parlor. Beside it is a threadbare, camelback sofa where a woman with flowing black hair is sprawled. She's dressed in a sleeveless, V-neck gown. Its emerald organza shimmers in the soft light cast by a nearby floor lamp.

A wide grin spreads across her face, her snowy white teeth brilliant beneath cherry red lips. Her greedy eyes drink in the sight of me. "Moloch, my love, what have you brought me?"

Moloch puts his arm around me like we're old friends. He wags a finger at her. "Now, Bia, you know this belongs to Raum."

She sashays across the room. "Just a little taste?"

With a rough hand, he pulls me close. "Rules are rules."

She stomps into an adjacent room. A series of door slams

follow her through the house and upstairs.

"Well, I guess it's just you and me," Moloch says.

"Still no Raum?" I try to sound indifferent, but the truth is, the prospect of being alone with one of them—let alone both— is too horrifying to consider.

A scraping sound from beneath the floorboards gets both of our attention and Moloch's eyes brighten. "I know just the thing to pass the time."

We cross the parlor and exit through a door to the right that leads into an L-shaped kitchen. Pots and pans hang from hooks on the exposed brick wall over an open hearth. A butcher-block table stocked with too many knives for comfort sits against the opposite wall.

At the far end of the kitchen is a heavy cellar door that creaks like a bad horror movie sound effect when Moloch opens it. A bare bulb hangs from a frayed wire overhead, bathing the stairs in a harsh light.

I freeze in my tracks, hit with the memory of following Delphine to her underground lair, where she attempted to imprison me during a previous, ill-fated trip into the city.

"No, not again." My knees lock and my body stiffens.

Moloch's grip tightens on the back of my neck. "Walk."

My promise not to let him see me afraid evaporates into the air. "I can't."

He waggles his fingers in front of my face. "You know what happens when you make me angry."

The threat is enough to get me moving. The wooden steps creak beneath our feet. It grows cold and damp as we descend, the air earthy and pungent with mildew. At the bottom of the stairs is a wide passageway with stone pillars on both sides, spaced a few yards apart. A series of bulbs dangle from the ceiling and cast long shadows in this dank space.

"The boy who whispered sweet nothings by the soft fountain light," Moloch muses. He pulls me close and laughs as I whimper. "I hope you like the weak, silent type, oh love of his death."

"What did you do to him?"

"You'll see."

There are heavy wooden doors to our left, and on the stone block wall to the right are chains and shackles—one set for each of the seven doors.

He's brought me to a dungeon.

Moloch hauls open the last door on the left and shoves me through. I scramble to dart out after him, but he pushes it shut too quickly. The sturdy oak barrier that now separates us should afford me some sense of relief, but I find none. I pound my fists against the door and scream—for myself, for Bobby, for Clara and my guards, for every nightmarish second of these past days.

"Enjoy," Moloch calls through the door. His boots click against the stone floor, back down the hallway. The faint sound of creaking stairs and a slamming door leave me alone to face whatever horrors this room holds.

I lean forward against the door, and a gasping sob escapes me. A doorknob is all that stands between me and escape. There is no lock, but I am no less imprisoned. He has me under his control, but my awareness of the fact does nothing to change it.

A moan from behind me sends my heart into my throat. I stifle a scream and spin to face whatever's next.

CHAPTER THIRTY-FIVE

I hardly recognize the gaunt shell of the boy who owns a piece of my heart. He's shirtless, and his torso is raw with cuts. His flesh is a palette of bruises in varying stages of healing. A thick, heavy scar marks the spot on his chest where Moloch inexplicably plunged a white-hot metal rod. The remnants of his jeans are tattered and dirty. His feet are bare, swollen, and purple.

He leans against the back wall, his legs splayed in a physical manifestation of his vacant stare. His eyes are dull, the spark of perpetual curiosity that has always set them alight extinguished.

"Bobby," I gasp.

He has no reaction to my voice. There's not a hint of recognition, not even a flinch.

I kneel. "Bobby, it's me." I reach for him, hesitant. There isn't a visible inch of him that's undamaged, so rather than touch him, I lean forward and kiss his forehead. "We're going to get out of here. I promise. You're not alone anymore." The words stick in my throat, strangled by fresh tears. "There are agents looking for us right now. They'll find us, and we'll go back to the towers where we can get you better."

I tear a strip from the bottom of my shirt and dampen it in the trickle of water running down the wall beside us in this dank cell. With a gentle hand, I dab the fresh blood that's dripping from his nose. My makeshift rag grows dirty, but I do my best to wipe clean Bobby's grimy, battered face.

I pull him into my arms. "Everything is going to be like it was before." I stroke his hair, caress his face. My lips press against the back of his hand. "Say something. Please, Bobby."

His body is limp in my arms. He stares into space, giving no indication he can hear me, or that he even knows I'm here.

Cradling him, I lie against the wall and bargain with the universe. "Please give him back. He didn't do anything to deserve this. He was just trying to help me. Good has to be stronger than evil. Please."

This empty, damaged shell can't possibly be the same, sweet, brilliant boy who mustered every bit of courage he had to tell me he loved me. This can't be all that's left of my adventurous friend who showed me the stars in an empty sky.

"Bobby." I hold his face in my hands and kiss his cheek. "You're still in there. You have to be. Please come back."

A sliver of light pushes through a crack in the corner above us, a tiny fragment of the outside world that's followed us into this evil place.

His chest rises and falls with quick, shallow breaths, the only sign he's still with me.

I try again, desperate for a reaction. Even anger. "I did a

terrible thing. I let Mack see your journals. He's an agent, and he's trying to find you, but that's no excuse. I know what your research means to you. I was trying to help and didn't know what else to do."

My tears smudge the remaining grime on his face.

"Please, Bobby. Yell at me. Tell me I betrayed your trust. Say you hate me for what I did. Tell me you don't love me anymore, that I didn't fight hard enough to save you. Just say something. Anything."

I hold him close and fight the darkness, still hoping for a miracle. The sound of my rambling, desperate voice is painful, but the sound of Bobby's silence is worse. "I wish we'd been on the train together. Maybe I could have made it better for you if we'd been together from the start. You didn't want any of this. You just wanted peace. Darkness. The end."

Bobby loved me without expecting anything in return. He bolstered me. He challenged me. But his spark of curiosity, his ability to find intrigue and learning in everything he came upon—it was all for nothing.

"It doesn't have to be this way. You can find joy again. I've seen it in you. We can't let them beat us. Please, Bobby. Now is the time to fight. I can't do this without you."

He's trapped in a dungeon because he fell in love. When he found his courage, when he let his guard down and loved, the universe wasted no time in crushing him.

I run my fingers through his matted curls. "I love you, Bobby. Maybe not the way you want me to. I don't know yet. We haven't gotten the chance to find out, but we never will if you don't come back to me."

Two boys love me, and in return, I've brought them nothing but pain.

I hold Bobby and cry. There's nothing else to do.

Minutes pass. Hours, perhaps. Our sliver of light retreats as the day begins to fade into night.

Mack and Clara may not be able to find me, but DSR finally does. I close my eyes in surrender.

Gwendolyn Jackson stands before the open, bi-fold doors of a walk-in closet. Her hair is disheveled, and her bloodshot eyes are puffy from countless tears. She grips a man's button-down shirt to her chest and inhales deeply, breathing in the scent of the fabric.

I totter at her feet and tug at her pant leg. "Mama."

"Not now, baby," she whispers. The shirt drops from her hands and lands at her feet.

The phone on the bedside table starts to ring, but she ignores it.

"Mama," I say, louder this time. The soft rubber hammer I hold in my hand lights up and makes cartoonish noises as I hit it against her thigh. "Ma-ma, ma-ma, ma-ma," I chant to the rhythm of the banging.

The phone stops ringing, and the answering machine in the next room beeps.

"Hello, Mrs. Jackson. This is Major Lowenkamp with the Department of Veteran Affairs. I just received word of Sergeant Jackson's passing, and I want to offer you my condolences. Bill was a good man and a good soldier. If there is anything I can do to assist you and little Desiree, please don't hesitate to contact me." He leaves his number and urges her to return his call.

I fall to the floor and cry.

Gwendolyn pulls a framed photo from the bureau next to the closet. In the picture, she and a handsome man in a dress uniform are exchanging vows on a beach. The sun is bright and the sky is a brilliant blue. She and my birth father beam at one another, captivated by the moment.

Her fingers run across the photo and stroke the image of his smiling face. My unanswered cries aren't enough to pull her from the memory, but the doorbell jars her back to the present. She carefully puts the photo back in its spot on the bureau and scoops me up in her arms.

She opens the door to a man and woman in uniform. The man looks to be right out of basic training, young and eager. The woman's graying hair gives her an air of authority and seniority that matches her body language. Gwendolyn looks at him, but he defers to his senior colleague, who holds out her hand.

"Hello, Mrs. Jackson, my name is Marianne Standish, and this is my associate, David Williams. We are with the Army Chaplain Corps. May we come in?"

Gwendolyn shifts me on her hip and walks back inside, leaving the door open. "Do whatever you want."

She plops me down in a playpen in the small living room and sits in the armchair next to it.

"May we sit?" David asks.

"Like I said, do what you want."

Marianne takes the spot on the couch nearest to Gwendolyn. "We're just here to see if there is anything you need, or anything we can do to make this difficult time a little easier for you."

Gwendolyn's face is slack, her voice fatigued. "It's too late for that. You killed my husband with silence and apathy."

David leans forward. His face is creased with worry. "Ma'am, we understand you're very upset. We can only imagine how hard this is for you. Is there anyone we can call? Any family members who could offer support?"

She sits up straight in her chair. "Bill was an only child, and his parents died years ago. My parents are gone, too. I have a sister in Detroit, but we don't talk. So, no, you're not pushing this off on anyone else." She turns her sad eyes to me. "Desiree and I are all that's left."

David and Marianne look at me and smile. "She's beautiful," Marianne says.

Gwendolyn holds up her hand. "Don't. She's been sentenced to a life with no father and a broken mother. So don't tell me how wonderful she is when we all know her life is going to be hell." She picks me up. I start to cry again, and she pats my back in a robotic motion. "I think you both should leave. Now."

CHAPTER THIRTY-SIX

The morning brings with it fresh fear and no change in Bobby. He's still slumped against the wall, staring into space without so much as a glimmer of awareness.

Our sliver of light returns. It's a tiny beam upon which I can pin my fading hope for a chance of things getting better, of an end to this nightmare. I take Bobby's hand and let the ray slash across our skin.

"Look, Bobby. There are some things they can't take away, even down here. We're like the light. They can't contain us, not completely. Mack and Clara are going to find us soon, and this will all be over."

I scoot closer and lean my head against his. The wall is cold on my back, but Bobby radiates an unnatural heat. "Do you remember the first time we met? I couldn't stop staring at your ID bracelet." I turn his wrist.

ERROR. PLEASE SEE SGA TECH REP.

"If you can hack the unhackable, if you can mess with something that isn't even real, you can come back. I know it. Whatever they did to you, we can fix it."

A shrill, high-pitched beep from my bracelet startles me. The message has changed.

RANGE ERROR.

Are we so far off the grid that it's killed my bracelet?

I double-check Bobby's ID, but his message remains the same.

The sound of approaching footsteps kills my curiosity. I fall silent and huddle against Bobby.

The door swings open. Moloch and Bia saunter into the cell, his arm wrapped around her waist. Bia crouches before us, looking elegant and evil in a tailored, black dress. "How sweet." She runs a finger down Bobby's cheek. He doesn't even flinch.

"Don't touch him!" I yell.

Her perfectly plucked eyebrows rise. "Or what?" She looks over her shoulder at Moloch and laughs. "She thinks she can save him."

"The heart is foolish." He crosses his arms. "But we have things to do today."

"Quite right, darling." Bia tucks one of my braids behind my ear and strokes my face. "We have to get you ready."

I recoil at her touch. "For what?"

She stands and offers me a hand.

I cling to Bobby. "I'm not going anywhere with you."

Her smile fades into irritation. "Don't give Moloch a reason to make you hurt. He enjoys it enough as it is, and he's just itching for an excuse. Isn't that right, love?"

Moloch's gleaming eyes are his answer.

"Now come along." She holds out her hand again. "Moloch will keep your beloved boy company while we're gone."

I stand on my own. "Don't hurt him," I say as we pass through the door. My voice shakes; whether it's more from fear or fury I can't say.

"It takes so much work to get a reaction anymore that it's almost lost its fun. Almost," he says.

"Poor baby," Bia says to Moloch as she leads me away. The door closes behind us, and she takes me back upstairs.

As we pass back through the kitchen, I give the biggest knife on the butcher block table a longing look.

She wags her finger and tut-tuts at me. "Those will be of no use to you, darling."

She leads me through the parlor and to the stairs.

"Where are we going?"

"Upstairs to the dressing room."

"What for?"

"We have to get you ready. I already told you that, and I do hate to repeat myself."

A sinking feeling makes my feet leaden. "Ready for what?"

She slips her arm through mine like we're girlfriends, and we begin to climb the stairs. "Why, for Raum, of course."

My body stiffens to the point of immobility.

"It is an honor," she chides. "You should be thankful. Few are chosen to serve him."

"Serve him? What...what does that mean?" I stammer. Something sinister grabs my heart and squeezes.

"He'll show you soon enough."

I begin to shake so hard that Bia has to drag me up the last two steps. "Is he here?"

Her expression darkens. "He's encountered some difficulties, but he'll be joining us shortly."

Difficulties? Like Clara kicking his ass, maybe?

At the end of the upstairs hall is a small door that leads to a soft pink dressing room with gauzy curtains and bright windows. A vanity table with a fluffy purple chair sits in the middle of the room next to a large rolling case stocked with an assortment of makeup. Racks and racks of clothes and a huge collection of footwear line the walls to either side of the table.

I stumble to the vanity and fall into the chair. "This room, in this place"—I start to laugh, because I'm sick of crying—"it's ridiculous."

"This house does need a woman's touch," Bia admits. "But I have to take it one room at a time, and this one is all mine." She closes the door and fetches a basin of fragrant, soapy water. "Let's start with the grime. You need a good scrub." She sets a towel down next to me. "Lose the shirt."

I wrap my arms around myself. "What?"

Bia rolls her eyes. "We haven't the time for modesty, girl."

This is neither the time nor the place for a fight, so I disrobe. I'm torn between disgust and pleasure as she washes the grime from my skin. Bia is repellent, the situation awful, but the water is warm and the soap's scent is calming—too much so, I realize. My head begins to swim. My eyelids droop.

"What did you do?" I slur.

"Just calming the seas." She smiles like the cat that ate the canary. "Don't worry, the effects are short-lived. Won't last much past getting you to him, doctor's orders. Raum likes his girls with a little spunk. Fighting and biting, as he puts it."

I know I should be afraid. I know I should resist, but somehow, the message gets lost between my brain and my body, and I completely forget what it is I'm supposed to be scared of.

Bia dresses me in a sleeveless, floral-print top with lace accents sewn into the bodice. She matches a simple but sexy pair of dark wash jeans and bejeweled sandals to complete the ensemble. My muddled brain tells me I'd have loved this outfit, had I any choice in the matter. It's feminine and pretty while managing not to be too girly. It looks just like something my mom would have picked out for me.

Next, Bia gives me a manicure and pedicure in a warm coral polish. I comply without a hint of protest, unable to muster the will to care that I'm her own personal doll to dress and primp. I can't even be bothered to concern myself with the stark reality of who she's doing this for.

As she's putting the finishing touches on my makeup, the door bursts open and Moloch storms in. "Change of plans. We're leaving."

Bia frowns. "We're almost done." She outlines my lips and fills them in with a deep burgundy shade.

Moloch grabs her arm and pulls her to her feet. "Now." He gives her a shove toward the door.

He crouches down before me and studies my eyes. For the first time, I see the details of his face, the light glinting off his coppery hair, the flecks of brown in his sinister eyes. The voice in my head that's afraid, that cries out a warning, is so faint as to barely be heard.

His fingers run down my cheek. "Ah, very good. You'll be no trouble at all." He takes my hand, and I follow him out the door.

I'm swept down the stairs that I was so unwilling to climb a short time ago, a fact I can remember, but the reason for my resistance eludes me.

Bobby is standing at the bottom of the staircase wearing the same vacant stare. His lifeless expression triggers something in me, cutting through my haze of cooperation with a flash of awareness. A glimmer of danger and evil strikes me, and my steps falter. A whimper passes my lips as I try to pull free of Moloch's grip.

"We'll have none of that," he says, his words hitting the midpoint between gentle and dangerous.

My mind stirs, but my body is helpless to act in its own best interest. The tension in me goes slack, and I follow without further protest.

He nods toward Bobby and tells Bia, "You take him. He'll be no trouble."

"But I like trouble," she protests.

"There will be plenty to go around."

We pass through the kitchen, this odd entourage of ours. Moloch leads the way with me in tow, and Bia follows close on our heels with a catatonic Bobby at her side.

At the back of the kitchen is a door leading outside into an alley that runs behind the brownstones. Nothing good ever comes from my travels down Atman City alleys, yet my body carries on without hesitation.

Bia slinks after us, her arm hooked through Bobby's like they're a couple out on the town.

"Where are we going?" I mumble through heavy, clumsy lips.

Moloch smiles. His eyes are bright with an assured cockiness that could only have come from millennia of experience.

It must be incredible to feel so alive in death, to be powerful beyond measure.

I try again. "Where are you taking us?" The words are nearly intelligible this time.

"We have plans for you."

I stumble as my thoughts return to Raum's promise. *"You belong to me, and I will not be denied what is mine."*

My brain tries to fight my all-too-willing body, but the task is impossible. My knees stiffen, and my steps slow.

Moloch stops the procession to study my eyes. He leans in close, and I want to lash out, to fight, to grab Bobby's hand and run, but I can do nothing.

"Save your fight for Raum. Believe me, you'll need it." His eyes gleam. "And he'll thank you for it."

He takes my hand, and we're on the move again. My awareness ebbs and flows. My feet are leaden, but they carry me step after slow step down the alley, past houses in varying stages of decay. Protests fire off in my mind like fireworks, building to a crescendo.

I come to a sudden halt and find my voice again. "Wherever it is we're going, you'll never get us there. The whole City Guard is out looking for us, not to mention every agent in ACEA. You've probably got half the Admin staff after you, too."

Moloch grabs me by my shoulders. "You seem to be under the mistaken impression that we're the quarry."

"Not we, *you*."

His grip tightens, but I take it. *I will not make a sound.*

He turns to Bia. "You didn't give her enough."

She scowls. "You weren't there. I gave her plenty." She runs her fingers through Bobby's curls and stares deep into his vacant eyes. "Soon she'll be just like this one. If you can't handle one mortal girl until then, one little sheep"—her eyes lock with Moloch's—"then you're not much of a shepherd."

"Mind your place." Moloch turns his attention back to me. "In order to find us, your saviors must first know where to look." His hands squeeze even harder. He whispers into my ear, "And they're looking in all the wrong places."

CHAPTER THIRTY-SEVEN

We emerge from the shadows into a busy street and blend seamlessly into the crowd. It's foolish to hope for a City Guard member to be present on this particular block—one of millions in the vast city—but I search nonetheless, my eyes for the first time actively seeking Atman Blue.

Moloch has brought us to a run-down, afterlife version of Times Square. Blinking neon signs tempt passersby with promises of THE PLACE TO MEET YOUR BASE DESIRES and THE CITY'S WILDEST NIGHTS, GUARANTEED.

The buildings at the center of the square soar toward the sky, surrounded by shorter, squat structures that fan out in all directions. A towering billboard proclaims what must be the local motto: BRING OUT THE DARK.

The clientele of this district is frightening to say the least, a ragtag collection of souls who look like they've leaped from the covers of some twisted graphic novel. A woman passes close by, her arms dancing with tattoos of demons and fire. Her long hair is heavily greased and runs down her back in clumps that look like snakes. The skimpy leather outfit she dons is studded with spikes and chains, and leaves little to the imagination, accentuating every curve.

Her arm brushes against mine, and she stops, sudden and furious. "Watch yourself, girl," she snaps, stepping closer.

"I…" I backpedal, but have nowhere to go in the dense crowd.

Moloch puts his arm around me. His hand hangs casually over my shoulder and I fall back under his spell, enchanted by Bia's nefarious potion. Unaffected Dez screams in my mind, begging my body to come to reason, but my arms slip around his waist. I huddle against him, seeking shelter from the crazed woman before me.

"She belongs to another," he warns. "Move along."

The woman straightens, forgetting me as she turns on Moloch. Her words come out like venom. "And if I don't?"

He exchanges a knowing look with Bia, who begins to laugh. She runs her hand down Bobby's chest. "Do it," she urges, giddy.

"For you? Of course." He bows and turns back to my latest antagonist. "Fall," he commands.

And she does.

She crumbles to her knees, gripping her head and screaming.

"Stop," I whisper. My arms tighten around his waist, and I bury my face in his chest.

He holds me close and strokes my hair. "Odd batch you made," he tells Bia. "Keeps coming and going with her."

"The potency may have been a bit off this time. But if someone hadn't been distracting me..." She laughs.

They leave the woman in a heap on the ground, forgotten. We walk down the street to a ticket window in front of a sketchy theater at the end of the block. A marquee above reads ALL SHOWS, ALL TIMES, NAME YOUR PICTURE spelled out in broken letters.

Moloch steps up and tells the man behind the window, "Four tickets to *Passages*."

The man has dirty blond hair and a series of teardrop tattoos running down his gaunt face. His five o'clock shadow looks closer to midnight. He eyes Moloch suspiciously. "Passages?"

"You heard me."

"If you say so." He slides four tickets through the window. "You'll be in theater six. That's all the way down on the right."

Moloch snatches up the tickets. "You've been a tremendous help."

"Enjoy the show."

The theater is just as run down as everything else around here. It's a relic of reds, from the carpet to the walls.

We pass the unmanned concession stand that smells of popcorn, and I'm hit with another pang of homesickness. Moloch's arm is still around my shoulders, but I let go of him and fight to get a bit of myself back.

"Have it your way," he says. "For now."

He lets me go and I fall back next to Bobby. Our fingers intertwine, but his hand is as slack as his mind. I whisper in his ear, determined he's still in there somewhere. "We're going to be okay. Mack and Clara are going to find us. We just have to hang

Sounds of films I can't quite place come from the theaters as we pass. An action movie with gunfire and squealing brakes in one, a woman professing her love in another.

We enter the darkness of theater six, an empty, dank place with ratty seats and garbage strewn on the sticky floor. Old popcorn crunches under our feet as we make our way down the stairs. The floor lighting is largely broken, leaving only a few bulbs to illuminate our path.

A flickering projector plays a film on a ratty screen, and I immediately recognize *Casablanca*. It's my mom's favorite movie. I could never for the life of me understand why Ingrid Bergman would still be pining after a surly, old drunk like Rick, but Mom always said I'd understand when I was older. *Too bad I never got the chance.*

Moloch leaves Bobby and me in Bia's charge and heads for the first row. *The worst seats in the house.* I silently curse his terrible choice, but as it turns out, he has no intention of sitting down. He moves over to the end of the row and runs his hands along the wall, in search of something. The fingers of his right hand catch on a seam, and he pushes his palm flat against it. A panel pops open.

He motions to Bia.

She hooks her arms through Bobby's and mine and brings us down to him. Her touch makes my skin crawl, but I am helpless to resist.

"Here we go," she says, all smiles. She hops up and down like an excited child as Moloch swings open the panel and disappears into the wall.

Bia gives me a little push. "After you."

I look to the tattered movie screen and say goodbye to Bergman and Bogart as they say goodbye to each other. With my stomach in knots, I step into the wall.

Moloch pulls me toward him to make room for Bobby and Bia. "I told you everyone's looking in the wrong places."

Bia pulls the panel shut with a click.

The space is cramped and dim, our way lit by overhead recessed lighting. There's just enough room to walk single-file, but it's a tight squeeze. Moloch's shoulders brush against the wall studs as he passes, sending bits of sawdust tumbling to the ground.

Thanks to the close quarters, there is little Moloch and Bia can do to me, at least for the moment. Doesn't-take-crap-from-anybody Dez, the one who has gotten me in plenty of trouble already, takes her cue and decides to come out and play, anxious for the chance while my body is cooperating.

"So we're just going to hide in the walls until, what, ACEA and the Council get over this whole major breach thing? Or, are you hoping Bobby and I will progress enough on our own inside these walls to get our tickets, so we can forget all about it, like some sort of big do-over? Either way, it doesn't seem like much of a plan."

Moloch looks over his shoulder at me. "Raum's going to enjoy ripping the bold from you, girl. And I'll enjoy watching."

Our journey through the walls is short. Too short. After my ill-advised comments, we travel no more than a few hundred yards to the outer edge of the building where the wall ends in a staircase wide enough to descend in twos.

Fabulous.

My dad's oldest brother Harry fought in Vietnam. He's haunted to this day by memories of the elaborate network of hand-dug Viet Cong tunnels that run beneath the country. Uncle Harry was part of the U.S. military campaign to flush out the tunnels, and on rare occasions would tell me about his days below the jungle. Moloch has brought us to what seems to be a slightly wider, afterlife version. Hopefully this doesn't have all the booby traps, vermin, and warfare.

The soft glow of our ID bracelets provide the only light sources in this cold, damp nightmare, but my eyes quickly adjust to the dark. The walls are so close that traveling side by side requires us to huddle together. Moloch has to stoop down to avoid hitting his head on the low ceiling.

We zigzag through a series of turns. Try as I might to keep track, I lose all sense of direction. Even if we could get away, I would be less than useless in getting us to safety.

"Not so brave now, are you?" Moloch's face is even more frightening in the dim glow of my bracelet.

Bia and Bobby start to lag behind. His shuffling, robotic steps are not conducive to subterranean travel. Bia's temper flares. She chides him for his uncooperative, slow strides, but it's no use. He reacts to her verbal assault no more than he's reacted to anything else.

"Moloch," she snaps. "Let's switch. Let me take the girl for a while."

Moloch calls out, "If you can't handle one mortal boy, one little sheep, well, you're not much of a shepherd."

Bia hurls a tirade of curses at him, but he just smiles. "The line between love and hate can be almost indistinguishable, don't you think?"

I look at Bobby then back to Moloch. "Seems pretty clear to me."

"Even a bold girl such as yourself is little more than clay meant to be shaped by a craftsman. You're rough and without form, but in the right hands, you will become a thing of beauty."

His knuckles brush against my cheek, but this time, I have the control to slap his hand away. "I hope Mack takes you out first."

"That's because you haven't gotten to Raum yet. You'll be begging for my kindness soon enough."

I've officially reached my limit of Raum threats. There's only so frightened a person can get. I'm scared, no doubt, but I'm also tired and angry. Angry for what they've done to Bobby, angry for what they did to my guards, angry for what they may have done to Clara, and angry for whatever it is they're planning to do to me.

I refuse to take another step. "You keep talking about Raum and hanging this threat over my head, yet where is he? It sure seemed like he was supposed to join us in the woods, but that didn't happen. Then we went to that crappy bar, and he wasn't there, either. No sign of him at the house, and then we left in a big hurry with your 'change of plans.' You so sure he hasn't been vaporized? Mack has a pretty itchy trigger finger."

Moloch raises his hand, ready to strike.

"Go ahead," I say. "I'm done being afraid."

His hand drops, and he grabs my arm. "You've only begun to know fear, child."

CHAPTER THIRTY-EIGHT

A rickety ladder creaks beneath my feet as I climb behind Moloch toward the light. We emerge from the ground through a well-disguised trapdoor. Although reluctant, I take the hand he offers me and allow him to pull me above ground. It's a visual blowout. My overwhelmed eyes take several painful, blinking minutes to adjust to the daylight.

We're standing on the bank of a tree-lined canal at the base of a stone bridge. A small wooden boat tethered to a post a few yards away rocks gently in the current. The canal's surface reflects a perfect, photographic image of the colorful maples on both banks. The trees are unnaturally tall, towering hundreds of feet into the churning blue sky.

Bluebirds dart between the branches, an odd and beautiful sight in such dense terrain. Their brilliant plumage shines in the light, making for a dazzling display against the bright, fall colors of the trees.

How such beauty and ugliness can coexist seamlessly is beyond my comprehension.

Bobby would love the bluebirds.

I'd do anything right now to hear his take on their presence outside their natural habitat of open grassland, to have my brilliant, inquisitive Bobby back. Maybe seeing them will trigger something in him, some recollection that will bring him back to me.

A tirade of curses from below grabs my attention.

"Climb, you useless boy," Bia screeches.

Moloch stands at the trapdoor and looks down the ladder. Amusement brightens his eyes. The light glints off his coppery hair, and a gentle breeze tousles his locks, but this time I'm immune to his allure. All I see beside me is a harsh-featured nightmare.

"Come on, shepherd," he chides. "Control your charge." He throws an arm around my waist. "I'm having no trouble with my little pet."

My hands grip tight in fists.

Bia slaps Bobby across the back of the head. "Climb."

He doesn't budge.

She paces back and forth behind him and spews a venomous rant, but he stays motionless at the base of the ladder, unaffected by her rage. She stops to stare into the light at Moloch, furious.

"You couldn't have left something? Some bit of this worthless child that could at least follow simple commands?"

Moloch shrugs and smiles. "What can I say? At times I'm a little too good at my job."

Bia grabs Bobby by the shoulders and forces him to turn

around. She slaps him hard across the face. "I will not be ignored, you insolent brat."

An angry red handprint blossoms on Bobby's cheek, but a series of rapid blinks is his only response.

Bearing witness to one more second of his abuse is more than I can stand.

Stop being a coward. You can't just stand by and watch this.

My voice cracks like a bullwhip, sharp with fury. "Leave him alone!"

Not waiting for forgiveness or approval, I lie on my stomach at the top of the ladder and dangle my arm down into the depths. "Come on, Bobby," I say gently. "Take my hand."

The daylight cuts a path through the darkness, down to where he stands. He turns his gaze skyward and stares at me with vacant eyes that contain not even a sliver of recognition. Gone is the drive, the perpetual quest to unlock the mysteries of the universe.

Bia crosses her arms and falls silent, content to be a mere spectator to whatever might unfold. She rolls her dark eyes, casting a clear vote on what chance she thinks I have in reaching Bobby.

"It's me, Dez," I say, trying to reach across the void of Moloch's creation. The struggle to keep the tremor from my voice is taxing, the ache in my chest overpowering.

Our night in the park is only a few days gone, but those days seem an entire reality ago, a whole other existence that no longer applies to either of us. How could everything go from so right to so very wrong in such a short span of time? How can this be all that's left of him?

With tremendous effort, I manage to push back my sorrow

and focus. "This isn't how our story ends. Take my hand, and we'll get through this together, I promise."

Perhaps it's just my hopeful imagination, but I could swear a glimmer of recognition lights his dull eyes, if only for an instant.

"You gave me your heart, and you showed me the stars. Let me show you the way out." I reach for him, despite the physical and emotional distance between us. "Don't be afraid, Bobby. I'm right here."

His movements are so slow as to be almost undetectable, but somehow his foot winds up on the bottom rung of the ladder.

Bia opens her mouth to speak but stays silent.

Bobby lifts his arms and shifts from stationary to moving in quick order, as though he's just remembered how to climb. He reaches the top of the ladder and steps by me like I'm not even there.

Bia slithers up the ladder behind him. Once she's above ground and back in control, she smiles at me. "You do have a way with the useless."

I step toward her. Pure, undiluted rage has taken the place of my fear. "Want to find out what else I'm good at?"

Bia begins to cackle, a sputtering sort of laugh that ramps up to a crescendo. She doubles over and laughs for several long, drawn out moments before righting herself and wiping away tears, still howling with sick delight.

Fed up well beyond the threshold of common sense and self-preservation, I lash out and shove her with both hands. My sudden motion catches her off guard and sends her to the ground. For an instant, I'm taken back to one of my first days at Atman when I kicked a floormate's chair with similar results.

The thing that seemed so big then, a loudmouth boy made cruel by a nightmarish upbringing, is nothing more than a trivial inconvenience when compared to all this. I'd trade these two for Herc any day. He was angry, he was bitter, he could even be cruel, but he was never evil to his core. It's a distinction I never would have made before, but now it's all the difference in the world.

Bia lunges at me with frightening grace, but Moloch steps between us and cuts off her path to my throat.

"Enough," he roars. He pushes her aside with one hand and wraps his free arm around me. I'm no match for his strength. Despite my kicking and flailing, he lifts me from the ground effortlessly and drags me back several paces.

Bia makes another charge, but Moloch stops her in her tracks with nothing more than a deadly look. "We haven't the time for this pettiness." His authority is absolute.

She shakes with rage. "I will not be disrespected by the likes of her."

"The blame rests at your feet alone. Your weak concoction has clearly worn off, and far too soon. If you'd done what you were brought in for—"

"How dare you," Bia snaps. "You forget who you're speaking to."

"As do you. Do not make the mistake of interrupting me again."

She falls silent, her eyes alight with anger. I can almost see the gears grinding in her mind as she considers her next move.

Moloch's arm squeezes painfully around my waist as he turns his attention to me. "I can still make him hurt, girl. You may not be afraid for yourself, but if you have any love for what's left of that boy, be afraid for him."

He drops me to the ground and walks toward the boat without looking back, leaving me gasping and shaken. Chastened, I hurry after him with an angry Bia on my heels. She leads Bobby, who is back to obedient, ever-silent compliance.

Moloch hops into the boat in a fluid motion that doesn't create so much as a ripple in the water. He stays on his feet and waits for us to catch up.

He holds out his hand to help me into the boat. I refuse his assistance and step aboard, clumsy but on my own. I stand on wobbly legs and send the boat into an unsteady back and forth tilt.

"Sit." He pushes me down onto the bench seat at the back of the small skiff and helps Bobby aboard.

Bia, like me, refuses his extended hand.

Moloch shakes his head. "The only one with sense enough to accept help when offered is the one without a thought left in his formerly brilliant mind." He unties the boat with an adept hand and pushes the oars into the water.

I lean against Bobby's shoulder, trying to draw strength from his presence despite his emotional and intellectual vacancy. If I close my eyes, I can almost imagine we're enjoying a lazy Saturday together.

The downside to this arrangement is that I don't feel safe enough to keep my eyes closed long, and am forced to stare into the faces of doom while I cling to whatever remains of my sweet Bobby.

Moloch's muscular arms ripple as he rows, taking us on a swift course down the canal. He catches me staring, and his mouth spreads in a wide, gleaming grin.

"It's almost as though we're on—what is it you call it? A double date? I've only recently become aware of such a thing, but it does have its charm."

"It's going to end on a bang when Mack gets ahold of you," I say.

"Oh." Bia purrs. "I guess Daddy doesn't like it when we keep you out past curfew?"

It's impossible to keep her from getting under my skin, and now that I'm free of whatever potion she had me on, the effort to keep my mouth shut is futile. I know I should stay quiet, for Bobby's sake and my own, but I can't do it.

"You're disgusting."

Bia clucks her tongue. "Moloch, my love, I do believe we've upset the poor girl."

He pulls in the oars, content to drift in the increasing current. "What a shame."

"Let me ask you something," I say.

Moloch pulls Bia closer. "You clearly have no desire to protect the boy you seem to love. I have to admit I find it fascinating. So ask away. But make it count."

Shut up, a voice in my head warns, but I can't bring myself to obey. "If you're so powerful, so undefeatable, why are we sneaking around underground and taking this circuitous route to wherever the hell it is we're headed? Why are we avoiding the City Guard and ACEA like you're scared to death of them? No pun intended."

Out of nowhere, Moloch backhands Bia with a sudden and severe blow across her face. "If you ever again fail at a basic task,

I will make you pay."

She doesn't react or make a sound; she simply stares down at her hands folded in her lap.

She's old and powerful enough to not feel pain or suffer normal damage, I know. But the psychological effect of that kind of attack isn't something I imagine you could ignore, no matter how long you've been around.

"It was a simple potion," he seethes.

A tiny scrap of sympathy wells up inside me, and I curse myself for it. I compare this situation to Herc again; a cruel boy for sure, but one created by circumstance.

"Was there ever any good in you?" I ask her.

She doesn't answer.

"If there was, it's not too late to find it again."

"One more word, girl," Moloch warns, "and I will make you regret it. I promise you that. I've already given you more warnings than you deserve." The oars splash back into the water, and he sets to work rowing again.

I take Bobby's hand, still hoping for any sort of reaction. There is none to be found, so I lean against him and watch the afterlife go by. The canal angles off to the right toward the outskirts of a densely populated sector of the city. To our left, rolling hills give way to craggy, mountainous terrain. The day's light is beginning to fade as Moloch leads our well-timed approach.

"Almost there," he says.

But where is that?

CHAPTER THIRTY-NINE

Two men stand on the stone wall of the canal in the fast approaching dark, awaiting our arrival. One appears quite elderly, thin and gaunt with a yellowed beard. His younger, clean-shaven companion is shorter and stout, with dark features. Moloch throws the line to the younger man, who ties off our boat without a word exchanged.

The boat bumps and creaks against its mooring as everyone aboard, save Bobby, prepares to climb out. Moloch springs onto the wall, his display of dexterity another reminder of his superhuman abilities. He looks down at me and smiles, making it clear the show was just for me. His fingertips wiggle as he holds out his hand to Bia.

This time she accepts his help, her tiny hand swallowed up in his as she steps delicately from the boat, her eyes lowered.

She does not deserve my pity.

Moloch doesn't bother to offer me a hand, opting instead to

grab my arm and yank me out. He hands me off to the elderly man, who smiles kindly and offers me his arm.

I surprise myself by taking it.

Once Bobby is removed from the boat—a slow process involving much maneuvering and prompting—we proceed behind a row of stone buildings a few yards from where we've docked. We ascend a set of stairs cut into the side of a steep, grassy hill. The steps are uneven, rough-cut stone and make for treacherous footing, made all the worse by the uneven light of the torches along our path.

The old man pats the back of my hand that rests on his arm. "Not far now, dear," he says kindly.

I want to ask where it is we're headed and why he's being so nice, given the circumstances, but I don't dare speak. The consequences of Moloch's anger are still fresh in my mind, his ability to inflict crushing pain a strong enough deterrent to keep me silent.

The dark-featured man leads the climb and brings the procession to a stop about two-thirds of the way up the hill. He taps his foot on the step, drumming out a strange rhythm with the toe of his boot, and an earthen entrance in the side of the hill slides open.

"Is he here yet?" Moloch asks.

The dark man shakes his head. "Not yet. Soon." His voice is deep and rough like gravel.

Moloch frowns. "Take our guests to their chambers." He grabs Bia and pulls her away from Bobby, urging her down the stairs.

She stops a few steps down. "What about the boy?"

A dangerous look clouds his face. "I am quite confident that Morris and Bates are fully capable of seeing them to their quarters."

Her mouth hangs open for an instant, but she follows him down the steps without further protest. They disappear into the night.

"Come along, dear," the old man—*Morris? Bates?*—tells me, and we follow Bobby and his new escort into the entrance in the side of the hill.

My whole body pitches forward in reaction to the din of the entry closing behind us. It takes only a moment for my eyes to adjust to the light, but fully adapting to the new surroundings is another matter. I shake from the culmination of anxiety, dread, exhaustion, and the ever-spiraling nightmare that has been these past few days.

We're in a small grotto where another staircase climbs up out of sight. The walls drip with condensation, and small pools of sulphurous water bubble to either side of us.

The dark-featured man hesitates at the base of the stairs, but my escort says, "After you, my dear Morris."

Well that clears that up, at least.

If I didn't know better, I'd think Bobby was relieved to be rid of Bia. He picks up the pace with no prompting and clambers up the stairs with what seems to be a spring in his step.

At the top of the steps, Morris takes a torch from the last sconce. His boots echo off the close walls as he leads us through a short, narrow corridor at ground level and into an abandoned blacksmith shop.

Beside a hearth sits an anvil and workbench scattered with tools and covered in a thick layer of dust. I drag my index finger across the bellows as we pass. The dirt is at least an inch thick. *Gross.* I wipe the grime on the pretty top Bia so carefully selected for me, satisfied by the long, dark streak it leaves. A small act of rebellion beats none at all.

Why did they ever need a blacksmith in the afterlife? Was there a big demand for swords and armor at some point?

The splintered door at the front of the shop opens with a grunt of effort from Morris. We step into a back courtyard of a small castle, where the grounds are neatly manicured and well-lit by security lights. A tall hedge runs the perimeter behind a display of stone statues—a hideous collection of gargoyles and banshees in frightening poses, perched on pedestals.

Decorative topiaries hug the castle's back wall, which is thick with ivy. A path of river rock leads to a back entrance—a tiny, arched door that each of us has to duck to get through.

Plank flooring creaks beneath our feet as we enter the castle single-file, via a dusty, crowded storage room. Built in shelving lines the walls, crammed with an amazing assortment of items, none of which seem to have any sort of order or connection to each other: a half-flat basketball, garden tools, a collection of paperback books, and, strangest of all, a full set of ski equipment.

Another shelf is overflowing with glass bottles and jars of all shapes and sizes, filled with liquids, powders, and an assortment of unidentifiable substances. I wonder if one of them contains Crosby's magical healing salve.

Without the benefit of Charlie's ability to ignore all pain and injury, I found myself on the receiving end of a vicious beating at the hands of Herc's murderous father a week after I arrived. Crosby carried me back to the dorms and brought me a salve that gave me instant relief and healed my injuries.

Maybe there's something here that can fix Bobby.

If ever there was a time for Crosby to swoop in and save the day, this is it. But my ever-sinking heart is coming to realize that if there is a way out of this, I'm going to have to find it myself. Moloch's underground travel, combined with the enormity of the search grid, has pretty much assured we won't be found.

I need to get us out of this. But I can't do it without Bobby.

I have to find some connection, some part of the banter Bobby and I so enjoyed if I am to have any hope of bringing him back from whatever place his mind has retreated. And there's no time like the present.

I stop at the shelf and grab a dusty, spherical bottle with a cork stopper. "Bobby, you suppose we've found the supplies of the Three Witches? Eye of newt and toe of frog? This looks suspiciously like wool of bat to me."

From my words sprouts a tiny miracle.

Bobby reaches toward the shelf with a steady hand and picks up one of the containers. It's a pretty little corkscrewing blue bottle filled with a dark liquid and has a metal stopper covered in tiny jewels. He holds it close to his face and swirls the bottle in a slow, smooth motion. He watches the contents stir.

His eyes brighten, and he lets out a satisfied sigh.

Tears fill my eyes. "Bobby?"

Bobby looks up from the bottle. His eyes stir with a glint of recognition when they meet mine.

He opens his mouth. In confusion? To speak?

I'll never know.

Morris snatches the bottle from his hand and gives Bobby a rough shove. "Keep moving, boy." He slams the bottle back onto the shelf, which sends the whole lot tumbling in a clattering commotion.

Bobby retreats back to vacancy. His expression goes slack, his body placid, as though he's settling comfortably in to a new set of clothes that don't fit him at all.

"Bobby, please," I whisper. "Come back."

Bates puts a hand on Morris's arm. "There is no need for such hostility. These children do not need punishment, not from the likes of us."

Morris glowers but doesn't speak.

"Our task," Bates continues, "is to deliver them to their quarters. Nothing more."

"And their task is to do as they're told."

While they're distracted in conversation, I slip Bobby's chosen bottle into the pocket of my jeans. It's a bit of luck that he picked one small enough to fit, and that Bia selected a top for me that hangs down to my upper thighs, effectively concealing my pockets and their contents.

Both men turn to me at once, but I disguise my clandestine move in a display of hurried cleaning. I right several of the bottles. "Just thought I should fix the mess we made."

"Never mind that," Morris growls. "We've wasted enough time as it is." He lumbers toward the exit.

Bobby and I follow, obedient in both our movements and our silence.

I can't speak, can't process the agony that's hit like a lightning strike. To come so close to reaching Bobby to then have it torn away by the cruel words of a stranger, to have hope extinguished with a shove…

I can't do this anymore.

CHAPTER FORTY

The sunny, Friday afternoon in late June when I stared into Aaron's casket was the worst day of my life. Before me laid a plastic, thin replacement of my friend, a shell cast off and left behind. I pleaded with him to open his eyes, to sit up and say it was all a joke, to go with me down to the creek to skip stones one more time. "Tell everyone they're wrong," I begged. I stood before his chemical-laden body, a young girl, foolish enough to believe that if I wished hard enough, I could take away the truth and bring back my friend.

I couldn't save Aaron. No one could.

But I'll be damned if I'm going to let Bobby slip through my fingers. This time, I have a chance and a choice. He's not gone, not completely. He can't be.

The corridors wind along in a single, continuous blur as I struggle to find my spark, my drive to seek better than this fate they've chosen for us. Bobby may not be able to defend himself, but I can at least try.

I got us into this, and now I have to get us out.

We've made our way to the second floor, up a winding set of stone steps. We passed a kitchen and a room full of artwork, a gallery of some sort, before coming upstairs. There were other rooms, too, but the details elude me.

Focus.

One room was decorated with fine tapestries. Another was a reading room with a large fireplace, and next to the hearth was an exterior door. It's an odd place for an exit, and a detail my semi-present mind latched on to.

That's how we'll get out.

With fresh resolve, I force myself to be present. I break my silence. "What is this place, anyway?"

"This is Nergal Manor," Bates says. "Only the highest ranking members—Earls, Princes, Lords, and the like—have access to these facilities when they visit the city. Few are allowed the opportunity to set foot on this hallowed ground. It is a great honor you have been given, sweet girl." He speaks like he's a curator at a museum talking about Impressionism or Ancient Egypt, rather than the kidnapping and torture of underage souls.

"Given? Nothing has been given to me. I have been taken. I have been forced. Bobby's been…" Just a glance at Bobby is all it takes to finish the awful sentiment for me.

Bates shakes his head. "Soon you will understand."

"Why haven't the ACEA and City Guard stormed the gates?"

"A millennia-old truce prevents their presence on our grounds, although we were generous enough to grant them full access this morning. They conducted an exhaustive search with our blessing and have moved on, satisfied."

"I'm pretty sure any truce you may have had went out the window when a couple of super demons decided to kidnap underage souls."

Morris looks back over his shoulder. His grip on Bobby's arm tightens. "Enough talk. We're almost there."

"Where is that?"

Ignoring Morris's warning, Bates explains, "You are being brought to the personal chambers of Raum himself."

Ice trickles down my back. I swallow back nausea, dizzy from fear. "Is he here?"

"He has given instructions to have you waiting for him upon his arrival, which should be quite soon."

At the end of the corridor is a huge set of wooden doors made from thick, vertical timbers. Two heavy iron rings take the place of doorknobs and hang from leering brass imps that seem to watch our approach.

Morris and Bates each take a ring and heave the doors open.

I grab Bobby's hand.

Bates holds out his arm, inviting us to step inside. "You may stay together, for now."

Bobby follows me into the room, his hand slack in my tight grip. The doors close behind us without another word from either man, and we're alone again, in a different sort of prison this time.

The space is easily five times the size of our suites back in the towers. At the center of the room is a huge bed with a heavy, wrought iron frame and blood-red bedding.

I shudder.

Luxurious crimson draperies hang from the walls alongside

large oil paintings depicting scenes too awful to give more than a passing glance.

Raum must have used the same decorator here as he did in the house where Moloch and Bia kept us. The artwork is reminiscent of the foyer's stained glass ceiling, although I can't bring myself to look too closely. My darting eyes picked up enough—depictions of torture, dismemberment, and sneering demons. It's enough to turn my stomach.

Floor-to-ceiling bay windows at the far end of the chambers grab my attention.

"Come on, Bobby. Let's go check it out."

I lead him across the room, hoping the expansive view will give me some sort of idea of where we are.

The windows look out upon a brightly lit plaza, and beyond it, nothing but unidentifiable city sprawl as far as the eye can see. At the center of the square, two dead, leafless elm trees twist and bend toward the sky. Between them sits a large sphere that glows blue and green. Tendrils of light pulse and twist within.

The gate.

A rush of energy makes my head spin. "This can't be real, Bobby. We can't really be looking at the Gates of Hell." I squeeze his hand tight. "I need you. I need to hear you say this is all your imagination, that your bored mind is running wild. You have to be our guide if we're going to have any chance of getting back to the dorms. I don't know the city the way you do."

Wrapped up in fear and distracted by the gate, I've failed to notice the most glaring detail of all: the square is crawling with City Guard and ACEA agents.

Bates lied. They haven't gone anywhere.

I let out a triumphant shout that trails off in a wail of relief. My fists pound against the glass. "Up here," I scream. "We're up here!" The closest guards can't be more than a hundred yards away, and it's no more than twenty or thirty feet down to ground level, yet not a single one of them looks in our direction.

Undeterred, I scream even louder and jump up and down waving my arms. My hands smack the glass hard enough to make the windows shake.

"It will do you no good," a soft voice from behind us says. "They cannot hear you."

Startled, I turn to face a diminutive girl who seems to have materialized out of nowhere. She looks to be in her late teens, although for all I know, she could be centuries old—millennia, even. Her long, dark hair falls in soft curls well past her shoulders. She's barefoot and wears a flowing, sleeveless dress. Her hair and vivid blue eyes combined with her overall features, from the dimple in her chin to her high cheekbones, make for a striking resemblance to Charlie. They could be brother and sister. Twins, even.

"Wh-who are you?" I stammer.

She bows her head. "I am Asha, one of Raum's handmaidens." Her voice carries the hint of an accent, a slight trill to her 'r's and a softness to her 't's I can't quite place.

"What do you mean they can't hear us? They're only a few hundred feet away."

Her graceful strides carry her quickly across the room. She stands next to me and taps her knuckles against the glass. "Soundproof. And camouflaged from the other side. We can see out, but they cannot see in. From out there, the windows are invisible. All they see is a stone wall."

I rest my forehead against the glass. My body slumps.

Asha takes my hand. "Come." She gestures to a pair of high-backed chairs by the window. "Make yourselves comfortable. I am to keep you contented until Raum's return." She tugs at my hand, but I don't budge.

She turns her efforts to Bobby, who follows her obediently to a chair and sits.

She returns to me. "May I offer you something to drink? Are you hungry? I know you are new, so you must be."

"I want to get Bobby back to the towers."

"I am afraid that is not possible. Raum has chosen you. It is your destiny to be bound to him, to serve him." She places her tiny hand on my shoulder. "You are very tense. Shall I draw a hot bath for you?"

Her resemblance to Charlie makes my heart ache. *I need to get back to him. There's so much to say, so much to fix.*

"You could come with us. I know agents who will keep you safe. You deserve better than this, Asha. We all do."

She pulls free from my grasp. "This conversation is not permitted."

"How long has Raum had you? How many centuries have you been stuck with him? The Council would never let him treat you like this, not if they knew about you."

"My fate was chosen long ago, and it is my duty to serve." Her practiced words don't match the sad look in her eyes.

She has to want more for herself.

"Do you know what he's going to do to me?" My throat constricts. "You have to help us. Please."

"I am sorry. I—" She turns and heads for the door. "I will be back soon to check on you. Make yourselves comfortable in the meantime."

Her petite stature is no match for the massive doors, but somehow she manages to pull them open and hurry from the chambers.

The vacant look in Bobby's eyes is painful to witness, and I don't think I can take one more second of him staring blankly at the wall. I pull him to his feet and lead him back to the window. My cheek presses against his chest and my arms wrap around his waist. I stare out at the agents and guards milling about the square.

"The city you love is right out there, Bobby, and I'm right here. You just need to come back. I saw a glimmer of you back in that storage room. Give me a sign, some sort of hint that you're in there, because I'm running on empty."

The storage room. I shove my hand into my pocket and grab the bottle I stole. I hold it up so Bobby can see it. The light filters through the blue glass and gets trapped in its dark, viscous contents.

"What do you suppose is in there?"

I offer him the bottle, but he only stares at it, showing none of the interest it sparked in him just a short while ago. I put it in his hand and close his fingers around the corkscrewed glass.

"Take it. It meant something to you. Find that spark and come back to me, Bobby. I can't do this alone."

He shuffles over to his chair and sits back down, clutching the bottle to his chest.

I sit cross-legged on the floor before the bay windows. With nothing else to do, I look out onto the square and watch eternity go on without us.

There's nothing more isolating than being completely alone in the presence of another, especially when it's someone who has given you his heart.

And for what?

Bobby hasn't made a motion or a sound since I gave him the bottle. He holds it tight but makes no other indication he's aware of where we are or what we face.

The gate casts an eerie, pulsating glow on the square and its occupants. The agents and City Guard members continue their occupation, stopping and checking each and every passerby.

Yet, here we are, just a few hundred feet away. And they have no idea.

Despair is a lot like a hurricane. It starts off small, far out in the ocean, and builds to a powerful storm. When it makes landfall, all you can do is board up your windows and hope to ride it out.

But how?

Help isn't coming, and even if I could get us out of here, where *is* here? Could I sneak us out to the square unnoticed? Would the dozen or so guards and agents be enough to fend off whatever fills this castle? If I can't get us to the square, and we have to strike off on our own, how would I find our way back to the dorms?

Everything in my life and death has lead to this, and I have only two choices: do nothing and prepare for whatever Raum has planned or run. There is nothing else, and there is no more time.

This is your moment. This is the time when you fight.

Bolstered by the prophetic words of Charlie's letter, my decision is made.

"Come on, Bobby. We're getting out of here."

CHAPTER FORTY-ONE

I pray for silence as I push against the chamber door, and my reward is a loud, sustained creak. The heavy door swings open much farther than the just-enough-to-squeeze-through width I had planned.

I press my finger to my lips. "We have to be absolutely silent," I whisper, as though there's any chance Bobby would make a sound.

Together we slip into the hallway, and I push the door shut behind us to another thunderous groan. I cringe and wait for the inevitable end to what must be the shortest-lived escape in history, but nothing happens—no rush of footsteps, no Asha sounding the alarm, no Morris and Bates appearing to drag us the five feet back into the chambers. All that surrounds us is silence.

We stick close to the wall as we make our way down the corridor, Bobby mirroring my every move with mindless obedience.

A few short days ago, he took my hand and led me through the sprawling metropolis of Atman. I was like an awed child following a seasoned veteran through the city he knew and loved. Now I've taken his hand to lead him through this nightmare, but I'm nothing more than a scared girl in over her head and trying to survive the afterlife.

I pause to slow my rapid breath and calm my shaking body.

We'll never make it if you don't settle down.

The courtyard filled with agents is tantalizingly close.

We just have to get there.

A quick assessment of the hallway tells me we're still alone, at least for the moment. Ahead is the route to the main staircase, a temptation we must avoid. It may be the most direct path to the awaiting City Guard and agents, but we'd have little chance of passing by undetected.

Pinning our chances on a gut instinct, I lead Bobby down a narrow passageway to our left in the hopes of finding a service elevator or back stairwell where we'll have at least a chance of sneaking out, unseen.

The walls close in on us with every cautious step we take, until we're forced to squeeze single-file down a steep stone staircase. My frantic heart races as we wind down the stairs. The tight, turning radius allows me to see only three steps ahead. At any moment, our flight could meet its end at the hands of one of the castle's staff—a servant, Morris, Bates...*even Raum.*

My hand shakes in Bobby's. I squeeze him tight, desperate for a reaction.

Please don't make me be alone in this.

A short breath escapes my pursed lips as I descend the final step of the staircase. I peek around the corner and see we're in a storeroom. Racks and racks of wine spread out before us, and wooden barrels line the walls. A pair of small windows high on the wall to the left is the only source of light in the cool, dim room, save for the glow of our bracelets.

"I don't think there's anyone here," I whisper.

The earthen floor is sandy and soft beneath our feet, making our footsteps silent as we cross the room to the door on the opposite wall. We climb four small stairs to the door and pause so I can listen, but it's too thick to hear through. There's nothing to do but open it and see what's on the other side.

Fear is alive in me, an organic entity wrestling for control. I take a deep breath in a fruitless attempt to quell the terror rampaging through me. My shaky hand grips the doorknob tight.

"Here we go, Bobby."

I open the door enough to peek through, and we're greeted by the sound of clattering dishes and the hurried work of food prep—knife blades clacking against cutting boards, sizzling pans, and a chef barking out orders.

I count twenty in the kitchen's staff.

"Less than two hours to go, ladies and gentleman," the burly chef calls out. "There is to be nothing but your best work tonight." He makes his way up the line, checking techniques and scrutinizing his assistants as he passes.

My breath catches in my throat when I see a young girl carry two big bags of garbage out a back door.

An exit.

And it's only a few yards away.

All we have to do is wait for our chance. A moment's

distraction is all it will take for us to slip by, undetected. We need ten seconds, at most. Ten seconds of not being noticed.

And then we're free.

The chef continues down the line, inspecting dishes and chastising knife skills. When he stops to taste something simmering in a large stockpot, his face goes red, and he throws the spoon at the assistant who made the mistake of being nearest to him.

"What is this?"

"I…I'm sorry, Chef," the assistant stammers. He takes a step back and lowers his head.

"You're sorry?" he roars. "Explain to me how I am to serve 'sorry' to our guests." He grabs the stockpot and hurls it to the floor, sending soup cascading across the kitchen.

Everyone freezes.

"Staff meeting, now!" he commands.

Each member of the kitchen staff files over in silence. They form a large circle around him, like moons in the orbit of a roiling planet, each one looking anywhere but at the furious chef.

He turns his wrath on a diminutive woman standing to his left. "Do the dead need food, Corisande?"

Her eyes grow big with fear. "Do we…need? N-no, Chef, of course not."

"So why do we cook?"

"B-because of the pleasure our lords derive from eating?"

He holds his hands out at his sides and addresses the group. "Because of the pleasure our lords derive from eating." He steps close to the assistant from the soup incident and stands nose to nose with the frightened man. "Is there anyone dead more than a week who shouldn't know this?"

The assistant hangs his head. "No, Chef."

"Do you know what happens"—the chef seethes—"when the masters of this keep are displeased with the quality of our service?" He lashes out with a sweeping arm and sends a crock of utensils clattering to the ground. "They take it out on me." His fearsome gaze scans his staff. "And I promise you, I will bring it down upon you tenfold."

Nineteen pairs of eyes focus on the irate head chef.

Now.

I press my finger to my lips once again. My heart pounds as I creep and Bobby shuffles through the wine cellar's door. Crouching low, we move toward the exit, using baker's racks and cabinets as cover while the chef continues to assail his staff. With luck finally on our side, we make our silent escape and pass through the exterior door unnoticed.

A large dumpster provides cover as I take in our surroundings.

Even in this emotional state, I can't help but ponder the ridiculous notion of afterlife garbage men, if only for an instant.

We're in a small courtyard with neatly trimmed grass and a dirt path that leads up its center to an outbuilding cast in the glow of sodium street lights. Faded, red clapboard siding gives the building the appearance of a stable, but the lack of animal sounds suggests it has fallen into disuse. A six-foot high stone fence surrounds the courtyard.

I'm a sprinter, not a pole-vaulter.

While I ponder the mechanics of getting Bobby to climb over the wall and give me an assist, I notice an iron gate to the side of the outbuilding, and the gate is ajar. High on this streak of luck, I hurry across the empty courtyard with Bobby in tow.

I peer around the wall through the gate, and the coast is clear. An open, grassy area spreads before us, with a tree line of tall pines a few hundred yards away.

"We must be on the opposite side from that hilly area where they brought us in," I tell Bobby. "If my sense of direction is worth anything, we should be pretty close to the square where all the agents and City Guard are patrolling. Should be over that way." I point down the long stone wall to the left, but it effectively blocks the view of what I hope is beyond it.

Bobby's auburn curls shine in the warm, yellow glow of the sodium lights, but his eyes are still dull and lifeless.

I squeeze his hand. "It's going to be okay. We just have to get to the square, and we'll be safe again. Then we can get you the help you need."

A hand lands on my shoulder, and I'm yanked backward, off balance. I don't need to see Moloch's face to recognize him. His iron grip is unmistakable.

"And where do you think you're going?" He drags me away from the gate and back into the courtyard.

"No! How did you find us?"

"Do you really think anything happens on these grounds without our knowledge?" He grabs a handful of my hair. "Don't you know it's poor manners to run off? This is your special night."

"Let us go," I scream, hoping we're near enough to the square to be heard. "It's Dez and Bobby! We're over here!"

"That will be enough." He clamps his hand over my mouth and drags me back toward the castle.

"Run, Bobby," I try to cry out, but he trails along after us.

CHAPTER FORTY-TWO

The hours creep along in Raum's chambers, where Moloch unceremoniously deposited us before posting a guard at the door.

The City Guard and ACEA agents continue their patrol as before, checking passersby but not venturing outside the square.

I've failed Bobby.

Moment after painful moment tick by until the chamber doors open, and Asha enters holding two large garment bags in her arms. Their size and black material gives them the appearance of body bags.

"We must get you ready now," she says, as though nothing has happened. Her voice is gentle but insistent.

My knees begin to shake and my stomach roils. "Bia already got me ready."

"There has been a change of plans. We must get you ready for dinner."

"I don't want to do this. Please."

"King Asmodeus is hosting a grand feast, and Lord Raum requires your presence."

"He's here?"

Asha walks across the room and lays one garment bag on the bed. Her every move is an elegant mix of caution and grace. She smooths the bag and straightens it so that the bottom seam is even with the edge of the bed.

She carries the second bag into the bathroom before going to Bobby, who's been staring at the wall since our return. "Let's get you ready," she tells him sweetly.

He follows her to the bed, where she begins to undress him. He stands stock-still, making no objection as she takes off his shirt.

Asha runs gentle fingers along the scars that crisscross his chest. "Sweet boy," she whispers, but she presses on.

I look away as she begins to unzip his jeans, embarrassed for him.

When he comes back, he's going to have so much to forgive. We've all betrayed him in some way—most of all, me.

She dresses him in a black, double-breasted tuxedo and sits him on the bed to work on his hair. Her magical hands tame his unruly mop of curls in short order, leaving him neatly coiffed.

Despite the dread and fear taking me by storm, I marvel at her skilled transformation of Bobby. All that's left is to get his shoes on his still swollen, battered feet—he doesn't even seem to notice—and he's ready.

He looks both handsome and broken. My shattered heart suffers another blow at the sight.

Asha joins me at the window and kneels. "It is time." She leans close to whisper in my ear. "Don't give them a reason to make it worse for you."

With gentle hands, she slips my shoes from my feet and helps me stand. "Take a deep breath, Desiree."

My breathing is rapid and shallow. I gasp. It's all I can do not to cry. "What is he going to do to me?"

Her nimble fingers push back a few of my braids. "Somewhere in you is a beautiful memory. Find it and go there. They cannot take that from you." She taps her index finger against my temple. "No matter what he does, Raum cannot get in there if you do not let him."

I follow her to the bathroom. The marble floor is cold against my bare feet, the light a bit too bright. I shiver.

She sits me down before a large mirror.

"First, your hair." Her practiced hands pull my braids into an effortless, elegant updo in just a few short minutes.

"Perfect," she says with a smile.

Asha unzips the garment bag that hangs from a hook on the wall and removes a pair of black strappy heels from a pouch at the bottom. She pulls the bag away from the hanger, revealing a stunning, strapless evening gown. It's the color of sunshine, with floral net embroidery in a rich green that cascades down the front.

She does her best to ease my embarrassment as she helps me into a lacy bustier and silk stockings. "There is no need for shame. The human form in this realm is but a residual image burned into our souls."

She zips me into the curve-hugging gown and steps back to admire her handiwork. "You look fit for the elegant banquet that awaits you."

There is a hard knock at the door, and Asha glides across the room to answer it. She heaves the doors open, but all I can hear is the pounding of my dead heart.

Why did he bother knocking?

Raum strides into the room. Moloch and Bia trail after him, her dress swishing across the floor. She's dressed in a plum ball gown with a plunging neckline and back that leave little to the imagination. Sequins glitter in the light with every move she makes.

Raum and Moloch wear elegantly tailored tuxedoes, fit for James Bond.

Or the devil.

I freeze in place, perched at the edge of the bed next to Bobby. My hands clench the bedspread.

Raum's gaze falls on me. His dark eyes are unreadable. "Hello again, pretty."

Moloch gives me an *I-told-you-so* look, and he's right. As bad as he is, Raum is far more terrifying.

Raum snaps his fingers. "Take the boy down to the Great Hall. We'll be along shortly."

Bia walks over to the bed and takes Bobby from me, leaving me alone and immobile. A tremble starts at my fingertips and spreads like a virus, moving up my arms and down to my toes.

Asha follows the trio out of the chambers and pulls the heavy doors shut behind her.

"Alone at last." Raum unbuttons his jacket and slips his hands into his pants pockets. He stands before me, content to watch me shake. His eyes brighten. "I hear you've had quite an adventure."

"Where's Clara?"

He shakes his head sadly and purses his lips. "Such a shame. But there is a price to be paid for challenging me."

"She was protecting me."

His hazel eyes narrow. "You are not hers to protect."

"What did you do to her?"

"That agent of yours with the gun isn't the only one who can make souls vanish from this existence." He presses his fingertips together, blows on them, and spreads his hand open like he's pantomiming dandelion seeds blowing in the wind. "Poor, sweet Clara."

"No," The room begins to shift and spin. My mind rebels, refusing the incoming input.

I can't breathe.

I can't think.

A smile spreads across Raum's face. "I'm afraid so. I have to admit, it got quite ugly, even for my taste. My methods aren't as neat and clean as that fancy gun of his. She did put up a good fight, though."

"You're lying." I lean forward, wrap my arms around myself, and begin to hyperventilate.

"Save your strength, my sweet. You have a long, adventurous night ahead of you."

It can't be true. It isn't *true.*

"What do you want from me?" I ask.

"I do hate to repeat myself, but it *is* quite simple. You are mine." He reaches for me and runs his fingers between my shoulder blades.

I recoil at his touch but have nowhere to go.

He wipes away a tear running down my cheek. "You belong to me, and tonight we will complete the sacred ritual that was so rudely interrupted."

I sit back up and find the courage to look him in the eyes. "I know why you're doing this."

"Oh, do you, now?"

"It's because you're scared."

He laughs and rocks back on his heels. He folds his arms across his chest. "Is that so?"

"Bobby and I saw you in Nero's. It was only a matter of time before he put two and two together and figured out what you were doing."

The mattress sinks as he sits down beside me. "And we can't have that, now, can we?" He strokes the back of my neck.

My skin crawls. "Too late."

Raum sighs. He drops to one knee and takes my hand.

I resist, but it's no use. He's too strong, both physically and emotionally.

He kisses the back of my hand. "There's no reason we can't still have our fun, my love." He stands. "Now come. Asmodeus wants to meet you."

He leads me out of the chambers and into the hallway. He offers me his arm, and I take it, if for no other reason than the fear of what will happen if I don't.

My mind reels.

Clara can't be gone. She can't be. She shouldn't have to pay the price for my mistakes.

He just said it to scare me.

Anger quells a fraction of my fear. "Are you for real?"

He frowns. "I'm not certain I understand the question." He reaches across with his free arm and squeezes my hand hard enough to transmit a clear warning.

"All this pomp and ceremony, for what? To terrorize a couple of kids? Don't you have anything better to do?"

He pushes me into an alcove. A small window looks out over a garden, but my view of the green oasis is short lived. He presses me against the cold stone wall and leans in close. His body is an immovable force, a weight pressing on me with unmatched strength. He's solid as rock. The scent of him and the visceral fear he creates will never leave me.

Not even in the span of eternity.

I have nowhere to go, no place to retreat. There is nothing but him and me.

He presses his lips to my forehead and speaks. "There is an order to the universe, and it will not be disrupted by the likes of you. I will always be the wolf, and you will always be the lamb."

Asha's words come to me. *"Somewhere in you is a beautiful memory. Find it, and go there."*

The warm waves lap against my feet. I dig my toes into the soft white sand, enjoying the break from the cold winter of Wisconsin.

We wade into the water until it is just below our knees.

"Now shuffle your feet," my mom says. "Use your toes, but be gentle. The living ones are dark and have wiggly bristles on the bottom. If they're alive, we let them go, okay?"

"How do you know this stuff?" I ask.

Mom smiles. The wind tousles her auburn hair. "My Aunt Molly used to bring me out here to dig for sand dollars every year when we'd come down for a visit. Sanibel Island was always her favorite spot, but Clearwater's good, too."

My toes push just under the surface of the sand, and I hit the jackpot.

"Mom," I shout. "I found one."

"That's enough," Raum warns, dragging me back. He pulls me close, his grip too tight. "We have no time for daydreams."

He takes me downstairs to the library, where I'd foolishly thought I could hatch an escape. The room is octagonal, its walls a deep mahogany with built-in bookshelves that reach the ceiling. An arched doorway at the far end of the room leads into a large solarium, and on the wall opposite from where we entered is the fireplace.

For an instant, the absurd thought of making a break for the exterior door that is so tantalizingly close dances through my mind. I could run to the square and get help. Maybe Bobby and I would have a chance. Never mind the floor-length gown weighing me down and the stiletto heels making each step a challenge. My wardrobe alone makes the maneuver an impossibility; the demon clutching my waist is just the icing on the cake.

Raum, as though he can read my mind, leans in and brushes his lips up my neck. "So close to freedom, yet so far away," he whispers into my ear. "Even if you could run, you know there is nowhere I can't find you. We're bound, sweet one."

A man with silver hair and a deep tan steps down from a rolling ladder. He puts a hefty book on a side table beneath a Tiffany lamp and buttons his tuxedo jacket.

His smile as we approach is the most intimidating, evil facial expression I've ever seen.

Raum bows in deference to the man. "My King."

"It's good to see you back in the fold," the man tells him. "I trust all is well?"

Raum considers his question for a moment. "I'm sure we will

MICHELLE E. REED

face some measure of negotiation with the Council, but I see no lasting impact."

"I hope she proves worth the trouble." He turns his attention to me. "Have you found our accommodations to your satisfaction, Miss Donnelly?"

I am scared mute, unable to move, speak, or breathe. This man's very presence immobilizes me, and I don't even know who—or what—he is.

"We had little choice, Asmodeus. She and the boy saw too much."

Asmodeus sits in the wingback chair next to the side table. He folds his hands in his lap, leans back, and takes in the sight of the two of us—an odd couple, for certain.

"I am well-aware, my troublesome Earl. However, from what I hear, you've gotten needlessly carried away. Entering administrative facilities? Destroying ACEA agents?"

Raum holds up a finger and smiles. "Just one. I may have maimed a few others, but they'll recover."

"No." I moan, soft and weak. *It can't be true.*

Asmodeus studies me, his icy blue eyes radiating power and danger. He turns his attention back to Raum, envy in his gaze. "She looks like a fighter."

"Please let us go," I beg. "You took us to keep what they were doing in the pods secret, but the Council already knows. If you let us go, it'll be better for everyone."

Raum grabs my arm and twists. "I did not give you permission to speak."

I bite my lip but can't help crying out.

"That's enough," Asmodeus commands. "Save your fun for later. We have a feast to attend."

CHAPTER FORTY-THREE

The Great Hall certainly lives up to its name. The marble floor's black and white checkerboard pattern leads the eye to the front of the hall and the massive, raised oak table with seating for fifty. Exposed stone blocks lead up to a soaring vaulted ceiling. Along the walls to both sides of the table is an impressive collection of armor, shields, and swords.

We are the first to arrive, and we make our way up the red velvet carpet that leads to the front of the hall. Asmodeus takes his seat at an intricately carved, throne-like monstrosity at the head of the table.

Raum pulls out a chair and motions for me to sit. He pushes the chair in like the perfect gentleman he isn't before taking the open seat between Asmodeus and me.

The table is set with fine china and sterling silver flatware. The linen napkins are deep red, a bold accent against the delicate silver pattern on the dishes. At each place setting is an engraved pewter goblet, each one uniquely designed and depicting graphic scenes from the underworld.

Raum catches me staring aghast at my goblet and leans in to get a closer look. A series of severed heads circles the lip, their faces frozen in horror. Beneath them, imps and lions claw and tear at their bodies.

"Lovely, aren't they?" he says. "The detail is exceptional." He holds up his goblet. "Cheers."

He takes a long pull and then looks at me expectantly. "Drink."

I don't even want to touch my glass, much less drink from it. "I—"

"Drink," he says again, his expression darkening.

My fear of the grotesque goblet and the thick red liquid it contains—*please don't be blood*—pales in comparison to my fear invoked by his angry look.

I take in a sharp breath and pick up the goblet. Its heft is surprising as I lift it to my lips. The sweet, pungent scent assails my senses before the liquid passes my lips.

The drink is rich and fiery, and the first sip sets my head reeling.

Time slows to a crawl.

My eyelids are leaden, each blink a slow and arduous task.

I can feel the wood grain beneath my fingers, yet my hands feel like they're floating a foot above the table.

I'm back at Clearwater Beach with my parents, clutching my first sand dollar in my hand.

"Look Dad, I got one."

"Cool, kiddo." Dad smiles big, despite his sunburned cheeks.

"Jim," Mom scolds. *"Put on some sunscreen. You're getting burned to a crisp."*

"It's just my damned Irish complexion. I'll be fine."

"That's a dollar fifty you owe the curse box when we get home," I say. *"And we're only on day two."*

Someone is holding my hand.

I hear a conversation but can't make out the words.

I open my eyes to raucous laughter. Turning my groggy head in slow motion, I find Bobby sitting to my right, with Moloch and Bia beside him.

Every seat at the table is taken.

Where did they all come from? And when?

Raum takes the goblet from my hand, smiling. "That's enough. I can't have you dropping out for another hour. Not on your big night."

"An...what? What time is it?"

The dinner guests roar with laughter.

A portly, bald man to Asmodeus's left drops a half-eaten turkey leg onto his plate and drags a napkin across his face. "How much did you let her drink?" he asks Raum. Bits of food fly from his mouth.

Raum gazes at me with a strange look in his eyes. Pride, is it? He takes my hand and gives it a kiss. "She took a single sip."

I snap out of my stupor and pull free. I tuck my hands into my lap.

Raum pulls me close, a stiff smile on his face. "Do not make the mistake of insulting me in front of our guests again," he whispers through clenched teeth. "And smile."

He takes my hand, and this time I don't fight him. I plaster a shaky smile on my face.

"Be convincing now or pay later," he warns.

Asmodeus holds up his goblet in a toast. "Now that Raum's guest has returned to us, the evening's festivities can begin." He looks at the portly man's chewed up turkey leg and half-empty plate. "Well, the rest of us may begin. Morax has never been one to stand on ceremony."

Polite laugher rolls around the table as the guests—a scary collection of souls—dig in to the feast. The men are all dressed in tuxedoes and the women in elaborate gowns, but dressing to the nines does little to mask the evil present.

"How did they all get through the gate?" I ask, confused.

"We come and go as we please," Asmodeus says. "And the City Guard and ACEA Agents believe we've come to broker a truce with the Council."

I stare at my plate, which is heaped high with turkey and what I believe is some sort of game animal. The thought of eating right now turns my stomach, but Raum's warning leaves me little choice. I begin to pick at a vegetable dish and take tiny, slow bites.

A woman sitting across from Bobby with silver, curly hair pulls a bite of carrot off her fork. She watches me with bright green eyes. "She has the appetite of a bird." Her emerald gown shimmers as she leans forward. "Such a delicate young thing, Raum."

Raum shoots me another of his looks.

"Thank you," I say, swallowing back fear, shame, and a simmering fury.

Movement from Bobby grabs my attention away from my

latest tormentor. He reaches into his pocket and pulls out the bottle I gave him. He sets it on the table beside his plate, and as he stares at the dark liquid the bottle contains, the shimmer that might become a spark returns to his eyes.

"Bobby," I whisper.

"Your toy moves, Moloch," Raum says. "What's that he has?"

Moloch pulls his gaze from Bia's cleavage long enough to cast a glance in Bobby's direction. "Where did you get that?"

Bobby reaches for the knife next to his plate, his gaze still fixed on the bottle.

Consequences be damned, I squeeze his arm. "Bobby?"

For the first time since Moloch dragged him off into that dark, awful night, Bobby looks me in the eyes.

Raum grabs my arm, but I ignore him.

"It's me. It's Dez."

With a slow, deliberate hand, Bobby drags the blade of his knife across his index finger. Blood springs from the wound. He stares at it for a moment before scrawling something on the table.

Bia frowns. "What is he doing?"

Moloch reads Bobby's message and laughs. "There will be none of that, boy. Have I taught you nothing in our lessons?"

Ignoring the pain radiating up my arm from Raum's intense grip, I lean across Bobby's plate to get a better look. He's written out a single word in blood.

ELEOS

"What does it say?" Raum demands.

"My Latin's no good," I gasp, having reached the limit of my defiance as well as my pain threshold. "He wrote out just one word. *Eleos.*"

"That's Greek," Raum scolds. He looks around me at Bobby. "You've come to the wrong place for mercy, young one, although you certainly are afflicted."

"Enough distractions," Moloch says. He grabs the corkscrew bottle from the table and hurls it at the wall, just missing Morax. The bottle shatters and the liquid trickles down the wall.

The light in Bobby's eyes flickers and vanishes.

Tears well in my eyes. I stifle a sob.

Raum stands. "If you would all be so kind as to excuse us for a moment." He pulls me to my feet and takes me through the door behind Asmodeus's chair, into the kitchen.

The servants scatter at the sight of us and hustle through a door in the back.

Raum pulls the pocket square from his tuxedo jacket. He takes my face in his free hand and begins to dab at my eyes. "Let us get one thing straight, pretty. I will have no more of this, do you understand me? If you let a single tear fall in front of my guests, this night will not end well for you. As bad as you may imagine what is to come, I assure you, I can make it worse."

Without waiting for a reply, he shoves the pocket square into his pants pocket and leads me back to the table, just as a string quartet is setting up on the main floor.

The sound of tuning instruments transports me away from this nightmare, back to the days before.

Before death.

Before perpetual pain.

Before I knew nothing but fear.

Before I lost my future.

Raum looks at the quartet, and back to me, intrigued. "Do

you play?"

"Not in months. Not since before..."

"The sweet release of death?" he taunts. "Come." He takes me over to the musicians and stops at the first violinist, a tall, thin man with thick, curly black hair.

The man bows. "Lord Raum, may I be of service?"

"Let her play something."

"But of course." He offers me his violin without question, which shocks me, even given the circumstances.

"I can't." I shake my head.

Raum gives me a furious look. "Are you refusing?"

"No. It's just—I play the cello."

The cellist lays her instrument down carefully and jumps from her seat. "By all means, Miss," she says.

Everyone at the table stops eating to watch us, intrigued.

Raum escorts me to the chair. "Be excellent," he says.

No pressure or anything.

He heads back to his seat as I get situated.

I adjust the cello's endpin. The simple task calms my frayed nerves and steadies my shaking hands. I tighten the bow, and the tension starts to leave my body. The act of picking up the instruments feels a bit like home.

I don't think; I just play the only piece fit for a situation like this. The Sarabande from Bach's Cello Suite No. 5 in C minor. It's sorrowful and haunting, and I know it by heart.

I've never before played on such a perfect instrument. The notes come with ease; the rust I'd feared from being out of practice is nonexistent. I close my eyes and drift away with the music.

Until the screaming starts.

CHAPTER FORTY-FOUR

My eyes spring open.

Screams permeate the Great Hall, muffled by the heavy doors but loud nonetheless.

My bracelet lets out a piercing squeal, which goes unnoticed by everyone but me. I spare it a quick glance.

PROXIMITY LOCK

Asmodeus snaps his fingers, and the head servant, a short man with dark hair, rushes to his side. "Tavi, go silence that girl. I will not suffer such foolishness in the midst of a feast." His eyes burn with irritation.

Tavi bows. "Right away, my King."

Before he can reach the doors, a servant girl runs in, wailing.

My heart rushes into a frantic rhythm.

Right on her heels is Mack, leading a squad of agents in full riot gear. Six of them fan out behind him in a V-formation, and the sudden realization of who they are makes me cry out.

The seven agents with Departers.

All drawn.

Close to a hundred agents and City Guard swarm in behind them.

The cello hits the floor with a thud. I leap to my feet. "Mack," I scream.

Mack and the other six agents rush forward, but Raum is on me in an instant. He pulls me back toward the table.

"We really must stop meeting like this," he tells Mack.

"Let her go, Raum." Mack shifts his weapon to his left hand and reaches into the thigh pocket of his black fatigues. He pulls out a document and holds it up high over his head. "I am here under the authority of a joint order of the Atman Council and the Grigori Watch."

He tosses the paperwork across the room. The pages flutter as they arc through the air and land a few yards shy of our feet.

"I've told you before, and I will only tell you one more time," Raum says. "The girl is mine." His grip around my waist tightens.

Asmodeus holds up his hands to quiet his agitated dinner guests, all of whom are on edge from the drawn Departers. "Silence," he barks. He stands and slowly adjusts his cufflinks. With an easy, deliberate stride that belies the building tension in the hall, he steps down from the table and walks over to pick up the order.

"That decree," Mack says, "bears the official seals of both the Council and the Watch and contains a direct command for the immediate release of Robert Jeffrey Hammond and Desiree Anne Donnelly. As a designated officer of the court, I am here to collect both Mister Hammond and Miss Donnelly, and, under the authority granted by the Atman Council and the Grigori Watch, I am executing the arrest warrants contained within."

Moloch jumps to his feet and shoves off the calming hand Bia places on his arm. He looks down at Bobby. "Rise," he orders, and Bobby obeys.

He brings Bobby over and stands shoulder to shoulder with Raum. "They're not going anywhere."

Asmodeus begins to read the document Mack delivered. "Lower your weapons." His gaze remains locked on the decree. "There is no need for such threats."

Mack shakes his head. "Lowering our weapons is not part of the conversation. Not right now. Hand over Dez and Bobby, and we'll talk about what comes next."

Asmodeus looks up at Mack, amused. "Dez and Bobby? How very informal. Are these children friends of yours?" He returns to studying the document.

The doors burst open again, and a dozen more City Guard members file in with a large number of the castle's staff in tow, Asha among them. Upon seeing me, she casts her gaze to the floor. She shuffles along obediently, following the line of staff to the center of the hall.

Mack glances over his shoulder at the new arrivals.

The head of the Guard steps forward. "We've cleared the second floor, sir. As far as we can tell, everyone is accounted for."

Mack nods and trains his Departer on Raum. "It's time to get down to brass tacks. It starts with you letting the girl go. Nice and easy."

Raum's forearm slides around my neck. "Put your weapon down, or I'll make her hurt." His powerful arm constricts around me like a snake. "And I'm very good at that, aren't I, pretty?"

I cry out, just as much from fright as the pain.

"It's okay, Dez," Mack tells me. His eyes are calm, his focus razor sharp. "We're going to get you out of here."

I try to slow my shallow, panicked breaths.

"Let her go. Now. You are in direct violation of an order issued by your own governing body."

Raum strokes my cheek with his free hand. "Moloch and I do as we please. And what I'm about to do to this girl pleases me greatly."

Moloch drops a hand on Bobby's shoulder. "If you're wise, you'll leave before things get out of hand. Raum and I have never been good at sharing our toys."

"Hold on," Asmodeus commands. He turns his steely gaze on Mack. "This warrant..." His face darkens. "You don't really think I'm going to let you walk out of here with the two children, and Raum and Moloch, do you?"

Raum's grip on my neck loosens, and he pivots so we're facing Asmodeus. I can almost feel his blood boiling. They exchange a long, dangerous look.

"The arrest warrant is for you. Both of you," Asmodeus says.

"On what grounds? On whose authority?"

Moloch storms over to Asmodeus, grabs the order from him, and begins to read. "On count one, Lord Raum is to be brought before a joint council to face one count of capital and willful destruction of an Agent of the Atman Council, the late Clara Perkins, during the execution of her duties. On count two, Lord Raum is to be brought before..."—he skims through the warrant—"to face two counts of willful abduction of an underage soul and two counts of gross negligence and unlawful care of said souls. They're charging me with abduction, gross negligence, and unlawful care."

Raum turns his wrath on Mack. "You have no authority here," he snaps. Rage burns up his words.

"This is a legitimate document," Asmodeus tells him. "You told me we'd see no fallout from your dalliances."

Mack and the other six agents inch forward as the conversation between the demons escalates.

Raum's grip around my neck goes slack. He snatches the order from Moloch.

I slip the stiletto heels from my feet, slow and cautious. I hold my breath and pray he doesn't notice what I've done.

My eyes lock with Mack's, and he gives me an almost imperceptible nod.

With a quick, sharp inhalation, I slip free of Raum and run. My gown is tight and heavy, but I've caught him in a moment of distraction, which gives me just enough time to bolt to the safety of Mack and his agents. I collapse against him in a heap of tears.

He holsters his Departer. "Okay, Dez, you're okay. We're going to get you out of here."

The agent to his left steps up and takes his place as triggerman.

"What's your next move?" Moloch taunts. He pats Bobby on the head like a dog. "This one doesn't run."

My heart sinks with realization.

I've abandoned Bobby.

Again.

"Let him go!" I scream. "Just let him go."

Raum pulls his dagger from a sheath in his waistband and

strides over to Bobby. "I will gut him like a fish. Right in front of the girl." The steel glints in the light, a sight all too familiar to me. He points the tip of the blade in my direction. "You belong to me, and I will tolerate no more disobedience."

"Put the weapon down," Mack's second in command orders. His voice booms with authority. His Departer emits the same high-pitched squeal that Mack's did in the park when all of this began.

All my fear, my anger, my rage from these past days, it all bubbles to the surface in a toxic brew and boils over. I scream, wild and unhinged.

I've been a victim too long, helpless. Powerless. Raum and Moloch have stripped away my sense of security, control, and my very sense of self. I've been taken, and rescued, and taken again. And it ends now.

Bobby, broken.

Clara, gone.

Innocence, shattered.

Love that never got a chance.

Pain that will never heal.

Conversations we'll never finish.

Thanks they'll never hear.

Wrongs that will never be righted.

It's all too much. I have nothing left, so I do the only thing I can think of. Taking everyone by surprise, myself included, I grab the Departer from the holster on Mack's thigh.

"Dez, no," he bellows.

But it's too late.

It feels so natural, so intuitive as it comes alive with a squeal.

The Departer is an organic extension of my hand, thrumming with life and surrounded by death. My index finger flips the safety as if I'd done it a thousand times before. I step around the agent in front of us.

And I pull the trigger.

I've never fired a weapon before, but my aim is true.

The look of surprise and rage on Raum's face disappears in a blinding flash of light. He shimmers in a halo of luminescence for an instant, and with no fanfare or fight, he vanishes.

It's so quiet, so simple. An ancient being, a prince of creation, gone with the pull of a trigger.

The hall falls into stunned silence.

"Dez, what have you done?" Mack whispers.

Asmodeus and his guests are as still and as statues. No one so much as blinks. Moloch stares at me, too stunned to speak.

Not an agent or officer of the City Guard moves.

Not a member of the castle's staff makes a sound.

I am every bit as satisfied as I am terrified by my action. I take a step forward on unsteady legs and train Mack's Departer on Moloch.

"Get away from him," I say slowly. "Now." My voice shakes, but I don't care. He will not control me. He will not terrorize us. Not anymore.

Moloch takes a cautious step back, and with this small move, the glimmer of awareness that's been so elusive returns to Bobby's eyes. He looks at me and holds up his still-bleeding hand.

The Departer shakes in my unsteady grip. My arms quake from my shoulders to my fingertips. "Bobby, I'm so sorry."

He looks from the Departer to me and nods.

A rush of terrible, cruel awareness hits me.

I know what he's asking me to do.

"Bobby, no. We can fix this."

Our eyes meet and utters his first word since our painful reunion. "Please."

My own words to Mack in Bobby's suite echo in my mind, the terrible truth I've known from day one. *He's never belonged here.*

All he ever wanted was darkness. The end. And I'm the only one who can give it to him.

Tears stream down my face and blur my vision.

I level the Departer on him. "*Eleos,*" I whisper.

And I fire.

CHAPTER FORTY-FIVE

Mack's reflexes this time are quicker than my resolve. He crashes into me just as the Departer fires, sending a wild shot into the wall. He takes me to the floor and wrestles the weapon from my hand.

"No," I cry, fighting for control of the gun.

"Stop. Just stop," he commands, but I keep struggling, desperate to get the Departer back and honor Bobby's wish before I lose my courage.

"It's over, Dez."

Two ACEA agents rush forward to subdue me.

"It's what he wants!" I cry out as they pin me.

A quick-thinking agent rushes up and grabs Bobby as the hall erupts in chaos.

I'm pulled to my feet, an agent at each arm, amid shouts and screams echoing in all directions.

With his Departer and his command back under his control,

Mack begins to bark out rapid-fire orders. "Line up. Formation protocol." The seven agents with Departers form a single, straight line and push the rest of us behind them.

Moloch lunges toward us, wild fury burning in his eyes, but Asmodeus restrains him.

"This will not stand," Asmodeus roars. "Hand over the girl to face justice."

"We both know that's not going to happen," Mack says. "We've all suffered losses, and now is not the time they will be sorted."

"Losses? She disintegrated the soul of an ancient Earl, and I demand you relinquish her immediately. You will not leave this hall without reparations."

"I have seven Departers here that say otherwise." Mack trains his on Asmodeus.

"How dare you point your weapon at me!"

"We lost one of ours, and you lost one of yours. I'd say that makes us even."

"Are you comparing a low-ranking agent to the likes of Raum?" His eyes narrow, and he fixes his gaze on me. "You will pay dearly for this, child."

"Not today," Mack says. He takes a step and begins a slow retreat from the hall.

He and the other six agents with Departers fall into a tight formation and provide cover as the rest of us move toward the exit. I try to find Asha amid the chaos, but the two agents flanking me are so quick that the crowd is little more than a blur as we rush by.

We hurry outside and across the courtyard to the dozens of

awaiting personnel carriers with emergency lights still flashing. Bobby and I are separated into different vehicles and rushed off into the night.

The motorcade moves at high speed, sweeping through the darkened streets and back toward the safety of ACEA headquarters. The city goes by in a blur. The flashing blue lights above the vehicles cast an uneven glow inside the vehicle and onto the stony-faced agents surrounding me.

There is not a friendly or familiar face. The closest I get to a conversation is a, "We're almost there, Miss," from the woman sitting next to me when we're a few blocks from our destination.

✦✦✦

The face of a distraught, awaiting Crosby is the best thing I've ever seen. It means I'm finally safe.

But Bobby. I've failed him, again.

Crosby jumps up from a bench outside ACEA headquarters as we pull into the parking lot. He begins to frantically search vehicles until he spots me.

I push past the agents who have opened the door to let me out and fall to my knees.

Crosby rushes to my side. He pulls me up from the ground and into a hug. "Thank god," he whispers. "Are you okay?"

"I—I think so."

He puts his hands on my shoulders and looks me over before pulling me back into his arms.

"Crosby," I cry. "It's Bobby."

"It's okay, sweetie. Whatever happened, we can fix it. The important thing is that you're back, and you're safe. That's all that matters."

"What they did to him, there's no fixing—"

"I'm going to need you to step back," Mack interrupts from behind me.

Crosby looks at him, puzzled. "Mack, what's wrong?"

"Just step back."

"She's terrified. Just give her a minute."

Mack takes a deep breath. He rubs his face, frustrated, and locks eyes with Crosby. "Cros, I need you to step back. Right now."

Crosby's arm falls off my shoulders and to his side. He stares blankly at Mack as he steps away from me and gives him room.

Mack steps behind me and pulls my hands behind my back.

I feel cold steel against my skin and hear the ratcheting of metal but can't process what's happening.

"Desiree Donnelly, as a duly appointed officer of the Council, it is my duty to inform you that you are under arrest for the unauthorized disintegration of a soul."

The universe shifts and shudders. My world goes black.

ACKNOWLEDGEMENTS

The fact that the pages you've just read have made their way to publication is the result of the hard work and assistance of many people, and I would be remiss not to thank them for helping me along the way, from creation to completion.

Once again, my thanks goes out to Georgia McBride, a champion of new voices in young adult fiction. Thank you for believing in Dez's story from the beginning.

There is so much research that goes into the fine details of a story, research that may never show itself on the printed page, but rather informs the author in their writing. Dr. Jeffrey Dippmann at Central Washington University was kind enough to share with me numerous articles and a great deal of information on Buddhism and didn't shy away from the crazy question of, "Is there any scenario in which Buddhists would willingly make themselves part of a limbo existence?"

A big thanks goes out to my brother, Eric Stassen, for his musical expertise. You didn't even bat an eye when I made a ridiculously detailed request. "I need a piece that a solidly-decent-borderline-quite-good high school senior first-chair cellist could play from memory. It needs to be sorrowful and beautiful and haunting, and she needs to be able to play it without sounding like a rank amateur." In a matter of minutes, you offered up The Sarabande from Bach's Cello Suite No. 5 in C minor and told me to be sure to look up Rostropovich's performance (I encourage readers to do the same). Amid my tears, I knew it was perfect.

I am a stickler for details and am especially paranoid about the details of which I know little to begin with. Thank you to Dr. Laurel Brown for helping to assure Bobby and Dez's night of stargazing was accurate, and for loving the scene as much as I do.

I was blessed with an enthusiastic and talented editor, Bethany Robison, whose hard work and eye for detail helped guide this story into something more. Thank you for caring so much for this book and its characters.

I owe many thanks to Courtney Koschel and the entire Month9Books team. You make manuscripts into books, and I am so grateful that you've again put your talents and time into mine. Thanks also to the Georgia McBride Media Group family of authors for your continued support. You are all amazing.

I have two beta readers, Ríoghnach Robinson and Crystal Waters, who again have offer me vital feedback. I can't begin to tell you how much I appreciate you getting me through that first draft. Thank you for helping me find Dez's truth.

To the fans of the Atman City series, I simply can't thank you enough. Your enthusiasm and positive feedback have made the joy of writing even greater. It's an amazing gift (and a big responsibility) to be able to write a story you know people are eager to read.

I have amazing friends and family who have been incredibly supportive. Your enthusiasm for my publishing journey and for this series has been overwhelming. Thank you for sharing photos, status updates, and tweets, for telling your friends about my writing, and for your wonderful feedback.

I save my biggest thanks for my husband, John. I could never do this without your support and love. Thank you for always believing in me and for pushing me to try. I love you.

Michelle E. Reed

Michelle was born in a small Midwestern town, to which she has returned to raise her own family. Her imagination and love of literature were fueled by a childhood of late nights, hidden under the covers and reading by flashlight. She is a passionate adoption advocate who lives in Wisconsin with her husband, son, and their yellow lab, Sully.

OTHER MONTH9BOOKS TITLES YOU MIGHT LIKE

LIFE, A.D.

BRANDED

DAUGHTER OF CHAOS

PRETTY DARK NOTHING

INTO THE FIRE

PREDATOR

PRAEFATIO

THE LOOKING GLASS

OF BREAKABLE THINGS

A MURDER OF MAGPIES

LIFER

A SHIMMER OF ANGELS and A SLITHER OF HOPE

SCION OF THE SUN

CALL ME GRIM

GEORGIAMCBRIDE.COM

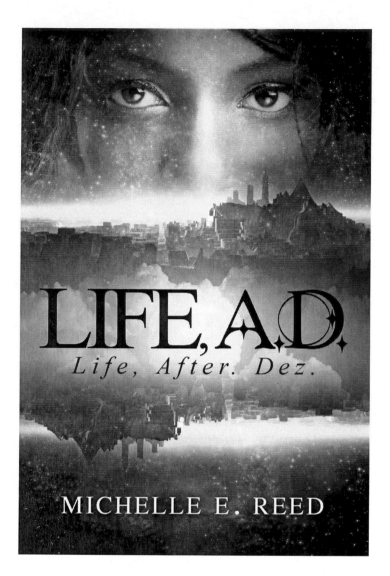

LIFE, A.D.
Life, After. Dez.

MICHELLE E. REED

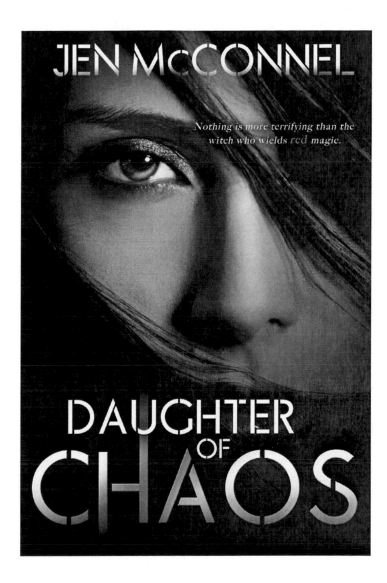

JEN McCONNEL

Nothing is more terrifying than the witch who wields red *magic.*

DAUGHTER
OF
CHAOS

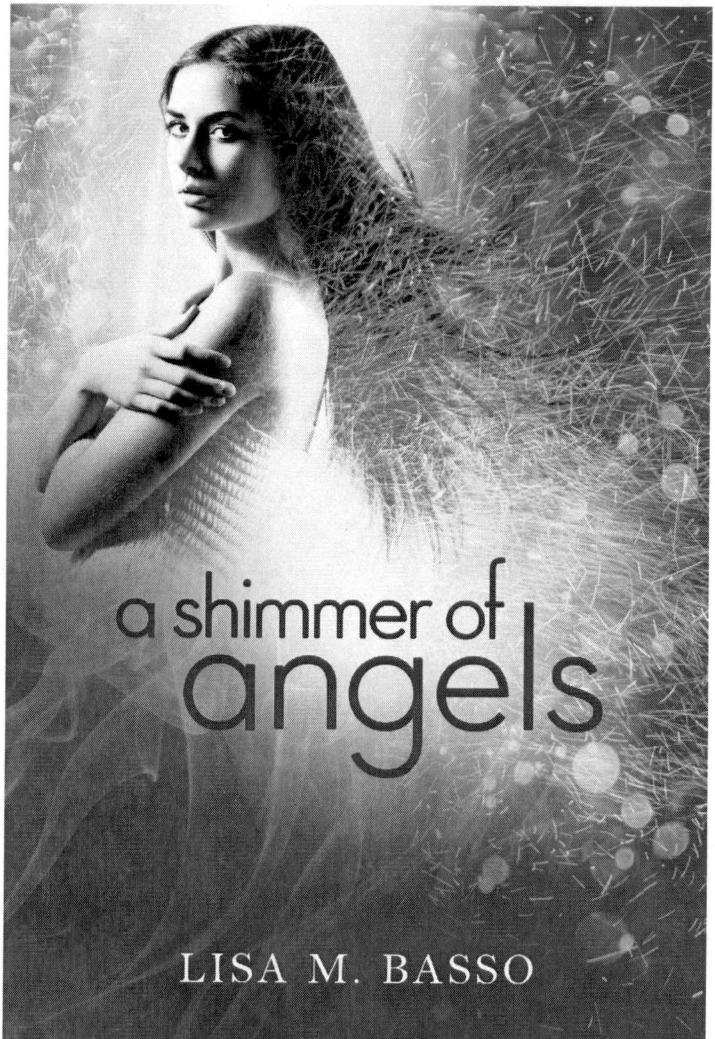
a shimmer of
angels
LISA M. BASSO

PRETTY DARK NOTHING

SOMETHING COLD AND DAMP BRUSHED AGAINST HER LEG.
IT FELT LIKE A HUMAN HAND, A DEAD HUMAN HAND,
THE MOISTNESS OF ITS EARTHEN GRAVE
STILL CLINGING TO ITS ROTTING FLESH.

HEATHER L. REID

PRAEFATIO

A NOVEL

"This is teen fantasy at its most entertaining,
most heartbreaking, most compelling. Highly recommended." –Jonathan Maberry,
New York Times bestselling author of ROT & RUIN and FIRE & ASH

GEORGIA McBRIDE

Find more awesome Teen books at Month9Books.com

Connect with Month9Books online:
Facebook: www.Facebook.com/Month9Books

Twitter: @Month9Books
You Tube: www.youtube.com/user/Month9Books

Blog: www.month9booksblog.com

Request review copies via publicity@month9books.com